BLUE INFERNO

Book Two

Salvaggio's Light

An Epic Contemporary Romance Serial

By C. L. Cattano

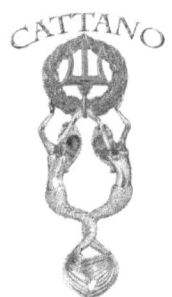

VAGARY PUBLISHING

Blue Inferno
Book Two
Salvaggio's Light

A Vagary Publishing Book

Published by:

VAGARY PUBLISHING

www.vagarypublishing.com
inquiry@vagarypublishing.com

Rogena Mitchell-Jones, Independent Literary Editor
RMJ Manuscript Services LLC *www.rogenamitchell.com*

ISBN 13-978-0-9980906-5-8

First Edition

WARNING

It is suggested readers of this story be adults over the age of eighteen.

This dramatic romance series has many scenes describing sex as well as intense emotional scenes and acts of violence.

This is a serial story with themes that flow from one book into another with lots of twists and turns. Reading this series from the beginning is highly suggested, or the reader may not be able to follow all of the story lines.

Go to the Salvaggio's Light Facebook page to join other readers who are talking about the series.
www.facebook.com/SalvaggiosLight/

Join the C L Cattano mailing list and check out my website at www.clcattano.com

Acknowledgments

AS ALWAYS, I need to thank all the people who read this book and the many re-writes until I was happy. Thank you to my great editor, Rogena, for all her hard work and to my significant other, Marie, for giving it a final read before release. I feel lucky to have so many people in my corner on this project. Thank you to all the readers and the feedback that made writing the first book in this series a great experience, and I hope you like this second book just as much. Thank you to everyone whose patience I tried while being unavailable as I finalized this book for publication!

In this book, I have introduced a new character named Annie Brown in honor of my real life friend Ann K. Brown, who died leaving our world sad, but a lot more glittery because of her work and whimsy. Ann was not only a friend for over twenty years—she was a great artist, photographer, and supporter of the LGBT community in Kansas City. Ask almost anyone in the community (especially the art and entertainment people) about Ann, and they will tell you how awesome she was and how much they miss her. She had more of an influence in my life than she knew, and I miss her too…

Dedication

For Marie – who took a second look and
saw beyond the orange.

Salvaggio's Light

An Epic Contemporary Romance Serial

Shattered Paradise
Blue Inferno
Secrets & Rivalry*
Wildling's Claim*
Sowers of Discord*

*Coming Soon

Love, which absolves no one beloved from loving,
seized me so strongly with his charm
that, as thou seest, it does not leave me yet.
— Dante Alighieri, The Divine Comedy

1

One week later...

IT WAS MID-MORNING on a mild California Sunday when Flynn Ogden pulled up to The Kiki Bistro and parked his dark blue, three-quarter ton Chevy truck, he had bought for hauling beach gear and dune toys, on the street. He grabbed his notebook from the seat and took it with him. He was meeting Eden for Sunday brunch to talk about what he found on her computer since he had taken it with him a week ago.

Eden broke up with Jake after she had received some information on him and a group he may be associated with called the Stewards. Since then, she had been harassed by Jake, and part of the harassment came in the form of emails. Flynn took Eden's computer to check it out and thought he would just find some basic information she could use to take to the police for a restraining order or something. Instead, he discovered other things he knew Eden would find concerning.

Flynn spent a lot of time over the last week diagnosing and pulling information from Eden's computer. He was uneasy about the fact Eden had been adamant they not tell Rafe about anything until she could fix things herself. Based on what Flynn had found, he didn't think Eden would be able to fix things herself. She would definitely need his help with Jake and the Stewards group. Even though Flynn thought it would be better to tell Rafe, he kept his word.

Flynn walked into the bistro and saw Eden was already at the table getting Bronte settled. When he made it to the table, they ordered, and Eden pulled out Bronte's bib to get her ready to eat. The waitress brought their coffee and juice for Bronte, and then he put his notebook on the table to go over what he found.

"So, I found something you might find interesting on your computer," he began. "Did you know your computer had been hacked into?"

Eden looked at him shocked. "What?"

"Yeah, it looks like it happened a while back when you were visiting some chat rooms," he said looking at the information he had written down about the file, including the date it was put on the computer. "It's strange because it is a pretty old file. It was loaded almost three years ago." He scratched his head. "It may have nothing to do with Jake. Whoever did it, though, could have gotten all your personal information, seen all of the pictures you have, and pretty much know all about you and what you were doing. Whoever was in your computer, they had access to it all. They could even turn on the camera to your computer remotely and see you as well as listen to your conversations." He took a sip of his coffee. "So you should probably change all your passwords. I can remove the file if you want. If I can't get the file off, you should buy a new computer."

Eden closed her eyes as her head spun and a sick feeling waved through her. "Can you find out who did it?"

"It's hard without some special software and stuff," Flynn explained. "I'll see what I can do. It was probably someone you actually talked with for a while online. They kept you online while they linked into your computer. Do you remember who all you talked with for long periods? You may have linked to them through a private chat room, or they may have asked you to do a link-up saying it was a private way to message."

"Oh, my god," Eden whispered weakly. "I think I'm going to be sick."

As if out of nowhere, Abby appeared like a genie. "Are you sick? What's the matter?"

Surprised by Abby's sudden appearance, Eden stuttered her response. "Abby. No, it's just an expression." She gave Flynn a signal to drop their conversation.

"Oh," said Abby with a shrug and sat down. "Well, I don't know if Flynn told you or not, but the art studio will be done by the end of the week. Annie's already organizing supplies and stuff. Rafe said Annie has let people know she'll be ready to have the first art class on Saturday."

"Wow, I'm not surprised. When she wants something, she works fast," said Eden as the waitress put their brunch plates on the table. Eden then began to feed Bronte.

Abby signaled the waitress to bring her order to their table and turned back to the conversation. "Well, you know Rafe. She can get what she wants from just about anyone. I swear she smiled at those contractors and they started working faster."

Abby looked at Eden for a moment and decided this was the perfect time to follow up on her plan to get her into Rafe's life again. Rafe had been hyper-focused on the art studio. Now it was only a matter of time before Julia got her hooks into her and convinced her to go out using her wildling ways for one of their damn wagers.

"You should go," she commanded.

Eden pushed her food around on the plate nervously. "I don't know." For the last few weeks, she and Rafe had barely spoken except to exchange Bronte. It was clear Rafe was coping with Greer being gone by trying to keep busy. Eden was just glad she hadn't seen a string of beautiful women coming out of Rafe's bedroom again.

"You should go see Bronte have an art lesson," insisted Abby.

"Yeah," agreed Flynn, "you said you wanted to be able to get along and do things with Rafe and Bronte." He hoped the more she was around Rafe, the more she would see it was best to tell her everything going on with Jake. Then Rafe would know why Eden had to do the things she was doing and they could help each other.

"See?" said Abby as the waitress served her brunch. "This is perfect," she said then took a bite of food. "It's Saturday at eleven. Go."

2

THE CHILDREN'S ART Studio was finally open for the first class. Rafe Salvaggio and Annie Brown had worked hard to have everything ready for all the new students and parents. The garage had been transformed into a colorful and inviting learning environment, and space was arranged for the toddlers and parents to work on the tarp-covered floor today.

Annie, the easygoing instructor, was making sure everyone was checked in and had supplies. "Okay, everyone, thank you for coming," Annie announced. "If you would pick a spot and sit down, I'll tell you what we'll be doing today."

Rafe carried Bronte to a spot and sat down on the floor beside her. Bronte was excited about having all the other kids around and was having a lot of fun.

Eden walked in and saw Rafe sitting with Bronte. It was hard to miss the two dark haired forms standing out in the sea of California dyed blond mothers. She went over and sat down next to them.

"Hi," she said to them both with a smile.

Rafe looked over at Eden, surprised she had come. "Hi," she answered back warily. She hadn't been prepared to face Eden today.

"Abby insisted I come," she explained quietly. "I hope you don't mind. I loved the painting you sent me, and I really wanted to see Bronte paint," she said fighting the feelings

Rafe's scent created in her and the reaction her body was having.

"I don't mind," she smiled and found she was happy to see Eden. It was nice being close to her and Bronte. She should not really have been surprised Eden was there. Abby had been hinting she should invite her, but she just kept putting it off. The way Eden seemed to be avoiding her stopped Rafe from saying anything whenever she would see her. She looked at Eden again then turned her attention to the instructor.

Annie was introducing herself and giving helpful advice to the parents as they caught her in mid-lecture. "If you didn't wear your old clothes, we have smocks for you in the cabinet," said the willowy instructor flinging her long brown hair back. "We will be getting messy. It's the best part of art with kids."

A few of the parents headed for the smocks while Annie tied her hair back out of the way.

"Some of you are going to be tempted to help your child make a logical design or use a certain color," Annie continued, "but I want you to try not to influence them. Let them experience and explore these new things."

Annie walked around the room making sure everyone had supplies. "Some children may want to just feel the paint while others may want to eat it," she said and smiled at the parental laughter. "It's safe to eat, as long as they don't over indulge." She laughed along with the parents at the comment about diaper art. "They'll be exploring the paint and some tools and supplies. It may just seem like a random mess, but they are learning. Your job is to tell them what they're doing, but not what to do. Name the colors they play with, the tools, and the supplies. You can also show them how to use everything. Are there any questions? No? Okay, let's get started."

"I think I'll go get a smock," said Eden as she stood up.

"Okay," said Rafe and turned to Bronte. "Let's pick some colors." After they had gotten colors, canvas, and supplies, Rafe opened the paints as Bronte started to play and learn.

Eden found a smock and sat down with Rafe and Bronte again. "She really knows what to do," she observed, amazed at what Rafe had done for their daughter.

"Yes, she does. She definitely has talent." She pointed to the paint. "Bronte, what color is this? You know it, can you tell me?" Bronte held up her small hand and made the sign for the ASL letter B then tilted her hand side to side twice making the sign for blue. "You're right, blue," Rafe repeated cheerfully and made the sign back to her.

"She knows sign language?" Eden asked, amazed.

"Just for a few colors and small words," confirmed Rafe as she nodded. "Blue was the first one Greer taught her." Rafe smiled remembering Greer telling her blue was not her color.

Eden smiled back at Rafe not realizing Rafe's smile was not for her. "That's amazing.

"It is," Rafe agreed. "I was thinking about enrolling us in a baby sign language class. I think it could be a good skill for her to learn."

"You should do it," Eden encouraged. "I think she's been using them, and I had no idea." She watched as Rafe and her daughter interacted in the art lesson. Soon she joined in, and they were all having fun in the lesson while laughing and creating together.

At the end of the lesson, everyone was cleaning up and discussing their children and their artwork with Annie. Eden helped Rafe put their paint and supplies away. "This is a great thing you've done, Rafe." She smiled. "I mean it."

"Thanks," said Rafe smiling back. "I wanted Bronte to keep having lessons. Greer knew Annie was available and needed a graduate project, and Annie knew a lot of other parents who were interested. It just all worked out," said Rafe with a casual shrug.

"Thank you, for letting me stay today," Eden said in appreciation. "I had fun."

Rafe looked at Eden and could see what being at the lesson meant to her. "Eden, you're welcome to come to all the lessons. Bronte loved you being here, and you should be able to see her progress. You should be part of it."

Eden felt a wave of warm happiness flow through her. She was so glad today went so well. "I'd like to. Thank you."

3

RAFE SALVAGGIO WAS up bright and early Sunday morning and in the art studio remembering how well the lesson went the day before. She was looking over Bronte's and the other children's colorful creations and making sure everything was organized and picked up. She gathered all of the paint covered smocks and put them in a basket for Annie to pick up and take to be laundered. She sat in one of the colorful chairs, pulled out her cell phone, and dialed.

"Hi, Beth. Is she busy?" She smiled into the camera as Beth signed to Greer and set up the phone to start their facetime conversation. "Greer, you wouldn't believe how great yesterday was. Annie was a hit with the kids and the parents. I think we went through two jugs of paint per kid. Putting in the shower was a genius idea, thank you." Rafe watched Greer look at Beth to make sure she understood what was said.

"It's so good to see your face! I wish I could be there," said Greer happy to see Rafe's smile. "Did Bronte like sharing her lesson?"

"I wish you could see the studio and the work in person too," said Rafe feeling how much she missed Greer and wished she was still here. "Yes, she loved being around all of the other kids."

"Are you wearing blue today," Greer teased with a wink and a big smile.

Rafe laughed at her teasing. "No, nothing blue is on me today." She winked back. "I couldn't stop thinking about you all day yesterday and all night last night. How are you doing up there?"

"There's so much happening I wonder if I'm taking on too much sometimes."

"I'm sure it is overwhelming, but I know you're up to the challenge," Rafe said confidently trying not to show how much she missed her.

"I'm glad you have faith in me!" Greer sighed, thinking of the huge commitment she had made and all the work she had to do for her new job.

"Of course, I have complete faith in you. Have you been taking time for yourself to paint?"

Greer shook her head and frowned. "There's just been no time. Maybe they will give me some free time soon."

"You're just going to have to take the time. You can't wait until someone gives it to you because it may never happen." Rafe insisted.

"Are you arguing with the teacher?" Greer laughed.

"No, I'm not arguing with the teacher. I'm encouraging the artist," Rafe said and smiled charmingly.

"Beth is telling me I have to go," said Greer. "It's the department's monthly Sunday brunch. We don't want to be late to our first one!"

"Okay, have fun! Bye," she said and watched as Beth picked up the phone. "Hey, Beth, wait. Tell her I said, just say, I miss you. Thanks, Beth. Bye."

4

RAFE SALVAGGIO WALKED down the palm-lined sidewalk under a bright blue sky toward The Kiki Bistro thinking about her short conversation with Greer earlier. She had a sunny smile on her face as she entered the busy restaurant to meet Letty, Julia, and Abby for lunch. She waved at Letty, who was behind the counter, and then headed where Julia was sitting by the window.

"Don't you look like the fox that ate the chicken?" observed Julia. "Why are you so happy?"

"Well, yesterday's art session was a huge success. Bronte made a painting for me and one for Eden to take home," she said proudly.

"Oh," Julia said and winked. "Eden showed up?"

"Yes." Rafe ignored her wink. "Annie came by to pick up the dirty smocks this morning. She said two more kids signed up for next week, so she has enough students to qualify her graduate project." Rafe's eyes sparkled as she continued. "And I talked to Greer earlier."

Letty came over from the bar and sat down. "I'm so happy to sit down and rest. I put in our lunch order. I've got to hire another waiter."

"Or maybe you need to let the waiters you have do their jobs," Rafe suggested with a smirk.

"Hey, you know I just like to be sure things are going just right."

"And it's why you go through so many waiters. You've got to give them *some* slack. Not everyone is you."

Letty laughed at Rafe playfully. "Like you have room to talk."

Abby made it to the table and plopped herself down. "So, what's going on?"

"The art studio is a success. So, I thank you for all of your help," Rafe said and patted her on her back.

"No problem," said Abby with a smile.

"And she talked to Greer so she can't wipe the smile off her face," added Julia. She quickly checked herself making sure her frustration and jealousy had not leaked out in her voice. Now, since Greer was gone, it might be her chance to finally get Rafe to consider the possibility of them dating. Julia knew she was not moving away, and she was definitely not going to leave Rafe for a man like Eden had. She just needed to be subtle about her intentions.

"How is she?" Abby asked as a waiter came over with the drinks Letty had ordered for them.

"She's good but overwhelmed. She's taking on a big job."

"It really is too bad about you two," Letty said sadly. "She's such a nice woman."

"Yes, she is. I miss her." Rafe saw Julia roll her eyes but ignored her. She turned her head and looked out the window. "Hey, there's Eden and Bronte. Eden!" She knocked on the window and motioned for them to come inside. "Come and sit with us," she said through the windowpane.

They watched as Eden wheeled in Bronte and approached the table. "Hi, girls," Eden greeted them as Rafe made room at the table. "Thank you," she said and smiled at Rafe in appreciation.

"No problem." She watched as Eden took Bronte out of her stroller. "Here, let me take her. *Ciao bambina, ti vedo!*[1] How's my B Girl, I didn't think I would see you today." She looked

---

[1] Hello baby girl, I see you!

over at Eden. "Was she exhausted when you got her home yesterday?"

"Yeah, she was." Eden beamed at the pair. "I barely got her out of her clothes and into her clean PJ's before she fell asleep. She took a nice long nap."

"What have you two been doing this morning?" Letty asked Eden.

"Nothing much," she said with a shrug. "We just took a walk in the park and played on the swings. She's getting so fast it's becoming a chore to keep up with her.

"Maybe you need to get her a leash," suggested Abby. Everyone looked at her in disbelief and horror. "What?" she screeched irritated by the looks they were giving her. "My parents used one on me when I was little. Apparently, I was a runner."

"Well, I think we can get along without a leash," said Rafe. "That just sounds terrible, doesn't it?" she said to Bronte in a silly voice.

Eden laughed. "I agree, no leash."

"So, Eden, Rafe was just telling us the studio was a success. What did you think?" Julia inquired being friendly to make Rafe happy.

"Oh, you went? Great," said Abby glad Eden had taken her suggestion, and her plan had worked. "Rafe, do you think I could interview Annie for my webcast?"

"I'm sure it would be okay," said Rafe as she nodded. "I should warn Annie in advance, though." She laughed because she had already lost one art teacher after Abby featured Greer on her webcast. "So, what'd you think, Eden?'

"It was excellent," Eden declared with a happy nod. "The kids were so responsive to Annie. She's a wonderful teacher."

"Rafe, it sounds like you've really done a great thing," Letty observed. "I'm impressed you got it all set up so fast and got the grant money to do it. Bronte is lucky to have you."

"Yes, she is," agreed Eden softly as she thought about how lucky it was Rafe had not let Jake take Bronte. She was still shaken by what had happened that night.

The waiter came back and this time, had their food order ready. He placed the food family style in the middle of the table and put small plates in front of each person. Letty nodded to him, and he retreated back to the bar.

"Well, more good news for you then," Rafe announced smiling as she filled her plate. She was very excited about her news. "We might be on the finalist list for the Jackson-Goyer Foundation Grant. They'll be calling to let us know if we made it in about two weeks. If we make it in, President Biggalow and I will be invited to go meet with the committee and make a final presentation on the Wednesday of that same week."

"Fantastic!" Julia exclaimed impressed. "Don't they pick four universities to give half a million dollars to each? It will be amazing if you get on the finalist's list. Universities from all over the world compete for those grants."

"I know. It's why this is so important for us. It'll jumpstart some major projects like expanding the electronic media arts department and maybe allow us to hire a couple of teachers for the department."

"It sounds exciting," Eden agreed amazed Rafe had gone into a completely different career and was flourishing.

Rafe nodded, grinning as she gave Bronte a bite of food. "It is, and there's something I need to talk to you about."

"Sure, what?" Eden was happy she and Rafe were getting along and were hanging out with all their friends.

"Well, like I said, if we're invited, the presentation is on a Wednesday, and I'm thinking about taking the rest of the week off for vacation since I'll be in New York." She looked at Eden her excitement about the trip growing. "I was wondering if you would be okay with me taking Bronte. I can get an *au pair* from the hotel to watch her while I'm giving my presentation and while I'm at the dinner. Other than those times, she'll be with me. And we would be back by Sunday sometime, depending on the flight I book. So, what do you think?" She looked at Eden expectantly the excitement glowing in her eyes.

Everyone looked at Eden as she shifted nervously, her happiness suddenly shrinking.

"Wow, I don't know. It's just... I've never been away from her for so long before."

Rafe touched Eden's arm to reassure her. "It really would mean a lot to me."

"The baby has been wearing you out lately," Letty reminded her. "Maybe a little free time would do you good." She looked around the restaurant and saw it was filling up.

"Looks like I've got to get back to work," she said and left the table.

"Sure, Eden," said Julia hoping to help knowing it was a good way into Rafe's heart, "a break every once in a while can be a good thing."

"Well, just let me think about it," said Eden as she rubbed the back of her neck. "I'm not saying no. I think I just need to get used to the idea."

"I'm sorry I dropped it on you so suddenly," said Rafe when she saw Eden was having some anxiety. "I just got a little excited. I want to take her to the children's museum and to Central Park, and then I want to drive up to Baltimore and visit Greer. I think she'd love to see Bronte again and it's *only* about a three to four-hour drive depending on traffic." Rafe hoped Eden's anxiety over being apart from Bronte would calm if she knew everything she planned to do while away.

Eden felt suddenly deflated and empty but tried to hide it. "Oh, well," she hesitated, "it sounds really nice. Like I said, let me think about it for a bit." She looked at her watch so she would not have to look at Rafe. "Hey, we have to go," she announced suddenly. She gathered Bronte up and secured her back in her stroller. "See you guys later. Bye, Rafe. I'll call you, okay?"

Rafe smiled warmly at her and Bronte, excited about her trip. "Okay, thanks for considering it. I hope you say yes."

Abby watched Eden as she smiled weakly and then as she turned and walked away. "Rafe, you really are hopeless!"

"Why?" Rafe asked looking at Abby puzzled as she took another bite of food.

"Why did you have to tell her you were thinking about seeing Greer?" complained Abby.

Rafe shrugged. "Why shouldn't I? She should know where Bronte and I are going."

"Rafe," Julia attempted to explain, "believe me when it comes to *other* women and a mother's baby, it can get ugly."

"Eden's not like that. I think she liked Greer, and she knows she was Bronte's first art teacher," Rafe reasoned.

Abby rolled her eyes at Rafe's thick-headedness. "She also knows Greer is your ex-lover."

Rafe frowned at Abby. "Why should that matter to her?"

Abby rolled her eyes again and looked at Julia. "Hopeless."

5

EDEN KINGSLEY WAS following an energetic and spirited Bronte around in the park as she toddled and played. Flynn had joined them and followed Eden as they talked about what he had found on the computer. She hadn't seen or heard from Jake, so Eden was feeling hopeful they would not need the information after all. To be on the safe side, Flynn helped her pick out a new laptop and set it up for her. She felt much better knowing she could turn on her computer and not be watched or overheard. They followed as Bronte decided to leave the swing set and slide behind, and go sit and play with her toy in the grass near a trio of palm trees.

"She's getting so big, and so smart," observed Eden as they sat on a bench near Bronte. "She was incredible at her art lesson yesterday. I'm glad Rafe is okay with me showing up for them every Saturday." She could not help the smile appearing on her face. "Yesterday was a *very* good day."

"Oh, yeah, why?" asked Flynn as he smiled, glad Eden was in good spirits.

"I finally got notice of our final court date for the adoption, and I took the paperwork to Rafe. She was beaming. I think I was too."

"Finally. Maybe Jake and those Stewards will stop harassing you once it is finalized."

"I hope so." She sighed. "I haven't seen or heard from him lately. Have you been able to find out anything more about who hacked into my computer?"

"Well, I didn't get to tell you this last time we met because I got distracted setting up your computer, but I found out the file was uploaded by someone with the username 'ChefDaddy.' Do you know who he is?"

"Shoot! Oh, my god!" she held her hand over her mouth feeling nauseous all over again.

"What?" Flynn asked with concern.

"Flynn," she groaned, "I had a really bad feeling when you first told me about the hacking." She looked at Flynn worriedly. "I don't know who he was exactly. I talked to him in one of the new parent chatrooms when I first started talking online about the inseminations, but," she shook her head, "then things just got—" she stopped again knowing she had no excuses. "Is there any way to find out who he is?"

"Not without going to the host company, and they have privacy policies. It would take a real good hacker or a subpoena to find out."

"I can't believe this. I'm so stupid," said Eden in distress, her good mood crashing into dust. "All of this crap—me having all those feelings for men I didn't know what to do with and hurting Rafe so much she couldn't even look at me, then hiding out from Jake, who I thought I knew and was what I wanted—it may have all started with me getting a 'cyber-f' or whatever they're calling it these days. What is wrong with me?"

"What are you talking about?" Flynn asked in confusion.

"Flynn, I was talking in chat rooms about our insemination process and this guy, ChefDaddy, started talking to me. At first, it was innocent, but then," she sighed, forcing herself to continue, "we ended up," she swallowed embarrassed, "we linked, and we typed sexual things to each other. He would tell me things he wanted to do to me and, well, I didn't stop it." She looked at Flynn's shocked face. "I know! It was wrong, and yes, I know it was the same as cheating. But I stopped, and I never did it again with anyone I swear!" she professed in distress. "I know! I'm a terrible person! All of this is my fault!"

"You didn't know," said Flynn sympathetically after he realized she was talking about a cyber-fuck. He knew people got taken advantage of online all the time, even computer savvy people.

"I should have known. It was all just too easy," she groaned in misery. "I start having feelings about wanting a man and find one online, and then soon after, a man shows up who's ready to get married and move away. One who told me everything I thought I wanted to hear and who practically cut me off from everyone I know."

"Don't do this to yourself. You couldn't have known those things would happen. It's called being catfished," he explained. "Then there's what Jake did. It's just, well, I don't know," he said as he shook his head because this group seemed not to pull punches.

"You don't understand, Flynn. Every time I was angry with Rafe, Jake was there to keep my anger on the surface until I almost did something even more terrible to her than leaving her," Eden explained. "Do you know how close I was to stopping this adoption? This is so messed up." Eden was beside herself with regret.

Flynn touched Eden's shoulder sympathetically. "But you didn't."

"I should have just stopped and taken the time to think things through or see someone professional before blindly following those new feelings." She looked up, and terror crossed her face. "Oh, my god! Flynn!" she hissed and grabbed his arm tight in fear as a dark shadow covered them.

"Hi, Eden, I just want to talk," Jake said calmly with a sad look on his face. "Why are you doing this to us? Did I do something wrong? I just need you to talk to me."

Eden backed away from him and looked toward Bronte. "Just please, stay away," she begged then jerked away and headed toward Bronte.

Flynn placed himself between Eden and Jake. "She doesn't want you around anymore. You should leave her alone."

Jake looked at Flynn and could not hide his revulsion she was spending time with some gay kid. He ignored him and called out to Eden. "Is this what you're moving on to, Eden?" he asked pointing toward Flynn. "I thought you wanted a real man and a real family for your daughter."

"Jake, you should leave. Please, just leave us alone," Eden pleaded trying to hide her fear.

Daniel walked out from behind the palm trees and started to lean down to pick up Bronte. "What a beautiful innocent child."

Eden spun to face Daniel and reached in a panic for Bronte. "Don't touch her!" They both reached down and took hold of Bronte balancing her between them. "Let go of her, let go of my baby!" She ferociously tried to pull her crying baby away from him, but Daniel was bigger and stronger, and he began pushing her back roughly. "No, no! Let go of her!" Eden screamed in terror.

Flynn ran and lunged himself at Daniel catching him off balance knocking him to the ground breaking his grip on Bronte. "Run, Eden!" he yelled. Eden spun away, barely holding onto Bronte, and sprinted away from them.

Angry Eden had broken free, Jake yelled at Daniel. "You take care of him! I'll go after Eden and the baby!"

Daniel jumped up, brushed himself off, and towered over Flynn. "Little man, you just made a big mistake," he growled menacingly.

Eden's adrenaline pumped through her from the terror of the immediate danger to her daughter. She ran as fast as she could while holding tightly to Bronte. Her heart was in her throat and fear burned through her body. She could hear Jake's heavy footsteps behind her getting closer and the gruesome sounds of Flynn and Daniel fighting. She looked back again and tried to see beyond Jake to find Flynn, but he wasn't there, and she couldn't stop her impulse to escape.

She looked up and saw her car. It seemed so far away. Tears of rage sprang from her eyes and blinded her to everything except her immediate need to take flight. Her lungs were on fire as she made it to her car, her anxiety making it so she was barely able to keep a breath in her body.

She pulled her keys from her pocket and frantically pushed the unlock button then yanked the door open. She threw herself and a crying Bronte violently into the car then slammed and locked the doors. She put Bronte in the passenger seat because there was no time to secure her into the car seat. She hastily put a seat belt on the baby as they both cried in fear.

She looked out the window and saw Jake moving closer. Shaking almost uncontrollably, she fought to insert her key into the ignition. She could hear the screams of her frightened child in her ears blocking all other sounds. Waves of fear were numbing her and seemed to freeze her body in place. Her sight seemed to be reduced down to almost a pinpoint, and every breath was a struggle. Her mind railed against her inaction and demanded she move, she run, she get away! But her body wouldn't listen.

Jake brought his hand down hard on the car, creating a menacing explosion of noise startling Eden back into action. She sucked in a painful breath and started the engine and put the car in gear then stomped on the gas as she held her arm out to hold Bronte protectively in the seat. She sped away from the danger at a high speed with the sounds of squealing tires and Bronte's cries echoing around her.

6

LOOKING OVER PAPERWORK in her home office, Rafe Salvaggio was helping the willowy graduate student art teacher with her graduate project budget for the studio. Annie Brown was sitting on the other side of the partners' desk working on her student list and updating contact information on her laptop. Things were going well, and it looked like they had all the paperwork in order for both the grant and Annie's graduate project. When Annie agreed to meet on a Sunday to work, Rafe had been impressed with how dedicated she was to her project.

"I think we'll have enough in the budget to add the sculpting supplies you want for the children," said Rafe as she looked over the numbers.

"Wonderful!" Annie was excited she was able to expand the project. "We have several kids who already have the motor skills to work with the materials."

"Well, we'll know for sure once—" Rafe was cut off by someone pounding on the door. "What the... Who could that be?" she wondered aloud at the interruption. "It's probably the neighbors wanting to swim," she predicted as she went to answer the door. She opened the door and was surprised. "Eden?"

Eden was crying hysterically and shaking. "Rafe, Rafe you have to help us! The park! Some men! Flynn!"

"Eden, calm down," Rafe said steadily . She led Eden with the crying Bronte inside to the couch. "What happened?"

Eden did not sit down and held Bronte closer. "I have to go back for Flynn!"

Rafe grabbed Eden as she tried to go back out the door. "Back where? Eden, what happened?"

"We were in the park by my apartment. Bronte was playing. Ja... a man tried to take her. Flynn was fighting with him and told me to run. He helped me get away, but I don't know what happened to him," she cried desperately needing to get back to help Flynn.

"*Merda!*"[2] Rafe got on her phone and called Jude for help. "Jude you have to go to the park over by Eden's place. I think Flynn may be there, and he may be hurt. I'm going to call the police. Okay, hurry!" She dialed again as she paced impatiently. "I need to report an attempted kidnapping and attack in the

---

[2] Shit!

Westside park," Rafe gave the police the park information as well as her own. "One person may still be there hurt. I have a friend here who came to me for help. I sent another friend to the park to see if she can find the person who may be hurt. Yes, she's safe here now. Okay, I'll be at this number. Yes, it's the correct address. I understand." She hung up the phone and went to Eden and Bronte.

Eden was finally sitting and rocking Bronte. "I'm sorry. I'm so sorry," she repeated as the memory of the man trying to pull Bronte away from her ran through her mind. Jake's angry face kept flashing in her vision as Bronte cried in her arms.

Rafe sat next to Eden and put her arm around her to comfort her and the crying Bronte. "It's okay. Jude and the police are on their way to find out about Flynn. Here, let me take Bronte and calm her down, okay?" Rafe reached for the crying baby.

"No, don't take her! Don't!" Eden cried and held Bronte tighter.

"Okay, it's okay. I won't take her." Rafe worried Eden might be on the verge of a serious anxiety attack. "Just loosen your grip so she can breathe and calm down."

Annie was shocked at what was happening and not sure how to react. "Is there anything I can do?"

Rafe shook her head. "The police will be here soon. Why don't you go ahead and go home? Everything will be fine."

Annie grabbed her things. "I hope your friends will be okay. Call me if you need anything."

"Thank you, I will," said Rafe then turned her attention back to Eden and Bronte. "Everything will be okay," she said and reflexively rubbed Eden's back and neck like she used to do when she had problems with her anxiety. "You're safe now, *bella*."

7

THE POLICE HAD been at Rafe Salvaggio's house for over two hours interviewing Eden and Rafe. They were finally satisfied with their notes for the incident report and were about to leave. Rafe had convinced Eden to put Bronte to bed, and the baby was finally asleep. Eden was sitting on the couch, pale and still not quite recovered from the terror she had experienced.

Rafe walked the police officers to the door. "Maybe she'll be able to tell us more tomorrow. She's very shaken up. She's always had some anxiety issues, and it makes things hard for her sometimes."

"Here's my card. Just call if she can tell us more," said the lead police officer.

"Thank you," said Rafe taking the card. "We will."

Rafe closed the door then went to the kitchen and poured a glass of red wine. She went back to the living room and handed the wine to Eden as she stood in front of her. "Take a few sips, bella," she said softly hoping the wine would put color back in her face. "It'll help calm you." She watched as Eden took a few sips then wiped her eyes. Rafe took the glass and sat it on the table. "Eden, maybe you should leave Bronte here tonight," she said gently. "I can get the sitter to come and watch her in the morning, and you can rest."

Eden grabbed Rafe's hand and looked up at her with terror in her eyes. "I can't go back out there. He may be out there waiting," she said as she trembled.

Worried and unsure about Eden's state of mind, she sat down next to her. "Who Eden?"

Eden hesitated because she knew she could not tell her about Jake, not yet, not now. She looked desperately into Rafe's eyes. "The man, the man from the park," she said shakily.

Rafe rubbed Eden's back and tried to console her. "It's okay. He doesn't know where you or I live. Do you want me to call Jake for you, or someone else?"

Hearing her say Jake's name sent Eden into another panic. "No, no, I don't want you to call him! I don't want you to call anyone. I, I just can't go out there!" she cried and clung to Rafe's hand tighter.

Rafe held onto Eden's hand with concern, and a decision took hold of her as her intuition kicked into action. "Okay, you can stay here. I'll just go and get the guest bedroom ready. You and Bronte can sleep in there tonight." She tried to get up, but Eden wouldn't let go.

"Wait. Don't let go yet," she said as she held Rafe's hand tightly. "Rafe, you know I'm not with Jake." Her eyes pleaded with Rafe to believe her. "I'm never going back to Jake."

"Okay, it's okay." Rafe brushed Eden's hair from her tear-stained face and then held Eden to her shoulder hoping to calm her. Eden put her face into Rafe's neck and then gently kissed her there. "Eden, stop." Rafe broke away and looked at her sadly. "I'll get your room ready," Rafe said softly and walked away.

"Oh, no, no," Eden groaned. "Dang it! What am I doing?" she asked herself softly. She could not believe what she had done—kissed her neck.

8

RAFE SALVAGGIO HAD spent the evening trying to keep Eden calm and help her through her anxiety until she was able to sleep. Eden finished her glass of red wine, took a warm shower, and then took some meds for her pain. For a while, Rafe sat next to Eden and let her hold onto her hand and arm, but she made sure the kissing did not happen again. She was worried about Eden and what had happened in the park. She was also worried about how Flynn was doing after Jude called and told her she was going with him to the hospital last night. Hopefully, Flynn would be able to tell the police more than Eden had been able to tell.

This morning, Rafe was up early to let Letty and Jude into the house. When they all gathered in the kitchen, Letty sat out some pastries she had brought and poured orange juice for each of them.

Rafe was sitting next to Jude at the kitchen island. "So how is he?" Rafe asked Jude who looked haggard.

Jude shook her head and yawned. She had been with Flynn most of the night. "He's fine. Some bruised ribs, a black eye, and some scrapes. He says he doesn't remember much. He says it's all a blur. I think he's most pissed about them wanting to keep him overnight."

"He may have saved the life of my daughter," Rafe said soberly.

"And Eden's," offered Letty wondering why Rafe was acting so odd this morning.

"Yes, and Eden's." Rafe finished her orange juice and looked at both of them. "Listen, can one of you stay with her and make sure she gets home okay? I called her office and told them she wouldn't be in today."

"Don't worry. We'll take care of her," Letty assured her.

"I'll come back later. I have a nine o'clock appointment," said Jude as she sat down her glass and got up from the table to leave. "Bye," she said and took a pastry to go.

"Bye, thanks, Jude," said Rafe as Jude made her way out of the house.

"Why are you in such a hurry to get out of here?" asked Letty suspiciously.

"I can't be here when she wakes up." Rafe shook her head with concern. "I think she would prefer it."

"Why would she prefer for you not to be here? She came to you for help."

"Letty, last night," she hesitated. "Last night, she was upset, and she started kissing my neck. I think she was just a little out of her mind. If I'm not here, maybe she won't be embarrassed or feel bad." Rafe ignored the confused look on Letty's face. "Call me when you find out more about Flynn."

Rafe grabbed her keys and a pastry and then headed out of the house, leaving Letty to take care of Eden and Bronte until Eden thought she could leave.

9

FLYNN OGDEN CHECKED himself out of the hospital just before noon. He walked out of the cold hospital and then kept walking into the warmth of the city for a while. He had to think. He had to think of a way to make sure he was not caught in a position like last night again. Those people Jake was involved with were more dangerous than Eden thought.

He stared into a store window for a moment then walked inside the pawnshop. Looking through display cases, his black eye and the cut across his nose were reflected in the glass—a reminder of what crossing paths with anyone from the Stewards and Jake would bring.

The tall slick sales clerk came over and just looked at Flynn without speaking as he leaned against the shelves behind him. He chewed on his toothpick with his arms crossed and waited. He knew the items in that particular case did not need a sales pitch. If someone wanted one, they would buy one.

"How much is this one?" Flynn asked and pointed at an item in the case.

"Good choice," he said and leaned over the case. "Let's see. It runs six hundred and fifty dollars."

"Do you have anything cheaper? I've got four hundred."

"Sure, come over here," suggested the clerk. "We have this one. It's marked four fifty, but I can sell to you for four. If you buy it with cash, I'll throw in some cartridges for target practice. We have a firing range in the back if you need one."

"So, how long do I have to wait?"

"It's a ten day waiting period. It gives you time to fulfill all the legal requirements for ownership."

"Okay, I'll take it."

10

ORANGE PAINT LIBERALLY covered all of Bronte's extremities from the art lesson with her teacher Annie and the rest of the kids. Eden Kingsley carried her possessively into Rafe Salvaggio's guest bathroom to clean her up from her messy artwork. It had been a week, but Eden was still a little shaken from her experience in the park, and she had a hard time letting Bronte out of her sight.

Rafe silently followed her inside and filled the tub while Eden took off Bronte's paint-covered t-shirt and diaper. She turned to take Bronte from Eden. As Eden reluctantly let go of Bronte, she ran her hand gently but purposely across Rafe's hand and arm. Rafe ignored it, put Bronte into the tub, and began to clean her up. *"Fateci lavare il bambina,"*[3] she cooed to her as Eden looked on with a drawn expression on her face.

Rafe was on edge and was not sure how to handle what was happening. Eden was acting strange again. She was touching her, looking at her, and generally making Rafe wonder if she had lost her mind. She had been doing this all week whenever they were in the same room. Eden was hesitant to leave Bronte and Rafe understood, but all the rest was a mystery, and Rafe just wanted her to stop.

Eden knelt down next to Rafe and began to help wash Bronte. She reached across Rafe to put the soap on the edge of the tub, their bare shoulders touched, their eyes met, and Eden leaned toward Rafe slightly. Rafe backed away quickly and got up to get a towel. She handed the towel to Eden then stepped back and pulled her phone from her pocket to look at the time. It was almost one o'clock.

Eden wrapped Bronte in the towel and dried her off. "So, do you have plans for today?" she asked softly noticing Rafe checking her phone.

"Yes."

"Are you meeting Julia?"

"No," Rafe said calmly not wanting to tell her she had a coffee date with a woman she met while at a networking event she attended.

"Oh." She paused. "So what time is the sitter getting here?"

---

[3] Let's wash the baby

"In about an hour or so," Rafe said getting annoyed with Eden's questions.

"Do you mind if I stay until she comes?"

"What for?" Rafe asked in exasperation. "Don't you have things to do? A new boyfriend or something?"

"No, there's no one," confessed Eden softly shaking her head. "I'd like to play with Bronte and make her lunch."

On edge but knowing Eden was still dealing with her fears and anxiety issues, she reluctantly relented. "Sure, okay. I'll just go get ready while you take care of her."

It only took Rafe about twenty minutes to shower and dress for the night out. She chose to dress casually in her favorite pair of jeans and her favorite super soft bamboo shirt. She had been sitting on her bed since the time she was dressed not wanting to leave her room. Eden was in the kitchen cleaning up after feeding Bronte, and Rafe had not wanted to interact with her alone again.

When Rafe heard the sound of the doorbell, she finally came out of her room and went to answer it. Thankfully, it was the nanny, Lydia.

"Hi," said Rafe with a smile and ushered her inside.

"Hi," Lydia said in her bubbly voice. "Where's Bronte?"

Eden appeared holding Bronte in her arms. "Here she is. She's had a bath, and she's had some lunch."

Lydia held her hands out, and Bronte reached happily for her. "Okay, any special instructions?"

"No," said Rafe quickly. "I should be back in a few hours." She held the door open as Eden gathered her purse and sweater.

"Okay, bye." Lydia waved then turned to take Bronte to where her toys were waiting.

Rafe closed the door behind her and made sure it was locked. She made her way to her car and Eden followed her.

Eden caught up to Rafe and touched her arm to get her attention. "Thanks for letting me stay," she said earnestly.

"No problem," Rafe answered working to control and hide her anger and uneasiness.

Eden looked at Rafe with soft eyes and then touched Rafe's arm again with the tip of her fingers feeling the softness of her bamboo shirt.

"You look really good." She looked down at the ground and fought to stop herself from touching Rafe again. She was not sure why, but she found herself needing to touch Rafe when she was with her. Maybe it was because it was reassuring to know she was close. She could see Rafe didn't like it. She tried not to do it, but it still just kept happening. She hated herself because she didn't want to do it, but she couldn't help it.

Rafe took a calming breath and looked closely at Eden. She was disheveled and pale with dark circles around her eyes, still showing signs of strain and anxiety from her encounter at the park.

Losing a little of her resolve and letting go of her anger, Rafe sighed. "Thanks." She looked at her phone again. "I've got to go, or I'll be late."

Eden watched Rafe go. "Have a good day," she called after her.

Rafe made it to her car and got inside without looking back. She looked out her window and saw Eden had finally gone to her own car.

"What does she want?" she asked herself then shook her head and took off for her coffee date.

11

MAKING HER WAY across The Kiki Bistro at dinner time, Letty Carver was checking on her customers. It was almost dinner rush, so she needed to make sure everything was ready to go and tables were set. She saw Stacey and Jude were already eating an early dinner, and it made her happy her place was a second home for some. She loved having regular customers she got to know on a first name basis because sometimes, it was like having an extended family. Letty saw Rafe walk in to join her friends and approached their table. "Hey, sweet Cugina! Eden was looking for you."

Rafe looked around annoyed. "Is she here?" It had been four days since her last strange encounter with Eden, and she had been doing her best to make sure they had space from each other.

"No, she and Bronte left about ten minutes ago." Letty saw the relief on Rafe's face, and it piqued her curiosity. "Are you avoiding her?"

"What, no," Rafe stammered, "What are you talking about?"

Stacey looked at Rafe and raised her eyebrows in disbelief. "Well, let's see, she walks in, you walk out."

"She sits down, you stand up," Jude joined in. "It's so obvious."

Rafe shifted uncomfortably in her seat. "Eden's been acting strange since the park thing," she explained while wishing they would all mind their own business and drop it.

"What do you mean, strange?" asked Letty as she sat down across from Rafe.

"Just strange," Rafe said quickly and tried to wave the conversation away.

Letty took a long look at Rafe and knew there was more to the story. "All I've seen is her being nice to you lately." She was glad they were getting along even if it was only for Bronte's sake, and she didn't want Rafe messing it up. They had lost enough time with the baby, and she didn't want to miss out on watching the baby grow up again. She knew things had been hard, but to fix things, Rafe had to make an effort too, even if she was still upset.

Frustrated Letty would not let it drop, Rafe lost some of her control and threw up her hands. "What she's doing is *not* being nice. She tries to stand too close, she goes out of her way to touch me on my hand or arm or wherever, and it's getting old."

Jude laughed and looked at Rafe slyly. "So, she's pulling a Rafe Salvaggio on you?

"What?" Rafe said shaking her head in confusion. "What are you talking about?"

"She's putting the moves on you," giggled Stacey.

Rafe did not see the humor and their teasing was not helping her mood. "No," she said firmly. "What she's doing is acting crazy."

"Now wait a minute," interjected Letty. "Maybe she's just trying to tell you something, Rafe."

"Tell me what?" she asked trying to keep her voice under control.

"I don't know." Letty huffed. "To thank you, maybe."

"Thank me for what?" Rafe retorted in confusion.

"Well, possibly for being there for her the other night," Letty said in her matter of fact voice.

Rafe threw up her hands again in frustration. "Then why doesn't she just say *thank you*?"

Letty put her hand on Rafe's hand to calm her. "Or, Rafe, maybe it's more."

"More what? What does she want? You think she wants us back together?" She pulled her hand away. "It's just not possible."

"Why not?" Stacey chimed in.

Rafe looked at Stacey as if she were crazy. "You're kidding, right? All of you know every reason why not."

Letty sat back and shook her head sadly. "So you're going to let all of those reasons get in the way of what you want?"

"What I want?" Rafe choked out. "I thought we were talking about Eden.

"I can't believe you." Letty sighed. "You really are turning into your father. You just can't, or won't, see and accept maybe someone wants forgiveness for a mistake. You deserve the forgiveness, but she doesn't." Rafe began to speak, and Letty cut her off. "No, you're just building up a wall of self-righteousness instead of being open to letting others have some control and pride in their life. You just turn a blind eye to any kind of peace offering they might try to offer."

"Letty, you're being ridiculous," Rafe countered. She shook her head at her because Eden was definitely not trying to give her a peace offering. She was not sure what she was doing, but it was not an offering.

Letty shook her head again. "I don't think so. You have the same passion in you that made all those women fall in love with your dad, and just like him, you're letting your passion turn into stubbornness."

Rafe was incensed. Her father had high standards, drive, and passion. Forgiveness has nothing to do with any of those things. Forgiveness doesn't fix mistakes, and Eden certainly did not seem to be asking for any type of forgiveness. And if she was, what was there to forgive? Rafe had no power to make her feel better about the choices she made, and it certainly was not her job to tell Eden her choice was a mistake warranting some kind of forgiveness.

Now it seemed to Rafe they were all attacking her for things Eden had done and making it seem like it was in her power to forgive and solve all of Eden's problems. It was just as crazy as what Eden was doing.

"Self-righteousness and stubbornness? Great, more things to add to my list of faults. Anything else?" she asked sullenly.

Letty could see the conversation was getting out of control and, Rafe was not happy. "Rafe," she said with sensitivity, "it's just you're cutting off all possibilities where Eden is concerned, and maybe it's a mistake. If she's doing all those things, she may be thinking about being with you again."

"When she sees you out with those other women, she does always make some excuse to leave," said Stacey, and Jude nodded her agreement.

Rafe looked at Letty calmly and tried to make her see the facts. "I am not who she wants. She has made it *very* clear," she said firmly. She looked at everyone at the table. "Remember those feelings she can't help having? They aren't for me. They're for men. In case you haven't noticed, I am not a man. She's moved on to men, and now she's broken up with her boyfriend, so maybe she just thinks I'll do in a pinch. Not going to happen."

Letty grimaced and shook her head at Rafe's stubbornness. "But she's not with anyone, Rafe. Specifically, she is not with a man. Maybe it means she doesn't feel that way anymore."

"Maybe it really wasn't men she wanted," Jude added. "Maybe she just wanted... you know." She grinned and winked.

Rafe rolled her eyes. "Jude." She groaned.

"Wait, what's wrong with that? I know I'd like it," Stacey confessed with a giggle.

Letty laughed and covered her grin with her hand. "You guys aren't talking about what I think you are, are you?"

"The strap-on!" Jude proclaimed in a deep voice.

"No," Rafe said flatly.

"No?" Stacey moaned with feigned disappointment. "Why not?"

"I don't use one," Rafe said and leaned back in her chair.

"Ever?" asked Stacey surprised.

Rafe sighed because she did not want to have this conversation. "No, I've used one. I just don't need to use one." She stopped and shook her head. "I'm not talking to you guys about this."

"Aww, why not?" whined Stacey playfully. "You can use one, but you don't," she said suspiciously. "Not skilled in that area?"

"Fuck you, Stacey." Rafe sneered. "I've been making love to women half my life. I can do things with or without one you've never even dreamed possible."

Stacey just laughed and pressed on. She loved when Rafe got started on a fusillade of creative curse words, and if things went well, she might get to witness it happen tonight. "So you guys were together for almost five years, and you never used one? Did you use other things?"

Rafe closed her eyes and fought to control her emotions. She knew they were teasing, but she was not in the mood. "We never used one, and I am not going to discuss what things we did use with you. If you want to learn how to fuck someone, go buy a book."

"I can't believe you," Stacey insisted happily ignoring her flippant remark. "You really must be some kind of miracle worker in bed," she said with a grin.

"Well, she didn't complain for almost five years," snapped Rafe angrily wishing Stacey would back off.

Letty saw her chance to get this conversation back to the actual problem. "So now since she has complained about needing something else, you refuse to give it to her?"

Rafe looked at Letty in disbelief she would even say that to her. "I didn't refuse her anything. It wasn't me she wanted. She is the one who changed, she is the one who stopped loving me, and she is the one who broke up our family!"

"Oh, Rafe," Letty sighed heavily, recognizing the signs they were getting nowhere. "You really are stubborn. You know you aren't completely innocent when it comes to the reasons you and Eden split." She looked at the frown on Rafe's face, and then she got up to get back to her customers.

Rafe watched Letty walk away as she ran her hands through her hair. *Why are they suddenly sticking up for Eden and giving me a hard time?* She saw Julia walk in and was relieved. *Finally,* she thought, *someone who had actually seen Eden acting crazy.*

"Hello, everyone. Why all the serious faces?" Julia asked as she joined the group at the table.

Stacey saw her chance to go back to her topic. "We just found out Rafe won't use a strap-on."

Julia made a disgusted face. "Ugh, I'm with Rafe. I guess I'm just a purist."

Jude laughed hard. "You're so full of shit."

Julia gave Jude a smirk and then ignored her. "So, who wants her to use one on them?"

Stacey moved close to Julia as if they were co-conspirators. "Eden, we think."

"Really?" Julia's said as her eyebrows arched and she looked at Rafe expectantly wondering if she was actually considering being with Eden again. She certainly hoped not.

"No," Rafe said in a flat tone.

Stacey took it upon herself to explain further. "Eden has been *nice* to Rafe, getting too close.

"Nice? Really?" Julia mused happy with Rafe's answer but wanting to join in the teasing. "Maybe you should just seduce her for old time sake."

"Another wager, Julia?" challenged Rafe crossly.

"Oh no, I've learned my lesson there," Julia sighed with regret at all the wagers she had lost with Rafe. "But maybe, if she wants you, and you still want her, seducing her would be good for both of you." She paused and looked curiously at Rafe and proceeded carefully. "Do you still want her?"

Rafe closed her eyes, shook her head, and tried a new way to reason with them. "Like Abby keeps reminding me, she's not just another one of my conquests I can use my 'wildling' ways on," she said making angry air quotes with her hands then crossing her arms as she leaned back in her chair. "And I don't think *she* wants *me*. Besides, putting on a strap-on doesn't make you a man."

"So true," Stacey piped in, "but from what I've heard it makes you better than a man." Everyone gave Stacey a surprised look, and Jude folded over in laughter almost falling from her chair.

Julia, who had let herself be infected with Jude's laughter, finally got herself back under control. "Since when do you listen to Abby?" she asked Rafe while wiping away her tears of laughter. "Maybe Eden would like to be one of your conquests. If you do this, and it doesn't work out," she shrugged, "then maybe it'll be easier for both of you to move on." She could only hope. "And if it works out," she winked, "then it could be a good thing too."

Rafe could not accept their suggestion as a good idea. "What if it works out either way for only one of us?"

"Then at least one of you can move on," reasoned Jude.

"I just don't think it's going to happen," Rafe said maintaining her opinion stubbornly.

12

RAFE WALKED INTO her house and sat her collection of shopping bags down on the dining room table. She had done some impulse shopping after dinner hoping it would make her feel better.

It hadn't.

She pulled out the plain brown box from inside one of the bags. She opened the box, pulled another box half way out, then opened it and looked inside. She looked at the new strap-on underwear—the sales clerk had told her was the latest thing—and the blue dong that came with the set. She then shook her head and shoved it all back in the box and put it back in the shopping bag.

"What the hell am I doing?" she asked herself realizing she had let her friends get to her tonight. "I can't do this," she said to herself. She turned and walked out of the dining room, leaving her purchase behind.

13

ABBY VAN FALKOV had met Rafe Salvaggio almost eight years ago at a party in West Hollywood for the grand opening of a new nightclub. Several people had pointed Rafe out, and it seemed everyone had a story about her. Intrigued, Abby put herself in Rafe's path and was rewarded for her efforts. They had left the party together, and Rafe led Abby to her house and into her bedroom.

Rafe smiled with just the corner of her mouth at Abby and then licked her lips. "Here, let me take your glass," Rafe said keeping her Italian accent on as she took the wine glass from Abby. She drank the last of the wine before dropping the glass onto the thick rug covering the wood floor.

Abby raised her eyebrows and swallowed nervously. "So, I'm curious. Why me? I mean, what made you want to bring me home tonight?"

Rafe gave a small shrug. "You made me laugh." She pulled Abby toward her and kissed her as they stood beside the bed.

Abby broke away for air. "Wow." She swallowed. "I was told you were intense—just not how intense."

Rafe gave a throaty laugh. "So, you know who I am?" she asked as she proceeded to remove her own top revealing she was braless.

"Who doesn't?" Abby squeaked as she got an eye full of Rafe's perfect olive skin and her well-formed abs.

"*Quello va bene,*"[4] Rafe murmured and began kissing her neck as she pulled off Abby's shirt.

Abby tried to maintain control of herself because Rafe's Italian accent was really turning her on. She had to find out everything she could about this woman. Knowing things about everyone was what drove her.

"Well, I was just wondering," she started, but her words were muffled by Rafe's kisses. Her body reacted as Rafe moved her hands over the front of her jeans and began to open them. "Oh, my god. You're really fast. I'd heard stories but, you know, you can't believe everything said out there. Oh," she took a short intake of breath at Rafe's hand entering her jeans. "I mean some people can really exaggerate. There was this one girl who said you—"

Rafe kissed her to cut off her words. "Do you always talk this much when someone is making love to you?" She moved her kisses to Abby's chest and to her lace bound breasts at the same time slipping out of her own pants.

---

[4] That is good,

"Ha," her voice broke, "no, I just. I just wanted to ask you. Oh, fuck that feels good. I mean..." She panted. "I'd really like you to use a, you know. A strap-on."

Rafe's only reaction was a small twitch of her lips. "No," she whispered as she kissed through the lace of Abby's bra and pulled down the shoulder straps.

"Mmm..." The moan came out of Abby uncontrollably. She was used to her lovers taking her cues and was confused at Rafe's reluctance. "Oh, if you don't have one," she said between heavy breaths, "I have one in my car."

Rafe stopped kissing Abby and gave her an amused smile. "You really are a funny little thing, aren't you?" Rafe said to the sweet freckled-faced girl in her soft, raspy voice thick with her Italian accent.

Abby wasn't sure what Rafe meant. She thought maybe Rafe did not believe her. "No, well," she explained," really, I do, have one in my car."

Rafe moved her face close. Abby could feel Rafe's breath on her mouth when she softly spoke. "Abby, I'm not going to use one. I can assure you I'm enough." She ran her warm hand down Abby's stomach and between her legs watching her reaction with amusement. "But if you think I'm not enough, I can stop," she paused for effect, "do you want me to stop?"

"Oh, shit no," was all Abby could manage.

"Good," purred Rafe as she pulled off the rest of Abby's clothes and kissed her neck and shoulders as her hands caressed her body.

"I'm just... just wondering. Well, why not?" Abby asked between her small catches of breath, not one to give up easily.

Smoothly moving to Abby's breasts, Rafe mumbled, "It just gets in my way."

"In your way?" Abby pressed.

Holding back a bit of exasperation, Rafe stopped and looked at Abby. "Close your eyes." She waited until Abby complied. "Very good," she said softly. "Do you feel that?" she asked as she pressed against her.

"Ye... yes," Abby cried out as the sensations in her body pushed her questions away.

Breathily, as she delved her hand into Abby's body, Rafe whispered, "So can I. We don't need anything that would distance us. I need to feel your every reaction. I need you to feel my passion. It can't happen if something is between us. We just need ourselves. You wouldn't add paint to a Picasso, would you?"

"Picasso?" Abby repeated weakly.

Rafe made her way down Abby with her tongue and lingered until she made her breathless again, then found her way back up slowly and spoke through her kisses. "If you added paint to a Picasso, you could make it look nice, but the Picasso would still be ruined. What's the point," she said heavily, "of ruining a masterpiece?" She kissed her on the mouth and ran her hands slowly but deftly over her body again.

"Master... piece?" was all Abby could manage.

"Yes," said Rafe softly, "we're creating a masterpiece right now."

"I don't..." Abby started.

"Shhh, listen," said Rafe in a thick sensuous accent as she caressed Abby's face and then continued exploring her body. "Making love is like creating a masterpiece, except when making love, you have to consider the feelings of the canvas, as well as the artist. Right now, you're the canvas, and I'm the artist. Just relax."

Rafe moved behind Abby and ran her hands down her back, then knelt as she gently left a series of burning kisses down Abby's spine to her lower back. "Usually, the canvas always gets all of the attention, all of the color and all of the feelings of the artist." She reached her hand through Abby's legs from behind and began a methodical exploration while her face was pressed against the curve of her lower back. "The closest an artist can get to a canvas is when the artist gives up all the tools and brushes and uses only their own hands and body."

She felt Abby suddenly go rigid and smiled with erotic pleasure for the sensation of her new throbbing discovery. She slowly withdrew her hand, allowing Abby to stay in her place, being careful not to touch her sensitive area again. She stood and kissed Abby on her shoulders and stepped around to face her.

She began kissing her body again and spoke between her kisses. "Then the artist can really learn the canvas and explore what can be done to it, to make it into a masterpiece. Every... time... it's touched." Rafe kissed Abby on her lips. "Abby, open your eyes," she said softly.

"I can't yet," quavered Abby. Slowly, Abby began to open her eyes, but it seemed any little movement took the sensation Rafe created in her to ebb away. When her eyes finally opened, she saw Rafe standing in front of her, her black curls in disarray and an impish smile on her face. When she looked into Rafe's steel gray-blue eyes, she could see a hungry glint in them, and it made her shudder with anticipation.

"Abby," she said again, "breathe."

Letting out a ragged breath, "Sorry," Abby apologized.

Rafe brought her lips to Abby's ear and whispered, "Can you still feel me?" She watched Abby as she could only nod slowly. Moving her body against Abby's, she locked Abby in place with her hungry gaze and reached down to feel the wetness she brought out of her as she spoke softly. "You see, as the artist, I'm giving you all of my passion. I can touch you," she said as she brought her wet hand to her mouth and ran her fingers over her own lips and then over Abby's. "I can taste you." She kissed her deeply and worked her way down to her breasts holding tightly to her arms and waist. "I can smell you." She placed her ear against her heart as she caressed her breasts. "I can hear you." She moved up until she was looking into her eyes again. "I can see you." She pulled her body tightly to hers and held her gaze until Abby was able to break away from it.

Reeling from the sensation of Rafe's fiery body against hers, Abby finally broke Rafe's gaze but not before she realized Rafe had just caused a sensation in her she had never felt before. She tried to name it but couldn't, and the concern showed on her face.

"What did you just do?"

Rafe smiled again. "I'm still doing it," she breathed, "*la magia zingara.*" She grinned, and still holding her close, she took Abby's hand, put her fingers into her mouth, and licked them. She then took Abby's dampened hand and placed it against herself and moved it down her own body and down between her legs. "Making a masterpiece."

Abby could feel the heat of Rafe's body flow through her hand, and the passion transferred crashed through her whole body. She could not help but lunge into Rafe's body and recklessly begin kissing her.

"I want you now," she moaned.

Letting out a soft roguish laugh, Rafe held onto Abby's upper arm tightly and returned her passionate kisses. "Now, the canvas comes alive and can give the passion back to the artist. That exchange is the only thing we need between us."

She pushed Abby down to her knees, and Abby began her own exploration. Rafe was on the edge. She pushed Abby from her and pulled her face up so she could kiss her as she forced her back onto the floor, and they reached for each other. Rafe retraced her steps back to the sensitive place of Abby's she had found earlier and touched it gingerly. She felt Abby's body rocking and writhing against her.

"I don't know if I can hold on. My god." Abby gasped. "How are you doing that?

"You can," Rafe said encouragingly as she squeezed Abby's shoulder tightly with her free hand. She moved her body with Abby's and could feel her own climax coming. "Abby, open your eyes," she whispered, "open them."

Abby forced her eyes open and found Rafe's hungry gaze enveloping her. She saw Rafe's open-mouthed impish smile again just before her lips covered her mouth. As they arched uncontrollably, and she released a cry of rapture, she realized the door to her soul had been opened, and Rafe just took a piece of it from her. As she slowly recovered from the trauma, she looked up at the grin on Rafe's face. "You actually are some kind of wild soul possessor, aren't you?"

Rafe laughed breathlessly as she rolled onto her back against the soft carpet. "That's a first. No one around here has ever asked me before."

Abby put her hand on her own chest. "I swear you tore out a piece of my soul." She looked at Rafe, and she just looked back at her with those smoldering steel gray-blue eyes. "I researched you. I know what your last name translates to," Abby confessed. Another wave of electric shock ran through her from her clit to her chest. "You know what... I don't care. I think I love you!"

Rafe laughed and sat up. "Abby, that wasn't love. It was technique." She got up, gently pressing her hand on Abby's abdomen, and headed for the kitchen. "I need more wine."

Abby felt the heat from Rafe's hand surge through her and surround her heart, then make its way back down through her body as it reacted in anticipation of the return of Rafe's touch. She put her hand on her stomach where Rafe touched her.

"Jesus, I think she just made me come again." But Rafe had just left her for some wine, her mind screamed. "She's definitely a soul possessing wildling!"

14

SINCE APPLYING FOR the Jackson-Goyer Grant, work had been hectic for Rafe Salvaggio. She and her department were working hard to be ready in case they were selected for the prestigious grant they had applied for just after she started working at the college. If they were nominated as a finalist, they would go to New York to give a presentation in front of the selection committee.

Rafe was in her office pacing the floor and talking into her phone's wireless headset. "I'll have the additional information sent next-day air to you today. Of course. Your consideration of our application is greatly appreciated."

Rafe's assistant, Brandy, looked in and signaled she needed something.

Rafe motioned for her to wait. "Not a problem, I'll add it to the information I am sending you. Our being picked to be on the final list for consideration is wonderful news. No, no, thank you. Thank you very much. Goodbye." She turned to her assistant. "What is it, Brandy?"

"There's a man outside who needs to see you," she said and pointed to the seating area. "He says it's urgent."

"Oh," Rafe said, distracted, "well, who is he?"

"Mr. Milts," she said reading from her notebook.

Rafe frowned, not recognizing the name. "Did he say who he's with?"

"No, he just says it's urgent." She shifted nervously because she knew Dean Salvaggio hated it when she was not well prepped for someone coming into her office.

"Okay, send him in," she said trying not to show her frustration at the unexpected interruption. She just hoped he would not take up too much time. They had a lot to do.

She wrote some notes on a piece of paper and handed it to Brandy. "I need you to send the things on this list to the Jackson-Goyer Foundation Grant Committee. The address is there. Make sure it goes out next-day air today. And Brandy, don't forget to make copies of what we're sending and put it in the file." Rafe was energized at the thought of going to New York. "Call President Biggalow and let her know we're going to be giving them the presentation Wednesday, so we need to book our flights. Then see if you can get Eden on the line. I need to see if she's made her decision about letting me take Bronte with me to New York." She walked around her desk to meet Mr. Milts as he walked in before Brandy told him it was okay.

"Rafaella E. Salvaggio?" he asked formally.

"Yes, I'm Rafe Salvaggio."

"This is for you." He handed her a packet of papers.

Rafe frowned and looked at the packet. "What is it?"

Mr. Milts just smiled. "You've been served. Have a nice day," he said and left quickly.

Rafe watched him walk away in confusion. She opened the packet and looked through the papers. "What the hell is this?" She shuffled through them more. "Injunction? Fuck!" She went to her desk and punched in a phone number on her phone angrily. "This is Rafe Salvaggio. I need to talk to Katheryn. Now! Katheryn?" She listened for a moment. "So you know about this? Does Eden? What the hell is going on? No, I'll be there in twenty minutes."

15

AT KATHERYN HARDAM'S Law Office the staff was well prepared for Rafe's arrival. They knew she was not as patient as most clients, and they were to make sure she was well taken care of whenever she was in the office. They also knew she was not only one of Katheryn's favorite clients, but she was one of the biggest and had been with the firm since it was formed.

Over the years, Rafe had become a top priority client as her restoration company grew and she needed more legal work done. When she came in, she never waited around in the waiting area. She always went straight into Katheryn's office because, as Rafe reasoned, she paid her enough she should not have to wait, and her time had to be more valuable if she was helping to pay for such a nice office. In exchange for this agreement, Katheryn had built a thriving business and gained a lot of wealthy clients, so Rafe's peculiarities were well worth any inconvenience.

Rafe had Katheryn on a permanent retainer because of all her business deals around the world. Katheryn currently had several lawyers and paralegals in her office who worked exclusively on legal matters on her behalf. Between selling her and her father's businesses, and all the real estate she inherited around the world, then selling her restoration business, Rafe kept the office very busy.

The entire building holding the offices had been restored and designed by Rafe's company. When Katheryn decided to open her own offices, she bought the property before it was finished based on what she saw and the plans Rafe had shown her. It not only served as her law offices, but it was a great investment because it was also income property, and she rented out the remaining offices in the building. The law offices were opulent with all of the old school wood and leather one would expect in the historic building. Katheryn even had a hidden bar in her office behind her bookcase left from when the place was a speakeasy.

Rafe stormed into the office, eyes blazing, and went past the receptionist and directly into Katheryn's office. Katheryn looked up as Rafe entered. "Ah, there you are."

"What the fuck is this?" Rafe demanded and threw the papers at Katheryn's desk.

"This would be an injunction filed against your adoption of Bronte based on moral standards and children's rights," Katheryn confirmed.

"Who the hell filed it and where's Eden? Does she know about this?" Rafe demanded as she shook with anger.

"I called Eden right after I talked to you. She sounded just as upset as you are and is on her way here. I suggest you sit down so I can explain what this seems to be about," she replied trying to get her client calm before Eden got there.

Rafe collapsed onto the leather chair in front of Katheryn's desk. "It means I won't be able to adopt Bronte, doesn't it? Why is this happening? Who the hell are these people?"

"It will delay things but don't give up hope yet. We have time to file an answer to the injunction," she assured Rafe. Katheryn looked up just as the receptionist showed Eden in and Rafe stood to face her.

"Rafe, Katheryn, what's happening? Who's filing this injunction?" Eden was clearly shaken. She was pale, and her eyes were red from crying.

Still enraged, Rafe all but screamed at Eden. "You don't know? Where's Bronte?"

"No, I don't," she said shakily under Rafe's angry stare. "Bronte's with Lydia at school."

Katheryn stepped between them to take control of the situation. "Both of you sit down." She motioned them to the large leather chairs in front of her oversized antique desk. After waiting for them to sit, she made her way around to her own chair. "Now let's just go over the facts," she said evenly and calmly. "This injunction has been filed by a low profile watch-dog religious group called *Stewards to the Protection of the Innocence and Morals of Youths.*"

Eden's eyes widened in recognition, and she tried to hide her familiarity with the name. "Oh, my god," she blurted, "Wha, I mean, who?"

Katheryn looked at them both with concern. "Somehow, this group got wind of your adoption petition and your situation. They, in their god-given wisdom, have determined this adoption is harmful to Bronte, and it would place her person in a hostile and immoral environment."

"Hostile and immoral?" Rafe shook her head in disbelief. "But I love her. She's my daughter."

"No, she's only Eden's daughter at the moment," Katheryn said stating the cold hard facts.

Rafe looked down at her hands and held back the pain caused by the truth of her comment. "Why us? They don't even know us," she said softly.

Katheryn opened up a file on her desk and flipped through it. "Well, according to their brief, they know you both fairly well. They have statements from several people who have had contact with you and who clearly define your and Eden's relationship as 'nonexistent and potentially hostile' and Eden's behavior as 'erratic.' Also, they describe you personally, Rafe, as quote, 'a sexual deviant who shows no restraint or sensitivity to the fragile sensibilities of the child,' unquote.

"What the hell are they talking about?" demanded Rafe as she threw her hands up in anger.

"And Eden," Katheryn continued, "one of the people who gave a statement was Jake."

Rafe looked incredulous at Eden. "What the hell?"

The color drained from Eden's face as she shook her head in denial. "Rafe, I didn't know anything about this, I swear. I didn't know he would do something like this."

Rafe looked at Eden with despair and mistrust. She didn't know if she could believe her. Jake's threat of this happening was still ringing in her ears. He made it very clear he was following Eden's lead.

Rafe grasped the arms of the chair tightly as she lowered her head and forced out the words she feared were true. "I'm going to lose her again."

Katheryn assessed her client's distress and then looked at Eden, who was shaking her head denying Rafe's words. She remembered the last time Rafe was sitting in that chair worrying about losing Bronte. At the time, she recommended they file for immediate court ordered visitation and take steps to force immediate adoption proceedings. She felt, under the law, it was within Rafe's right to expect the agreement she made with Eden to be legally upheld in a timely manner.

However, Rafe was more worried about how Bronte would perceive her when she got older if Eden resented her for dragging her through court and talked badly about her. Katheryn thought it had a lot to do with how people talked about Rafe's father, and Rafe did not want people talking about her the same way. So Rafe decided to keep paying child support and hoped Eden would keep her promise.

"Eden, you must understand, I have to ask you this." Katheryn paused to accentuate the importance of what she was going to ask. "Is this adoption really what you want for your daughter?" She stood to emphasize her words. "Do you, without a doubt, feel Rafe is the best choice to become Bronte's other parent? Because if you have any doubts, or agree with anything, or any person's statement in this brief, you need to speak up now. I really don't want to waste my time or my clients' money, nor cause her any further emotional distress if you have had, or currently are having second thoughts. Am I clear?"

Eden nodded her head under Katheryn's harsh stare and then looked away. She looked at Rafe, who had placed her elbows on the arms of the chair and was leaning over with her hands covering her eyes.

She got up and stood in front of Rafe. "Rafe," she said as she lifted Rafe's face so she would look up at her. She saw Rafe was blinking her eyes and trying to control her breathing so no tears would fall. She held Rafe's sad face in her hands. "Rafe, I know you. Bronte knows you, and she loves you. And I know you love her. You *are* Bronte's parent. You never lost her. I would never take her away from you." She stroked Rafe's face and wiped away the tear that had broken away from Rafe's eye despite her effort. "You have to believe me when I tell you I have absolutely no doubt you're not only the best person to be Bronte's parent, you're the only person I want to be her other parent." She turned to Katheryn. "I don't ever want to be questioned on my decision about the adoption again. I, without a doubt, want this. Can you help us fight them?"

Katheryn sat back down and flashed a cocky smile. "I'll have them for lunch. This is exactly the type of case I love to argue. I'll have an answer prepared before the end of the week, and we will counter sue for damages. If they don't drop the injunction, there will be a hearing, but it may not be for several months depending on the court schedule. I'll be in contact."

"Thank you," Eden said with relief flooding through her. She turned back to Rafe, who had wiped the remainder of the tear from her face. "Let's go, Rafe. Why don't you go home, and I'll get Bronte and bring her over."

Rafe stood up in a daze. She was still reeling from this whole mess, and she still did not think she could trust Eden. She looked at Katheryn. "Thank you," she said and made her way out the door in a fog of pain.

Eden started to follow Rafe but stopped at the door. "You go ahead, I forgot my bag," she called after Rafe. "I'll see you in a little while." Eden turned back into Katheryn's office and went over to the chair she had been sitting in. "Excuse me, my bag."

"No problem," Katheryn said absently as she looked through some papers on her desk. She looked up at Eden. "It was a big thing you did."

"No, it was the right thing, the only thing to do. It's what I've always wanted for Bronte, and for Rafe." She picked up her bag and opened it then shifted nervously. "I need to tell you something, but I don't want Rafe to ever know about it," she said quickly. "I can't keep causing her so much pain. I can't keep throwing these terrible things in her lap and expecting her to fix them. I have to be the one who takes care of this problem, because," she hesitated, "I'm the one who caused it." It took everything in her to look into Katheryn's eyes. "I need you to promise you'll never tell her what I am going to tell you."

Katheryn looked at Eden and considered what she had just said. "Are you sure you want to tell me? This could be a conflict of interest. Rafe is my client."

Eden rubbed her face and ran her fingers through her hair nervously. "I think, once I explain things, you'll understand and will do what's in Rafe's and Bronte's best interest. Please, promise me."

"Eden, I can't make you a blanket promise. I have to protect my client," Katheryn explained. "I can, however, assure you if the information you give me will cause no harm to my client by withholding it from her, I will use it to her benefit without telling her about it. But if not, I will make the information available to her without revealing you gave it to me."

"Okay, good," Eden said relieved, "that's good." She pulled out a file containing a large bulging manila envelope and a plastic bag with other letters and papers and then handed it all to Katheryn. "I think, somehow, this information can help stop the injunction and anything else they may have to throw at us." She watched as Katheryn looked at the contents and then looked up at Eden with raised eyebrows. "Katheryn, I believe any hope Rafe and I can just," she paused and fought to hold back her tears, "just at the very least, get along, depends on her not finding out about all of this."

16

EDEN KINGSLEY HAD rushed to pick up Bronte from school to keep her promise to Rafe. Everything she told Katheryn was on her mind. The fact the whole situation had escalated with the injunction against Rafe was unnerving. She never imagined Jake and the group would involve Rafe. She thought once there was a court date, they would go away, and Rafe would never have to know about them.

She pulled up to Rafe's house and began the unloading process of pulling out Bronte's backpack and unhooking the safety straps to get her out of the car seat.

All the things she read about the Stewards group online had been flooding into her mind since Katheryn called her about the injunction. Posts described them as ruthless and dangerous. She agreed. It was a relief to know Katheryn would use the information to help them with the injunction. She found it nerve-wracking though, not knowing if Katheryn would end up revealing the information to Rafe.

When Jude looked out her front door and saw Eden, she quickly made her way out of the house and over to the car. "Eden, hey," Jude said catching her breath.

"Hi," said Eden with a forced smile as she drew Bronte out of her seat.

"So what are you doing here, just dropping off Bronte? I'll take her in to Rafe," Jude volunteered.

"I can take her in, thanks," Eden answered as she picked up the backpack.

"Well," Jude hesitated, "I don't know if you want to go in there."

"Why not?" asked Eden concerned because she knew Rafe was expecting her.

Jude looked over at Rafe's house then back to Eden nervously. "It's just, well, something's going on with Rafe, and I think we should leave her alone right now."

Now she understood. She knew what was going on with Rafe. "I know what's going on, Jude," confessed Eden. "We've been to the lawyer's office. An injunction has been filed against Rafe's adoption of Bronte."

"Oh, man," said Jude sadly. "Still, maybe she needs to be alone right now."

"What's going on, Jude?"

"It's just," she hesitated and looked at the house again. "I've never seen her like this. "

A wave of anxiety ran through Eden. "You've never seen her like what? What's happened? Where is she?"

"She was in the studio, but she's back in the house now." Jude looked at Eden with worry. "Eden, usually Rafe is so, in control, you know. I think this situation with you and Bronte is pushing her over the edge. I think she is going out of control. It's scary, and I don't think you should be here. It may make it worse for her."

"What do you mean she's out of control?" Eden asked wondering what could make Jude so upset and worried about Rafe.

Jude looked at Eden with eyes full of distress then unleashed her worry. "She was in the studio for an hour just, just yelling and throwing things around. The studio is trashed now." She looked at Eden and bit her lip. "I'm not even going to tell you some of the things she was saying because I'm sure she couldn't have meant any of it. Then she was yelling things in Italian, and I'm sure it wasn't anything good. She's just... she's... I don't know," Jude choked. "Like I said, I've never seen her like this. I really think maybe you shouldn't go in."

Eden was torn. She was distressed about what Jude said because it sounded out of character for Rafe. But she also made Rafe a promise. "But I promised her I'd bring her Bronte. I have to go in."

Jude knew Rafe was already angry with Eden, and if Rafe really was expecting her, then maybe Eden was right. "Okay," she sighed, "but just go easy."

Eden made her way up to the house with Bronte on her hip. The door was unlocked, so she entered quietly. She found Rafe in the living room lying back on the couch with her eyes closed. She noticed Rafe had changed her clothes and was wearing her lounge pants and a low cut tank top.

"Hi," she said quietly. "We're here."

Rafe sat up and smiled at the sight of Bronte. "*Ciao bellissima bambina,*"[5] she said to the baby.

---

[5] Hello beautiful baby girl!

Bronte reached for Rafe, and Eden released her into Rafe's arms and put the backpack on the floor. She sat down on the couch next to Rafe as she held Bronte and watched them silently.

"Are you okay?" she asked to break the silence.

"Of course, I am. Why wouldn't I be?" Rafe said flatly. She turned her attention to Bronte. "Hey B Girl, *ti voglio bene*.[6] Look at this." She picked up a new toy and showed it to her. "What are you going to do with it?" She let Bronte take the toy, then sat her on the floor and watched her play.

Eden put her hand on Rafe's shoulder. "It'll be okay. It will," she reassured her. Her heart went out to Rafe, and she wanted her to believe everything was going to be okay. She didn't really know what other words to say, though. She watched as Rafe just closed her eyes, and when she didn't respond, she tried again. "Rafe," she said as she ran her hand over Rafe's back and moved closer to her. She fought herself and knew she should stop, but before the signal got through, she kissed Rafe lightly on her jaw and neck. "It will, I promise babe," she said softly in her ear and inhaled her scent.

"Stop," Rafe said firmly as she stood quickly and faced Eden. She looked at Bronte then back at Eden and spoke quietly. "Don't make me any promises right now, Eden." She bent down and picked up Bronte with her new toy. "I need to know," she said as she jiggled Bronte, "are you going to let me take Bronte to New York?"

---

[6] I love you.

Eden looked away from Rafe's stare with apprehension. "I, I don't know if it would be a good thing to do right now, with the lawsuit and everything," she said as she shifted uncomfortably. She couldn't tell Rafe the real reason for her refusal to let Bronte go. She couldn't tell her about the Stewards or Jake and the trouble she was in with them. She was frightened they would follow Rafe to New York now that they had involved her with the injunction.

Rafe swallowed her fury as she gently hugged and kissed Bronte. "Hey, baby, I think it's time for you and your mommy to go home." She handed Bronte to Eden. "I'm sorry you came all the way over here. I think I need some time alone. You two should go."

"I didn't mean to upset you," Eden said as she took Bronte. She stood and shifted the little girl on her hip. She wished she could give Rafe what she wanted, but it was impossible. The thought of not knowing where Bronte was along with the possibility of Jake and the other man taking her when she was in New York terrified her. To make things worse, she had kissed her, and she knew it made Rafe angry. It made herself angry. She berated herself again for kissing Rafe, for wanting to touch her and to be close to her. She didn't understand why it was happening. She just knew, right now, she had to try to think of a way to fix things between them for Bronte. "Don't you want me to leave Bronte with you tonight?"

"No, you should both go." She handed Bronte's toy to Eden then walked to her bedroom.

Eden slowly and thoughtfully gathered Bronte's things. As she left, she looked back toward Rafe's bedroom door and could not stop the tears beginning to run down her cheeks full of sadness, sorrow, and frustration.

In her room, Rafe began to try to calm herself by lighting her meditation candles. She sat down in her meditation position and closed her eyes. She breathed deep and began speaking to herself. "What the hell does she want? What do I want?" She began thinking about Bronte, and her heart shuddered in her chest. "Bronte, will the only place where you'll be my daughter be in my heart?" She thought about the injunction. "Who the hell are those people?" She took another breath and then shook her head.

Calmness is a very long way from here.

17

JUDE ATWOOD LOOKED out her kitchen window at the garage Rafe had transformed into an art studio. She could see Rafe was out there and debated on whether she should go visit her as she sipped her morning coffee.

She hated to see Rafe going through more problems. When Eden left to be with Jake and took Bronte with her, Rafe was in bad shape. Rafe tried to hide it, though, by working and being out of town all of the time, or by just not talking about Eden. They were all worried about her so Jude made a point to go hang out with her when she could. It was the least she could do for her. Rafe had been there for her when she was going through a breakup of her own.

Jude owned a massage boutique she had worked hard to create. She co-owned a different massage company with her ex-girlfriend, Chloe, a couple of years ago, but after their breakup, she had to start over. Jude envied Rafe and Eden because she had very few long-term relationships. As a masseur, she met many women who wanted a bit more than a massage. Jude, being a compulsive giver because of her need for affection, gave the women what they wanted, which was the catalyst for her breakup with Chloe.

Jude's lips twitched into a smile at the memory of Chloe. All she had to do was smile and flash her dark brown eyes for Chloe to follow her into the dark massage room. She met Chloe while working as a masseur for a big corporate company specializing in hotel boutiques. Chloe was a recent graduate of massage school and had just started at the company.

After hanging out together for a few months, they decided to go out on their own in the massage business, and they did very well. According to Chloe, though, Jude gave 'too good of massages' sometimes, meaning she ended up having sex with some of her women clients. Jude never really understood the issue. While she and Chloe lived together, it was supposed to keep expenses down. They never said anything about being exclusive, but Chloe said it was unspoken they were. Jude felt like she never got the memo, and it should have been spoken if it were true. It was not like she didn't care for Chloe. She did. She may have even loved her because it hurt when they broke it off. They just had different ideas of where their relationship was, and it was a big problem.

When they broke up, Chloe was so angry she took almost all of the customers, leaving Jude to rebuild. Now Jude was making progress with her new business and was keeping it respectable, even with the many clients requesting 'more' during their massages. She knew now it just wasn't worth the trouble, or the risk, to do things like that anymore. Now, when she met someone who wanted more than a massage, she took it outside the business.

Jude told herself, and everyone else, she didn't really do relationships because they were too confining. She hoped to find someone but was not overly worried about it because she knew she could always find temporary affection whenever she felt she needed some.

The thing Jude liked best about Rafe was there was never any kind of judgment. It had always been hard for Jude to be judged based on what was on the outside by people who never cared about what was on the inside. It was one reason for her defiant way of dressing and hairstyles at times when she was younger. Jude knew if anyone cared to look, they would see she understood herself well, and how her actions sometimes were a rejection of that understanding.

Rafe understood underneath all of Jude's defenses was a quiet, sensitive person. Jude didn't have to talk or explain her fear of abandonment, a fear she sometimes excused as a fear of commitment, or the fact it was an issue conflicting with her desire for a stable relationship. Deep down, Jude understood she had a fear of abandonment, but she tried not to think about it, so she didn't have to deal with the issue.

She saw Rafe pass in front of one of the garage windows and noticed it didn't look like she was upset today. Her empathy made seeing Rafe so upset yesterday difficult. It was even harder to be around because it affected Jude on an emotional level she had not been ready to cope with then. She was one of those people who had a very hard time dealing with overly emotional displays from people. They affected her deeply, and the emotions that threatened to pour from her scared her sometimes. As a defense, she built up blocks of indifference so her overly sensitive empathy was locked away until she could get it under control.

Jude felt, if it weren't for Rafe's encouragement, she might have just given up and not started a new company. She was grateful to her and wanted to help if she could. She looked out the window again, and despite her discomfort, decided she was finally ready to go check on Rafe and make sure she was okay.

18

RAFE SALVAGGIO DECIDED to work from home for the day since her mood meant nothing would get done at work. She handled everything for her trip to New York and made sure things would run smoothly while she was gone. The rest of the day, she took off to get her head back together and to clean up the mess she made in the studio. To keep herself from thinking too much, she was listening to Gianna Nannini's *Perle* CD. She was a popular Italian singer whose music she had found when she was younger and living in Italy.

Letting the door close with a bang, Jude entered and found Rafe sweeping the floor. "Nice music. Sounds like Latin or something."

"Yes, it's Italian," Rafe said as she put the broom aside.

"Huh, what's he saying?

Rafe gave a small laugh. "It's a woman singing," she said. "The song is, *Amandoti*."[7] She walked over and turned the volume down. "It kind of means, 'to love you' or 'loving you.' She's singing their love consoles her and what he wants, makes her life. She doesn't want to waste one more day or hour not loving him. To love him is her life."

"So it's a love song?"

"Yeah, it is." Rafe laughed bitterly.

Jude sat backward on one of the small chairs. "I thought I felt that way once," she said as she thought about the last real relationship she was in and sighed at the thought of Chloe. "But I think she's better off without me now."

Rafe nodded. "I get it." She took a deep breath and gave Jude a small smile of understanding. Jude had been a good friend over the last year. Sometimes Rafe felt she and Jude were similar in many ways. One thing they had in common was they both didn't like talking about things until they were ready. Right now, she was not ready to talk about Eden or the

---

[7] Loving you

injunction. "Greer liked this song a lot," she said knowing Jude would get the hint.

Jude looked at Rafe with confusion. "She listens to music?"

"Sure," Rafe answered matter-of-factly. "She can't hear the words, but she can feel the beat. Beth helped me tell her the words." She smiled at the memory of listening to music with Greer. "And this is a sexy Latin beat," Rafe said and raised her eyebrow.

Jude laughed out loud, happy Rafe seemed to be in a better mood. "Almost all Latin beats are sexy."

Rafe picked some papers up off the floor, and a small notebook fell out. She picked it up and looked inside and then flipped through the pages. She looked up at Jude. "Is this yours?"

"Oh, yeah," said Jude as color flushed up from her neck. "I've just been trying things out. I need to make some new marketing stuff for my massage company. I'm taking your advice and trying to build it back up after..." she let her words fall away. Rafe and everyone around already knew about what happened with her ex-girlfriend.

"This is pretty good," said Rafe. She looked around and grabbed a ruler and a pencil. "Here, let me show you something," she put the ruler on the page and drew a line across it. "I can see you're trying to draw something that needs perspective. This is called a horizon line," she said as she pointed at the line she drew. "The top of this line, you draw things that should be far away, so they will be progressively smaller from the horizon line. Then below they will be progressively bigger." She used the ruler and drew two lines from the ends of the horizontal line up to the middle of the page. "You see how you have everything the same width? Well, not having perspective is why it looks a bit chunky and off."

Jude watched with interest as Rafe fixed her picture and added perspective. "Wow. It looks a lot better. Maybe you can do some drawings for me."

Rafe chuckled. "I think you're doing well. You just need a few basic pointers. How about I see if Annie will help you with the basics, and in return, you can help her with her classes," she offered.

"Really?" Jude smiled. "That'd be great. I'd like that."

Rafe looked at Jude and sighed, "Listen, about yesterday, I'm sorry." Rafe knew what happened had upset Jude. From experience, she knew blocking her empathy was harder for Jude if she was close to the person in distress.

"Eden told me what happened," Jude said and waved her hand as if to wave away her worry. "I understand. I know how much Bronte means to you."

Rafe began picking up paint bottles and putting them where they belong. "It's not just the legal issues. It's my whole life lately. I think things are stabilizing and then shit like this happens."

Jude got up and began helping clean. "Yesterday, Eden said it wouldn't stop the adoption."

"She can't know for certain," Rafe said as she threw a paper towel hard into the trash can. "She's doing and saying a lot of things lately that don't make sense."

"What happened?" Jude asked uneasily at Rafe's frustration.

"Nothing happened. She's just doing some things that don't make sense," Rafe said shaking her head.

"Like what?" Jude pressed. "Still getting too close?"

Rafe nodded her head and frowned. "I don't know if it's just her trying to be nice or if she's just out of her mind or what. On top of everything, she first tells me I *am* Bronte's parent, and then the next thing, she doesn't trust me to take her to New York." Rafe picked up a stack of paper and straightened it up before putting it on a shelf. She stopped for a moment and sighed. "I just can't figure her out."

19

RAFE SALVAGGIO'S TUESDAY flight landed in New York after a five and a half hour flight time, and she disembarked along with the CCAD President Clarice Biggalow and their carry-on bags. Rafe spent the flight time going over her presentation for the grant committee. She felt ready for the most part but wanted to get to the hotel to make a few tweaks.

After disembarking, Clarice needed to go get a checked bag from baggage claim. Rafe had packed light, just her carry-on, and her laptop briefcase.

"You have everything for five days in such a little suitcase?" Clarice quipped. "How is it possible?"

Rafe laughed. "It's called experience," she said with a slight smile. "I used to travel so much over time, I just figured out what was necessary and what could be left behind."

"Believe me, nothing I packed could be left behind," she said and headed off looking for baggage claim.

Rafe smiled and followed her. "I'm sure you're right. I think we need to go left up here to get to the baggage claim."

Clarice looked ahead and saw someone waving a sign. "Do you know that person?" she asked Rafe. "She's waving a sign with your name on it."

Rafe looked where Clarice directed, and her face lit up. "Greer!" She waved back and quickly headed straight for her.

"I can't believe it. It is Greer!" Clarice exclaimed. "I didn't recognize her without her paint-covered clothes."

Rafe rushed up to her, hugging her and then gave her a short but passionate kiss. "How are you? I wasn't expecting to see you here. I was going to drive to you tomorrow night."

Greer motioned to Beth to interpret in the crowded airport. "I know. Beth said you sounded so sad Bronte wasn't coming, so I wanted to come to surprise you. Are you surprised?"

Rafe looked quickly at Beth then back at Greer warmly. "Definitely. Pleasantly."

Greer motioned to Rafe's bag. "Is this it?"

"Yes, but Clarice has one to claim, so we better get down there," she said and led the way happily.

After checking into the hotel, they all went out for dinner and a few cocktails. When they got back to her room, Rafe made a quick call to Bronte to tell her goodnight. Afterward,

Greer worked with Rafe for a few hours on last-minute tweaks to her presentation for the next day. Greer left her with a kiss goodnight so they could get some sleep, and Rafe fell into bed exhausted.

20

THE AFTERNOON EVENT for the Jackson-Goyer Foundation was in full swing. The presentations were running on time, and Rafe Salvaggio was presenting to the Jackson-Goyer Grant Committee, with the hope they would win one of the grants, and was giving her conclusion.

"Only with vision and forward thinking can we hope to protect the future of our young artists in today's world of political correctness, fundamentalism, lack of open-mindedness and backward thinking similar to the thinking of the dark ages." She paused for effect.

"We are forging the way for a new renaissance encompassing new revolutionary ideas, self-expression and a message of acceptance for all people, beliefs, and ways of living. Art education is more than putting pigment to canvas or memorizing facts. It is not only a look through the windows of the past, through which students can obtain knowledge allowing them to gain a broader understanding of the world that came before them; it is a reflection of the world in which they will live, love, and die.

"Protecting their reflection of the world, their artistic expressions, their modern artistic tools, their philosophies and their ability to create in a safe environment of acceptance and understanding is paramount to the future of these young artists. Thank you." Rafe smiled as she finished and was rewarded with an enthusiastic round of applause. She left the platform to take her seat next to Greer.

Greer clapped until Rafe sat down then leaned into her. "You were wonderful!" she said, and Beth began interpreting. "Much more entertaining than any of the others. They have to choose your school for one of the grants."

"You don't think I was too pretentious, or too technical when I talked about electronic mediums in art?" Rafe asked, nervous about how she was perceived by the committee.

Greer laughed, and Beth interpreted her signing. "Anything but. You had everyone enthralled. They were on the edge of their seats!"

"With enthusiasm or the urge to get up and leave?" she asked jokingly. She had presented plans for multi-million dollar restorations to investor groups but had never dealt with idealistic academics and was not sure how she came across while flaunting quite a lot of her rationalism at them.

"With adoration of your passion, I'm sure. I know I couldn't take my eyes off you," said Greer, and Rafe smiled in appreciation as she took a sip of water.

"Well," added Clarice, "now we just have to make it through dinner."

21

FINALLY FREE FOR the night, after making it through the catered, bland, chicken dinner, Rafe Salvaggio and her group were able to spend the rest of the night relaxing. Beth and Clarice were somewhere in the hotel taking time for themselves and taking advantage of the wine bar. Rafe and Greer were taking a walk in the nearby garden holding hands and leaning close to each other, happy to be spending the rest of the evening together.

Rafe made sure Greer was looking at her so she could talk with her. "I'm glad you were there with me today. I needed someone there more than I thought. It's always easier to relax when I know someone in the room."

Greer gripped Rafe's arm tight. "I was happy to be there for you."

They stopped under a tree dressed in lights. Rafe saw Greer was looking at her with her humor-filled blue eyes. "I'm sorry I couldn't talk to you more at dinner," Rafe said and gave Greer a small kiss. "I had to do a lot of sweet-talking to try and convince the committee to give us the grant."

"You were fine!" Greer assured her returning the favor and gave Rafe a kiss. "I was impressed at how you handled those pompous committee members. It was a side of you I've not seen. You were so graceful and confident—and very sexy."

"Sexy?" Rafe laughed. Greer nodded her head and smiled. Rafe leaned in and kissed her deeply, leaving her breathless.

"Wanna go to my place?" Rafe asked with a wink. Greer laughed and grabbed Rafe's arm holding her closer as they started back toward the hotel.

22

RAFE SALVAGGIO AND Greer Noble drove to Baltimore through the moonlit night after they finally left the hotel Wednesday. The unexpectedness of having Greer sitting next to her for the drive prompted Rafe to think about where their relationship might go. She loved the way Greer thought about her and had surprised her by showing up at the airport. There was something about knowing someone else thought about her and cared about her enough to do something special for her. Especially when she knew Greer expected nothing in return. It made Rafe want to give her something, though.

Maybe her heart.

Living in Baltimore and being close to New York would make finding work easy. She thought she might even be able to buy back into her old company and start doing the job she really loved again. It would be hard not being close to Bronte, but Eden was making it hard even when she was living close to her. She held onto Greer's hand and tried to imagine life with her.

They made it to Greer's house with little trouble. When they woke up on Thursday, they took full advantage of the mid-February weather that was actually a surprising sixty degrees.

They broke out the paint and canvas, braved the cold, and painted in the park. Then they took a walk, made love and then just spent time being together and doing nothing in particular. Two full days spent with Greer, one in New York the other in Baltimore, had been such an amazing reprieve for Rafe. She was able to forget about everything going on at home and just be in the moment and think only about herself and Greer.

Sadly, it did not last long. She ended up talking about her problems back home with Eden most of the night the night before. She wasn't sure what came over her. It seemed like everything had built up, and once she was finally able to relax, the floodgate opened. Greer was great and attentive, but Rafe still felt a little guilty spilling out her problems to her.

Waking early, Rafe and Greer had a light breakfast in Greer's warm kitchen. Rafe waited for Greer to look at her, enjoying watching her move around the kitchen. "Thanks for listening to me rant and complain about my life all last night. You must be sick of me already."

"Never," said Greer as she sat down at the table and took a bite of her food.

"I think you're a saint," Rafe said earnestly.

Greer laughed. "Nice. You think I'm a saint and Abby thinks you are a wildling. I guess opposites attract."

Rafe furrowed her brow and frowned. "Abby told you she thinks I'm a wildling?"

Greer nodded. "She thanked me one day for saving you from your rogue soul stealing ways." She grinned at the vexed look on Rafe's face. "What made her believe you're a wildling?"

"I guess she's just a really funny girl," Rafe said drolly. "I think she's projecting the translation of my last name, Salvaggio," Rafe guessed.

"Oh, what does it mean?" Greer asked sassily.

Rafe grimaced and put her fork down. "You know, you're the first person to ask me about my name. Even Abby didn't ask. She just looked it up and made some assumption. It's kind of a nickname from a long time ago based on the word selvaggio meaning *wild* or *wild man,*" she signed the letters for the Italian words and then signed the translation 'wild man.' "My name is an old spelling. It doesn't mean I am some soul possessing rogue or anything. It's just a name." She took a sip of her coffee. "You know, if it were an American name, it would be something like Wilde or Wildman or something." She chuckled. "My mom used to call my dad her 'wild love' based on it, and she'd called me her wild child." She laughed at the memory. "From her, it was sweet and loving. From Abby, it's, well, I don't know what it is."

Greer nodded her head in understanding. "Well, I find it interesting Abby believes you're a wildling, even if it is something she's saying because of your name. I don't think I've seen a wildling in you. The way she goes on about it and the stories she tells, I wouldn't mind meeting this wildling Rafe," she teased.

Rafe found her smile again. "Well, I guess when I'm with you, the wild woman inside me is just laying back waiting for a nice tummy scratch. You calm her, and she just sleeps inside her cage all safe and sound."

"Let's wake her." Greer laughed. "I think you should take her out of the cage. You hide away too much of yourself."

Rafe's eyes widened, and she grinned. "Really? So, just regular Rafe doesn't excite you?"

Greer cocked her head and smiled. "I would never say that. I'm just disappointed I won't be able to experience every side of you."

An immediate rush of desire ran through Rafe as she looked at Greer. "You know, I think we should change the subject. Beth will be here soon, and I don't think she'll like waiting on the porch until I'm finished with you."

Still smiling, Greer nodded in agreement. "She hates waiting on the porch." Just then, Beth entered the kitchen with a stack of papers and transcripts for Greer and put them on the counter. Greer looked at Rafe and covered her mouth to hide her smile.

Beth joined them at the table and signed as she spoke. "Good morning, you two." She turned to Greer. "Are you ready to go?"

"Yes," Greer said and got up from her chair to put her dish in the sink.

"Hey, Beth," Rafe greeted her. "Did you have fun on your extra day in the New York?"

"I did." Beth nodded happily. "I got to visit a few galleries and might show my work in them."

"Congratulations," said Rafe then ate the last of her breakfast.

"Rafe, what are you going to do while I'm at work?" asked Greer as she turned back to the table. "I hate that I have to go in, but it can't be helped. Luckily, it's Friday, and we'll have almost two more days together this weekend."

"I think I'll go to the Historical Society and Museum to meet the curator. Then I'll come and have lunch with you. What time should I meet you?" asked Rafe before taking the last sip of her coffee.

Greer got her bag to leave. "Just come when you're finished. You'll be my excuse for getting out of there." She gave her a kiss good-bye. "See ya!"

"Bye," said Rafe resisting the temptation to go after her and make her stay.

23

BACK IN LOS ANGELES Julia Hawthorn and Eden Kingsley had stopped in for a quick bite to eat for lunch at The Kiki Bistro. It was a beautiful day to be out of the office for a while. They were both happy it was Friday, and the workday was almost over.

Eden was glad to be hanging out with the girls again. She was especially glad to spend more time with Abby, who had been her confidant a lot when she was with Rafe. She missed spending time with them all and was happy they had welcomed her back.

There was a difficult conversation with Rafe when she called from New York Tuesday night and another this morning. Rafe didn't say much and just wanted to speak to Bronte. Eden offered to set up the Skype so they could see each other, hoping it would help Rafe not be as upset with her, but Rafe told her not to bother. It seemed like she was in a rush to get off the phone. Eden knew it was because Greer was there with her. She wasn't sure exactly how to feel about Rafe seeing Greer again. She knew Rafe was planning to see her and they cared about each other. She also knew they had to cut their relationship short. Maybe all the feelings she was fighting inside would not matter if Rafe decided to renew her relationship with Greer.

As Eden and Julia walked into the restaurant, they went over and joined Abby who was already at a table.

"Hey, guys. How's work?" Abby asked as they sat down. She closed her computer and set it to the side.

"Do you know they actually expect me to stay there all day except for an hour lunch break?" said Julia sarcastically.

"It's usually how a regular job works," Eden informed her, deciding to put all her worries away and join in the fun. "They pay you for the time you work in an actual office."

"Well, I work better when I'm not locked in a dreary building," Julia said dramatically. "I should start a blog!"

"Shut up!" Abby pouted, "It's a real job! I do make money, you know."

"You'll get used to never seeing the sun," Eden continued with Julia. "I got to meet with a horror film director today."

"Sounds like it was a cheery meeting," said Julia sarcastically.

"Actually, the guy really creeped me out." Eden laughed.

"Have either of you heard from Rafe? Isn't she supposed to be back in town Sunday?" asked Abby.

"She called Bronte this morning," Eden said with a sigh. "She didn't have too much to say to me."

"So, she's still upset?" Abby asked tentatively.

"Upset?" Eden scoffed. "I think it's more than upset. She didn't even call to tell us when she was leaving or stop over to say good-bye. She called to Facetime with Bronte when she was already in New York."

The waitress came and took their order. When she left, Julia looked at Eden. "Why didn't you let her take Bronte?"

"I guess with what happened at the park, and then the injunction, I was just afraid to let her go," said Eden as a wave of anxiousness flew through her at what had almost happened.

"You know Rafe wouldn't let anything happen to Bronte," said Abby.

"I know," said Eden despondently knowing she would have to lie to her friends. It seemed the guilt she was carrying because of what she was keeping from Rafe, and everyone else was getting heavier. "I just felt like I couldn't let her be so far away right now."

"Well, I hope she's calmed down by the time she gets back," said Abby.

"Me too," admitted Eden. "I know I have to make it up to her somehow. I don't know how yet, but I'll figure it out."

The waitress brought their lunches, and they ate in silence for a few minutes. Julia swallowed her food and looked out the window at a pretty woman who was walking by the window. "I just need her to be in a good mood so we can go to the clubs. She makes going so much more exciting," Julia said to try and lighten the mood.

Julia's comment razzed Abby. "Julia, I told you, you have to stop making her participate in those crazy bets."

"I don't *make* her do anything," Julia defended herself then decided to spin Abby up a bit more. "She has a god-given talent. I'm thinking of wagering with other people and placing my money on Rafe. I could make a fortune."

"So, you're going to pimp her out?" said Abby in outrage at the idea.

"Guys, come on," Eden interjected nervously. Talking about Rafe this way made her uncomfortable. She didn't want to know what Rafe did when she went out with Julia.

"Sorry, Eden," Abby apologized noting her discomfort, "but I'm trying to stop her from doing those crazy things."

"Maybe you wouldn't complain so much if the girls Rafe rejected came looking for you like Tess came looking for me," Julia said with a smug look directed at Abby. "Tess said Rafe was a real heartbreaker, and I got to soothe her broken heart," she said with a click of her tongue and a wink. It was not like she hadn't dated women Rafe threw away before, and maybe, if she couldn't have the real thing, then Tess would do.

"Of course, you did," said Abby as she rolled her eyes. She noticed Eden looking at her with confusion. "The girl Rafe did her *wildling thing* with the other night ended up coming back in and hanging out with Julia."

"She did?" asked Eden. She was surprised and wondered what happened. The girl looked eager to go with Rafe. She shook her head to get the memory out of her mind. She didn't really want to know. It was bad enough she found herself wondering what she was doing with Greer.

"We did a little more than hanging out." Julia winked again. "She was only here visiting, but I may see Tess again the next time I go to New York."

"Okay, we get it," said Abby in frustration. "You can stop showing off now. Besides, if it weren't for Rafe, you'd have nothing to brag about."

Julia smirked and ignored Abby's jealous remarks. "Eden, why don't you come out with me tonight?" suggested Julia with hope twinkling in her dark Mediterranean blue eyes. "Maybe you can reveal all of Rafe's secrets. You were with her for over four years, so something had to rub off."

"Sorry, Julia, I don't know any of those secrets," confessed Eden as she pushed her salad around her plate her hunger quashed.

"Of course, you don't," said Abby peevishly as she gave Julia a harsh look then turned to Eden. "Rafe would never do anything like that to you. She was different with you. She's different with Greer too," she revealed.

Eden stopped in mid drink and sat her glass down. "She is?" she asked gloomily.

"Yeah, she was like this cool breeze when Greer was around," said Julia pushing her silver hair back from her neck. "Did you know, when they broke up, Rafe said it was almost sweet?"

Biting her lip, Eden gave an almost imperceptible shake of her head. It was hard to imagine a sweet breakup with anyone, and she felt a wave of jealousy Rafe was getting along so well with Greer still. "You know, she's seeing her while she's gone. Do you think Rafe loves her?" Eden asked with apprehension.

Abby exchanged a look with Julia. "No, she doesn't love her. I asked her," said Abby.

"And she said no?" Eden asked with uncertainty and lowered her eyes to her plate.

"Not exactly," said Abby. She gave Julia a quick look and saw her shrug at a loss. Taking a deep breath, she decided to tell Eden what she knew. "She said she didn't know yet. But, then they broke it off. They wouldn't have broken it off if it was love."

Eden didn't know what it meant either. "Maybe," she said, "but she did go see her."

"They probably just have one of those weird lesbian relationships where they're really close but don't sleep together," Abby guessed then looked helplessly at Julia. "You know what I'm talking about."

"Abby, don't be stupid." Julia laughed and then looked inquisitively at Eden wondering what she was up to. "Rafe is single now. She can be with anyone she wants. Why do you want to know if she loves Greer? Do you want her back?"

Eden looked down at her plate again not meeting Julia's eyes. "No, no," she hesitated. "I just want her to be happy."

"You *so* want her back, don't you?" taunted Abby as she snickered.

"Abby, stop," pleaded Eden. "It's not funny. I really just want her to be happy," she repeated.

"Well, when she gets back, just try to be extra nice to her. She needs friends with all the stuff happening to her. If the injunction is upheld, her whole world is going to come crashing down," said Abby as Julia sighed and shook her head.

"The adoption is going to happen. I'll just keep filing petitions until it does, even if it means fighting every crazy watch-dog group in the country," promised Eden.

24

AT MIDNIGHT THE night was quiet, but inside his truck, Flynn Ogden's nerves were on fire, and the anxiety of waiting for something, anything, to happen was making him sweat. His ribs still hurt, and his face was healing, but the blow to his sense of well-being and safety for Eden and Bronte was agonizing. He looked out the front windshield of his truck and saw all of the lights were off in Eden Kingsley's apartment and the moon reflected off the dark windows.

If only he had not promised to keep things from Rafe. But a man was only as good as his word, or so he understood. It just meant he had to step in where Eden wouldn't allow Rafe to tread. By not telling Eden he was keeping watch over her, he now had a secret from both Rafe and Eden.

The whole time he had been working on the project for Eden, and waiting for his gun permit to go through, he couldn't help thinking about the abusive situation he had left behind when he left home two years ago, and the hope someday, his mother would reach out to him.

In Indiana, Flynn was raised by a single mother who was a drug addict and alcoholic. Though his mother finally did get clean, she could never seem to make good choices about men. The last boyfriend Flynn knew about was abusive and a drunk. He was just one in a line of many.

Flynn came home one day to find his mother bleeding with broken ribs and arm along with many bruises and cuts. He called the police, but his mother didn't want to press charges out of fear of repercussions, and the police stood by and did nothing.

After taking his mother to the hospital, he sought out the boyfriend and found him stoned and drunk. He kicked him awake, confronted him, and then proceeded to beat him up. The boyfriend was so drunk and stoned he had no idea who it was that beat him up. His mother found out what he had done and got angry. Flynn tried to explain he was trying to help her, and she told him she had not asked for his help.

Her angry statement was devastating to Flynn.

He did not think his mother should have to ask for his help or he should have to have permission to help her. But he found out the hard way he was wrong.

Because his mother was not able to work and bring money home for drugs and booze, the boyfriend soon tired of her and moved on. When his mother got better, Flynn told her he couldn't take it anymore, and since she kept refusing his help, he saw no reason to stay. He left town for California where he was able to feel free to be himself. It was nice to live in a place without worrying about his mother complaining or her boyfriend of the month verbally abusing him or beating him up for being gay or beating his mother up because he could.

The best thing that had happened to him since coming to California was finding people who accepted and respected him. He could be out, and no one gave him any trouble. He could tell, for the most part, who genuinely cared about him. He kept tabs on his mother through the landlady and made sure her rent and utilities were paid when necessary but never let her or the boyfriends know so they didn't start asking for drug and booze money.

When he got to California, Flynn found a great place to live and was able to get a job with a large IT company. He was proficient in several computer languages and had created several phone apps and small programs freelance for companies, as well. It was great to be in a place surrounded by others with his same interests doing a job he loved.

Flynn was happy Eden was letting him help her. He had kept his promise to help Eden by checking out her computer. She was a single mother like his own mother was. He saw she needed help to get away from a situation he saw as abusive with Jake and the Stewards group. He wanted, no, he needed to help her—like he could not help his own mother. Eden had done what his mother had not. She had asked for help. He vowed to give her his help.

Flynn looked in the passenger seat and saw the dark glint of gunmetal. It was just lying there, but he knew it was alive and ready to do his bidding. All he had to do was to pick it up and squeeze gently. It was what the instructor at the target range taught him.

What he experienced the first time he shot the gun was not like any other. When he shot his dad's gun, it was a lark, for fun at targets. His dad's gun was not as powerful as the one lying next to him. *This time would be different,* Flynn swore to himself. If there were another attack, he'd be ready.

Over and over, he told himself he could have no doubt, have no fear, and have no hesitation. He would watch over them all, and if it were within his power, nothing bad would happen to them. But, if it did, he knew what to do when bad things happened.

Inside Eden's apartment, Bronte slept soundly in her crib and Eden tossed in her sleep unaware of the night watch going on outside her home.

25

RAFE SALVAGGIO WAS on her own in Baltimore Saturday morning because Greer was at the hospital for an unexpected half day of work. It was the first time Rafe had spent any length of time in Greer's house alone, and she wandered through the now too quiet house looking at Greer's family photographs and her art collection. It was all familiar to her because it was in her apartment back in L.A., but, looking at it in a new environment made it seem different somehow.

She smiled as she looked at a picture of Greer as a little girl with braces and huge glasses covering her tiny face. It seemed to Rafe those were the girls who always grew up to be the most beautiful inside and out. She put down the photo and decided to take the paintings they had done a few days ago up to Greer's studio and have a look around. She had been encouraging Greer to get back to painting and wanted to see if her words of encouragement had worked.

She walked into the studio and saw a lot of old furniture used for props and several works in progress. She peeked under the covers Greer had put over the paintings to keep off any dust and liked what she saw. As she walked further into the studio, she saw a large canvas toward the back. When she stood in front of it, she was stunned. She knew instinctively it was a painting of herself, though most of the features of the woman in the painting were hidden in shadow.

It was a portrait of a nude woman in many, many shades of blue with a few small red lip imprints on her neck, breasts, and abdomen. The facial features not in shadow, the penetrating gray-blue eyes, and the lips, were done in striking detail. Rafe was especially moved by the way the eyes seemed to break away from the canvas and were alive with an intense hunger. The curly midnight blue hair framed the woman's features. Swirls of many lighter blue shades outlined the hard body with a luxurious softness.

Rafe looked through tear-stained eyes with wonder at the image Greer saw when she looked at her. She felt entranced by the way she had captured the emotions of sadness, heartbreak, anger and a need for closeness that were always just on the edge of breaking out. Dropping to the floor, she sat in front of the painting just looking and feeling the energy and intensity of the piece. It amazed her how one single color could have so many shades and hues and how they seemed to ripple and move as the light in the room changed.

Spellbound by the painting, Rafe slowly noticed Greer was sitting silently beside her. She didn't know how long she had been looking at the piece and thinking about all it meant to her. She turned her head, looked at Greer, and quietly whispered her words, as there was no need to speak loud. "I really love this."

"I can see that," said Greer as she wiped a tear from Rafe's face.

Wiping her eyes, Rafe laughed. "I've not cried like this in a long time. I don't know what's wrong with me."

"Stendhal Syndrome," said Greer tenderly. "Overwhelming beauty makes the soul swell with so much emotion a great pressure is built up and, when the soul bursts open, tears spring forth to release the pressure of the soul so we can breathe again. Though, it is kind of conceited when it's a painting of yourself making you cry," she teased and kissed her.

"I guess I never expected to feel this way outside a museum," said Rafe liking the way Greer explained the feeling she had inside herself. She recognized it now. She remembered the first time she felt that overwhelming feeling. It was when she was in a museum looking at art with her mother. It seemed like it had been a long time since she had felt that feeling. It had been a while since he had visited a museum to look at art. She was glad Greer gave the gift back to her. "When did you do this?"

"I started painting it almost as soon as I got home from the first time we made love," she said smiling and remembering their first day together.

"It's so beautiful," was all Rafe could say.

"I know. It's you," Greer said stroking Rafe's face tenderly with the tips of her fingers.

"Yes, it is. Is this really what you see?" Rafe wondered out loud.

"It's what I saw that day," Greer admitted softly. Rafe was too overwhelmed to speak and looked intensely into Greer's eyes. Greer edged closer and kissed her. "I see those eyes now."

Rafe felt a rush for Greer again inside her. "I think the wildling has come out to play." Rafe moved up onto her knees in front of Greer and single-mindedly began to cover her in hot kisses while, at the same time, feverishly removing Greer's shirt so she could touch her soft skin.

The power flowing through Rafe's kisses permeated Greer's senses making her helpless in her own flesh. She felt Rafe pull her up so she was standing. Swiftly, Rafe loosened Greer's pants and slipped them and her frilly silks down so Greer could kick them away. The cool air of the studio on her skin did little to subdue the heat Greer felt from Rafe's kisses and hands. She loved giving herself to her dark-haired beauty and experiencing the intense single-mindedness Rafe had when taking everything she wanted.

Without hesitation, and with a wild roughness, Rafe claimed Greer's limbs and muscles, bending them to her will. Kissing her, Rafe pushed Greer back onto the antique vanity until she had no choice but to fall between the high drawers and onto the vanity. Feeling the shock of the cold mirror against her naked back, Greer gasped.

Rafe drew her kisses away to look at Greer, and a fever took over her senses. She wanted to show her what she meant to her, what the painting meant to her. This was more than sex. This was a confession of how much Greer meant to her, and she hoped Greer would understand and feel the message she was sending.

Pulling Greer's legs up by her knees, she began her slow descent. She kissed and licked her body as she lowered herself between Greer's legs, using her own legs to force herself against and into her.

Greer's heart beat hard at the thrill of Rafe taking over her body. She ran her hands through Rafe's hair, as toe-curling pleasure was being caused with great skill by Rafe's mouth and tongue until she needed to kiss her mouth before she lost her mind. She pulled Rafe's head up so she could taste her and kiss her face and lips.

Rafe pulled Greer's legs around her waist and lifted her off the vanity while Greer clung to her and kissed her feverishly. She carried her to the overstuffed ornate chaise so prominent in many of the paintings in the studio and brusquely dropped her onto the soft cushions.

As Greer looked up from the chaise and watched Rafe, her body reacted in anticipation and appreciation as Rafe slowly revealed her toned, youthful body. Greer felt herself melt a little and her nipples stand at attention. *Oh, the confidence of youth*, she thought. The way Rafe teasingly ran her hand over her own body, so poised and self-assured, made Greer's mouth water. Rafe stood naked over her and smiled down with her impish grin that made so many promises. Greer wanted them all. She laughed and trembled knowing she would be lost to the wildling with the burning gray-blue eyes and had no idea if she would make it back.

Rafe took her.

26

CURLED UP TOGETHER on the oversized chase, Rafe Salvaggio kissed Greer Noble softly and gently. As they stroked each other's smooth bare skin, a peacefulness they both felt was a considerable juxtaposition from the wild lovemaking they had taken pleasure in not long before.

Rafe sat up and pulled Greer up with her, making sure she could see her lips. "Hungry?" she asked, and Greer nodded.

Rafe got up and handed Greer her clothes. After kissing her again, she picked her own clothes up and put them on. Reaching out, she took Greer's hand, helping her stand. Greer's knees would not hold her up, and Rafe grabbed and held her for a moment until she stopped shaking.

"Are you okay," Rafe asked softly looking into her heavily lidded pale blue eyes.

Greer nodded her head then put her fingers over Rafe's lips. She didn't want to miss what she was saying, and she could not focus at the moment. Leaning against Rafe, she willed the strength back into her own body while trying not to lose the pleasurable buzz echoing through her.

Rafe held Greer for a moment more, taking in the feel and the scent of her, and hoping she could feel how much she meant to her. After Greer had put her clothes on, Rafe led her out of the studio. They went into the kitchen where Greer fixed them drinks and got out some food. They took everything into the living room and sat close, facing each other in front of the fireplace and eating ravenously.

Greer leaned forward and kissed Rafe gently. "I think I did see the wildling that's supposed to be in you," she said and took the last bite of her food.

Rafe smiled curiously. "Did you really?"

"I think I more than saw it." Greer put her forehead against Rafe's and looked into her eyes. "I think I lost all control of my body, and I think I'm going to have a bruise on my ass from the vanity."

"Sorry." Rafe laughed. "I guess my inner wild woman will never go completely into the cage again. It's entirely your fault."

"How's so?" Greer asked and took a drink of her wine.

"I think it was the painting," Rafe teased.

"Just the painting?" Greer laughed.

"No. It was everything we did," Rafe said and kissed her.

Greer pulled back from Rafe's kiss. "You mean what *you* did. You completely took over!" Greer could not help her grin. "I'm supposed to be the teacher."

Leaning forward, Rafe kissed her quickly again. "You are my beautiful teacher."

Greer looked down, away from Rafe's happy face for a moment. The conversation she had planned would be a hard one because she truly loved Rafe. But there was no doubt they needed to have it. Greer knew she had to let Rafe go. Rafe was so young and had so many things going on in her life right now. She knew she could not wait around for Rafe. She needed to be free to find someone who was ready for her and who could love her now. Greer felt at her age, she had to feel sure and not waste time she could never get back waiting for something that may never happen. She loved Rafe but could feel Rafe was holding herself back, and Greer needed all of her if they were going to work. Based on their conversations about Eden, and everything else in Rafe's life, it did not seem like having all of Rafe would ever be possible.

She looked back up then and began to speak slowly and purposely. "Rafe, what we just did," she said hesitantly, "it was fantastic." She saw Rafe smile, and Greer touched her face. "And I have to tell you something."

Rafe waved her hand to cut her off not, wanting to hear what she thought was coming. It felt like Greer got the message she had been trying to send, and the reply was not good news.

"I know. It wasn't love. It was technique."

"Technique?" Greer said confused.

Rafe looked away from Greer's eyes then down at her hands. She sighed and looked back up at Greer. "Yeah, it's what I told Abby once, and I think maybe it's the reason she thinks I'm a soul possessing wildling."

"Well, I never would have thought to say *technique*." She paused, thinking, and then looked back at Rafe. "But yeah, I guess it's accurate."

"Okay then, it was fucking incredible technique!" Rafe laughed wanting to keep the good mood they had created.

"It was!" Greer laughed with Rafe. "It was!"

Rafe sobered and looked at Greer with a little pang in her heart. "You know that wasn't why I came to see you, don't you? I didn't come to check whether or not I loved you. I came because I just feel so calm when I'm with you. Am I selfish?"

Greer shook her head and smiled. "No. I'm glad you came."

"There are just so many confusing and painful things going on in my life," Rafe explained. "You really have been my saving grace."

"I'm here anytime you need me," Greer assured her.

"Thank you. I'll always be there for you too," she promised.

"I've been thinking about all the things you told me and, well, can I tell you what I think about it all?" Greer asked hoping Rafe would not think she was adding to her troubles.

"Are you going to be using one of your college degrees on me?" asked Rafe as she arched her brow and smiled.

Greer chuckled. "I think I may use more than one." She looked at Rafe somberly. "Will you talk with me?"

Rafe took a sip of her wine and nodded. "Of course."

"I have a lot to say. Do you mind if I call Beth to help me?" she asked.

"No, I don't mind."

"Okay, I'll be right back." Greer went into the kitchen and got her cellular phone to text Beth. When she was finished, she went back into the living room and kissed Rafe. "She's on her way. We have just enough time for a shower."

"A shower," Rafe said slowly and suggestively as she ran her hands under Greer's shirt.

Greer laughed and grabbed her hands and pulled her up. "No funny business," she said as Rafe followed her willingly to the bathroom. "Really." She laughed as Rafe kissed her and stripped off her clothes. "I don't know if I can take anymore."

Thirty minutes later, Beth arrived. Beth waited in the living room and heard Greer and Rafe as they made their way through the house. She looked up as they came into the room with their hair still wet from their shower. Greer blushed bright red when she saw Beth sitting there on the couch, and Rafe just looked at her with a cocky grin on her face. Beth had never seen her boss blush so brightly, and she wasn't sure how to react, so she looked away.

Greer took Beth to the kitchen to talk to her alone for a moment and to make sure everyone had a glass of wine while Rafe got settled in the living room. When they went back, Greer gave Rafe her wine and let Beth know she was ready. She sat down and looked very seriously at Rafe for a moment. She touched Rafe's face then ran her hands down her arms and over her hands gently. She then took a breath to clear her head and began to talk with Rafe.

"First," she started slowly, "I think you should consider taking the feelings you may have for Eden out from behind the wall you've built around them and take a good long look at them. You two have spent a significant amount of your lives together, and you have a baby together. Don't you think really understanding yourself and your own feelings will help you choose the path that will give you some happiness?"

Rafe shook her head and frowned, surprised Greer was starting with this after what they had just done in the shower. She expected something like this because of what she told her about Eden and all the things she had complained to her about the other night. She just hadn't expected it right out of the gate.

"Greer, I am sick to death of looking at my feelings. I don't know if my feelings for her are the same as they used to be."

"They don't have to be the same," Greer said through Beth. "It doesn't even mean you have to feel one way or another about Eden. This is about what you're really feeling. If you look at those feelings, you may be able to answer the question 'what do I want' you keep asking."

"What if what I want isn't Eden anymore? Lately, I really have been enjoying my freedom. I know she doesn't want me, and I think I'm finally becoming okay with it," Rafe revealed.

Greer shrugged and signed for Beth. "Then you don't want her, and you can both move on and find some happiness. There's nothing wrong with not wanting her at this point. What about the other question you've been asking? 'What does she want?' You said after her trauma in the park, she kissed you and has kissed you one other time since then."

"Yeah," Rafe confirmed, "and she keeps touching me and just getting too close." She wondered if Greer was jealous and wanted to put her mind at ease. "I think she was just out of her mind because, like I said, she doesn't want me, she wants men."

"Is that what you want?" Greer asked. "Her to be out of her mind because then you wouldn't be making the wrong decision about letting your feelings for her go?"

Rafe frowned as she thought about Greer's words. She fought her urge to cry out, yes, it was exactly what she felt. She had never wanted to let Eden go and never thought she would be in a position where she was considering living a life with someone else. But here she was, in Baltimore, with Greer, and had been seriously thinking about staying. But now she knew Greer might not love her either, so it was probably off the table too.

Rafe took a deep breath and shook her head to clear her mind. "I really don't know. I just don't trust Eden right now, even if she does think she has feelings for me."

Greer looked at Rafe with concern. "Why can't you trust her?"

"Well, mostly because she says she's not with Jake, but Jake seems to be everywhere," Rafe explained trying not to show the anger over him had being party to the injunction filed against the adoption. "Then there's the latest fucked up thing she is doing—saying I *am* Bronte's parent but then not letting me bring her to New York. Not to mention there is her erratic behavior about picking up and dropping of Bronte. Who knows what else she's doing. And I know she's lying to me about something because she's always looking down and averting her eyes," she raged, "and the way she lifts her chin." Rafe shook her head to calm herself. "Honest people don't do those things. On top of all the other problems, this whole kissing thing is happening."

Greer could tell by Rafe's words how aware she was and how closely she looked at Eden that she still felt something for her. She thought it was why Rafe always tried not to look at Eden or went to another room if she could when she was around. It was almost like she purposely chose to be ignorant about what was going on around her sometimes, especially if it might be uncomfortable. Rafe couldn't help being aware of Eden otherwise.

"Sometimes," Beth interpreted for her, "traumatic events cause people to seek out the security and safety of something, or someone familiar. Her terrifying experience in the park could have been the catalyst that opened Eden to the possibility she still has feelings for you, whether she showed them to you intentionally or accidentally," Greer explained.

"She's been having a lot of *feelings* lately," Rafe quipped. "And she made it clear when she left me she wants to be with men. So why is she doing this? I don't like it at all. I don't want her kissing me or touching me if she is fucking men, or anyone else, now. Maybe I was just the one who was there in the moment. It could have been anyone else she had any kind of feelings for or answered the door."

"You're referring to Jake, right? He's your rival?" Greer asked carefully. She decided not to point out the double standard Rafe was holding Eden to when it came to sex.

"He's not my rival," Rafe said annoyed.

"If you're going to try and get Eden back, then he is your rival," Greer explained.

Rafe shook her head and crossed her arms. "I don't know if I'm going to try." It seemed like Greer was now pushing her to get Eden back. *It must be true—she doesn't love me.* The thought brought a lump to Rafe's throat. It was hard to swallow even though she had been fairly certain it was the truth from their conversation earlier.

"Okay, you don't have to figure it all out right now." Beth paused to watch Greer sign then continued relaying her words. "You and Eden went through some very traumatic events. The inseminations failed, your father died, your breakup and all the other things leading up to where you are now."

"True," said Rafe, feeling like the affair would always be held over her. "I guess because I didn't go to someone familiar it blows your theory. I went to a woman I barely knew."

"You did go to someone you barely knew," she agreed with a nod. "But really, you went into a familiar behavior. Abby said you went back to the behavior you had before you met Eden," Greer signed, and Beth voiced. "Because of you did, I think it caused you all kinds of frustration when it came to Eden and her lack of responsiveness at the time. Reverting to your old behavior may have caused your infidelity. You're still in that state now. I knew it as soon as Abby thanked me for saving you from your wildling ways and told me those stories."

Unsure if her theories were true, Rafe decided not to argue. It sounded like another excuse everyone seemed to heap on her. She hated thinking about that time and what she was going through because it always seemed to lead to heartache combined with a headache.

"So, why is it different with you?" Rafe asked quietly wondering just how much Abby had told her.

"I think it has a lot to do with how we have to communicate," explained Greer. "We have to look at each other, pay close attention to certain details, and you've been learning a new language. It's hard work. I think the effort uses up the overabundance of passion and energy you're always exuding. Because it's all used up, you can be calm and clear."

Rafe smiled impishly. "So, how do I get calm and clear without you around?"

"A very good question," Greer teased. "But you need to find something outside of work and family you can put your energy into and burn it off. You used to burn off energy with your old job, and the job you do now is not as intense or stressful for you."

"So do you think the behavior thing is similar with Eden? She was only with men before me," revealed Rafe.

"I don't know Eden like I know you, so I can't say for sure," answered Greer. "But I don't think Eden would have kissed you if there wasn't something inside her causing it." Greer looked at Rafe and her sad face. Her heart went out to her, and she wished she could keep her with her, but she knew Rafe had to be clear about what and who she really wanted first. "You know, Eden's feelings may have been just as protected as yours are, and this trauma put a crack in her emotional wall. If she is trying to get close to you, it may be time to think about letting her back in your life and exploring the possibility of being with her again."

"How do I know she really has feelings for me or if it's just something temporary because of the trauma?" asked Rafe as she rubbed her temples afraid it was really the issue.

"There's the hard part," said Greer sadly and then signed again as Beth interpreted. "You can't tell her how to feel, and you can't force her to explain her feelings. She may not even know why she kissed you or seems to need to be close to you. Also, there is still the possibility her reasons may not change the fact she wants to be with men. You'll just have to be calm and patient and open to all possibilities."

"I think I've been calm and patient enough," said Rafe surly and crossing her arms.

"Have you?" Greer asked and saw the hurt look on Rafe's face. "You have all these questions you ask about Eden, but you've never asked her the questions. Why?" She could see Rafe could not, or would not, tell her the answer. "Patience isn't just about waiting for someone to change or something to happen. It's also about listening, really listening, to the answers to all the questions you have. But you have to ask them. Eden can't read your mind. If she doesn't know you have questions, or what they are, you may never get your answers."

"So, what are you saying? I need to corner her and start asking all these questions and hope she'll tell me the truth?"

"It's not an interrogation, Rafe," she explained. "You can't demand her answers or even the truth—because her truth may not be the answers you want. She may not even know the answers."

"How can she not know the answers? She did those things. They were her actions."

"True, but people do things all the time without knowing why. Asking questions may be the way to get her to think about why she did things. Her answers to why may be multi-leveled, and not just black and white. It could take a while for her to really understand it all herself." She looked at Rafe and could see she wasn't happy with what she was hearing. "Another thing," she began again, "every time you ask a question or ask for something from her, you have to give something back."

"What do you mean?" Rafe asked suspiciously.

"I mean you can't expect her to open up if you aren't willing to open up too."

"I'm open."

Greer chuckled. "No, you're not. You're not open at all." She touched Rafe's face and traced her frown. "It takes a lot to get things out of you sometimes. I have a psychology doctorate and look how long it takes me to get into your head. I imagine Eden doesn't beat you over the head like I do to get things out."

Rafe rolled her eyes. "It's easy to talk to you."

"Really?" Greer smiled and looked over at Beth. "Because communication with me is a lot of work. Just like we talked about. Plus, like now, I have Beth here. With Eden, you wouldn't have those hurdles." She watched as Rafe looked at Beth and gave a small shrug. "Why have you never asked her any questions about why she left?"

"I don't know," Rafe sighed. "I guess I figured if she wanted me to know, she'd tell me."

"What if she wants to tell you, but isn't sure if you want to know? This is a woman you've told me has chronic anxiety issues. Don't you think it would be hard for her to just start telling you some of these things? Especially knowing how hurt you were and how closed off you are sometimes."

"I'm not closed off," Rafe said annoyed. "I've always been there for her and given her everything she wanted."

"Okay," Greer said seeing Rafe's stubbornness on this issue was causing them both frustrations. "But you've never asked her your questions, and you've never opened up to her about how you're feeling."

"I think it's clear how I feel," said Rafe stubbornly.

"I'm not talking about your hurt or anger. You have more feelings than those few. Tell her why you told her to explore her feelings. Tell her what's going on inside your head and your heart."

Rafe ran her hands over her face and hair. She didn't know if she wanted to tell anyone what was going on inside her, including Eden. "What if I do decide to try and get her back and open myself up to her, and I'm wrong? My life turned upside down when I met her. I had never felt so much happiness or love for anyone—and I have never felt as much pain as she caused." She sighed. *I caused,* she thought as she swallowed trying to control her emotions. "I'm not ready to relive it again."

Greer touched Rafe's face gently. "You have to open up sometime."

Rafe sat back and put her hand out so Greer would stop. She wasn't sure about all of this. She didn't think opening up and being vulnerable was the solution. Eden had enough feelings without adding hers. Besides, as her father said, emotions just get in the way of seeing things clearly.

"I don't think vulnerability, at this point, is an option."

"Why not?" Greer asked curiously.

"I've been down that path, and I learned vulnerability is meaningless if the person you're making yourself vulnerable to doesn't care," explained Rafe. She had her first experience of meaningless vulnerability with her father and dealt with it for a big part of her life. When he did allow emotion into the equation, it was usually because he was playing hers and wanted something. He had seemed to soften not long before she moved away, and they got along better, but Rafe still wasn't sure if it was a real change or if he finally considered her an equal—or if there was something else behind the change. She chose to believe his change was real because she loved him.

Greer saw what she said was true. "Then don't be vulnerable, be passionate," she said and smiled.

"Passionate?"

"You've already brought the wildling out of her cage. Why not use it to help yourself find what you really want?" she asked and continued, "You've been keeping yourself from being a whole person for a long time. Don't you think you'd be happier walking around as who you are instead of locking parts of yourself up?"

"I have felt free lately, and I would like to keep that feeling."

"Then you should."

"To be the wildling or not to be the wildling... this is the question," Rafe quipped as she smiled at Greer. "There's just one problem. What if Eden doesn't like the changes in me? With her, I was always so," she hesitated, "gentle and careful. I've never done with her the things you and I've done. As Abby is always reminding me, Eden has never seen the wildling Rafe."

Greer smiled at Rafe, flattered the intimate part of their relationship had been distinct from her past relationships. "You have to decide if you can go back to living the way you were, as a half person, or if you want to stay whole," Greer advised. "You know, you can still be gentle and caring. You can't stop living because of the situation with Eden. And if you do reconcile, I really don't think Eden will mind the change, not if she loves you and you love her."

"I know the answer," Rafe said with resolve. "I have to be whole."

Greer smiled warmly. "Good for you. You're making a good start. I hope finding the answers to the rest of your questions is as easy."

Rafe gave Greer a wicked grin. "There's just one more problem. Abby is going to go ballistic when she finds out the wildling is back to stay."

Greer laughed. "Abby cares about you and Eden a lot. You'll just have to be firm but gentle with her. I think she just wants to save Eden from being hurt again like she was."

Rafe frowned and ran her hands over her face. "I wish she wanted to save me from being hurt. I never really thought about it much before, but I guess I owe Abby a long overdue apology. Maybe I'll get to a place where I can give it, and she'll be able to accept it. Right now, I can only concentrate on one problem at a time."

27

SUNDAY MORNING SEEMED like it came too soon, and it was time for Rafe Salvaggio to board her plane for home. It was a long sleepless night of talking about things Rafe felt unprepared to talk about, but she was glad Greer cared enough to try. It was a relief when Beth finally left, and they could spend the evening just being close and waiting for the hours to pass before it was time to leave.

Beth and Greer had come along to the airport to see Rafe off and were walking her to the gate. "I'm sorry you have to fly out on Valentine's Day," said Greer with a sly smile. "I hope you can visit again soon."

"Me too." Rafe chuckled as she pulled her carry-on to her, parking it close to her leg. They had a very nice Valentine's Day morning making up for the fact she had to leave. "You have to come back to L.A. and see what we do with all the grant money if we get it."

"You'll get it," predicted Greer.

"If we do, maybe I can hire you away from Johns Hopkins," Rafe said with a slight twitch of her lips as she tried not to grin at the thought.

"Believe me... I would take your offer seriously," Greer said with a laugh. She would take the job if it included being able to have Rafe, but she knew, right now, it did not.

"Well, I have to go." She pulled Greer close and kissed her passionately then smiled her impish grin. "Just the wildling checking to see if the cage door is still open."

Greer laughed. "Just make sure you let the wildling know she's not always in control, and I think you'll be okay." She kissed and hugged Rafe holding her close for some time, sad she had to let her go.

"Thank you for everything," she said warmly to Greer then looked at Beth and gave her a smile. "You too," she said grabbing the handle of her carry-on as she turned and walked into the terminal.

Rafe boarded the plane, found her seat, and laid back to relax with her eyes closed. She felt the air around her move and opened her eyes to the vision of a stunning brunette standing over her. The girl indicated her seat was next to Rafe's, and Rafe let her through noticing every part of her body and her sweet smell. The girl settled in, and Rafe stole a glance at her. Then she lay her head back, closed her eyes and began to laugh in a way she had not in a long time.

"What's so funny?" the stunning girl asked.

"Oh, nothing," Rafe said with a sigh. "I'm just happy to be in this seat right now."

The girl looked at Rafe puzzled. "Okay."

"What's your name?" asked Rafe.

"Emily."

"Emily, I'm Rafe. It's nice to meet you." She held her hand out.

"It's nice to meet you too," said Emily and took Rafe's hand.

"Emily," said Rafe as she looked intently at the girl, "what are you passionate about?" she asked warmly still holding her hand.

28

AS SHE DROVE along the hectic traffic-filled highway from the airport toward home, Rafe Salvaggio was smiling. She was feeling better about the world after visiting with Greer and the very interesting flight home. She took the exit toward her neighborhood and decided she would stop by The Kiki Bistro to see Letty and let her know she was home, and to get some dinner.

Letty spotted Rafe as she walked into the bistro she had decorated for a day of love. "There you are!" she said and hugged Rafe. "How was your trip?"

Rafe hugged her back and smiled at her warmly. "It was wonderful. I think we have a really good chance of winning one of the grants."

Letty chuckled because she had no doubt Rafe would get what she wanted. She had a way about her, always had. "How was Greer?"

"Greer is wonderful," she said and could not wipe the grin from her face. "She's done a painting for me and will be sending it to me soon. I can't wait for you to see it, Letty. It's just beautiful."

"Oh, what's the subject?"

Rafe winked at her. "Me."

"You go, girl!" Letty laughed and led Rafe to a table.

Rafe followed Letty and sat down at the small table near the kitchen and was set up with a candle and flowers for the holiday. Letty sat down across from her where she could keep an eye on the restaurant and waved a waitress over to their table.

Rafe ordered food and a drink for takeout then turned her attention to Letty. "So how has everything been while I was away?" she asked glad to be home.

"Well, Eden came in for a while with Flynn and Stacey before taking Bronte to her art lesson yesterday, and they were both fine," Letty reported. "She, Julia, and Abby were here Friday for lunch. I didn't get the chance to talk to them, but they all seemed okay. So all is well on the home front."

Rafe leaned back in her chair and frowned. "I'm glad everyone is happily getting along with Eden suddenly," she said sarcastically.

"Rafe, are you still mad?" Letty asked in disbelief.

"Yes, I'm still a just a little upset," Rafe said with hostility. "But you know what I find insane? Eden can screw me around royally, and everyone jumps up to absolve her and be her friend, but if I do one thing to disturb Eden in the slightest, I'm treated like a fucking criminal."

"What are you talking about?"

"I'm talking about Abby and them not caring if I get hurt or not by the shit Eden does to me. If I had done to Eden what she did to me, none of them would even speak to me. But they're all out happily having lunches together again, and it's okay because it's Eden," she said hotly.

"They care," Letty reassured her.

"No, I don't think they do," said Rafe as she shook her head. "It's a fucking double standard. Do they think I don't feel pain?"

"I'm sure they know it's painful for you," said Letty. Though she knew none of them grasped just how hard it was on Rafe when she came home to find Eden gone the first time she left after the affair. No one blamed Eden for leaving, but they never saw how hard Rafe had been on herself.

"What do you want? Do you want them not to see Eden again? You know that isn't reasonable."

Frustrated, Rafe tapped the table with her fingers. "I know, I just want everyone to stop treating me like I'm the only one who causes all the pain around here. Everyone is always telling me how I'm hurting Eden and fucking up. Do they ever tell her she's hurting me and fucking up?"

"Well, I know they talk to her about you. Your friends love you. This is why they're always telling you those things," she said sympathetically. She knew Rafe was talking about when Eden left the second time, taking Bronte without warning. Rafe was devastated and so sick Letty was very worried about her for a while. But now, since they were getting along, Letty didn't want Rafe to mess things up so they lost time with the baby again. "They're doing it because they want to help you. Believe me, Rafe, sometimes you're oblivious to what is going on with people. It's why it gets pointed out to you so often."

"I don't know what I have to do to figure her out. She says one thing and does another. She says she wants to be with men, but she kisses me. She calls me Bronte's parent but doesn't trust me with her. Which is it? What does she really want? I am so tired of guessing wrong all of the time. I wish she would just come out and tell me so I know," Rafe hissed in anger.

Letty was not sure how to make Rafe feel better about her situation. She thought she was doing better when it came to Eden since meeting Greer and having so much time apart. Since the breakup, Rafe had pulled away from everyone, so Letty was glad when Greer came along to get her back out with the living. Right now, she just knew Rafe had to get along with Eden for Bronte's sake.

"Rafe," Letty said calmly, "sometimes you're not the easiest person to talk with. Maybe, if you'd just back up and listen, or actually stay in the same room with her, instead of outright avoiding her, you could learn things through her actions about things she might feel like she can't say to you in words."

Letty remembered when Rafe seemed to always know what Eden wanted and heard what she had to say. Now it seemed like she treated Eden as if she were invisible sometimes.

"I hope you're not going to start getting all demanding and trying to push her to talk to you about things to get your answers," she said with concern. "You know, you two need to get along and make sure the adoption goes through," she reminded her and Rafe scowled. "You could also respond more positively when she wants to be close to you, instead of being all suspicious and trying to guess about things all the time." Letty paused reining back her opinion. "Try being quiet and listening to her again."

"No, you know, you're right," said Rafe and threw her hands up in concession because she was too exhausted to fight about it anymore. "I'm always the one who's trying to figure things out and define things. Maybe I should just start leaving it all up to her."

"I don't know if you have the patience," Letty said with a half-smile.

"Well, I'll just have to find it." Rafe shook her head again and stopped short to think about what Letty had said to her while the waitress came and set her food on the table. "I'm sorry. You know, you're not the first person who's told me some of those things," she sighed in exhaustion. "Thanks for the takeout and the advice Letty. I'll see you later."

29

TURNING INTO THE parking lot and parking her car, Eden Kingsley was on edge and wondering why Katheryn, Rafe's attorney, wanted to see her on such short notice. It had been about two weeks since she gave her the information about Jake, and she hadn't heard a word from her until today. She was gripping the steering wheel tightly and preparing herself for the worst news possible.

When she finally let go of the steering wheel and got herself under control, Eden walked into the office. Katheryn's assistant sent her directly to her office, and Eden was surprised to see Katheryn actually standing in her doorway waiting.

Katheryn closed the door when Eden was inside the office. "Thanks for coming over on such short notice," she said in a business-like manner as she went to her desk and sat down.

"What did you need to talk about. Is it something about the injunction?" Eden asked as she sat down nervously. "Is something wrong?"

Katheryn looked at Eden firmly and opened a file in front of her. "This doesn't directly have to do with the injunction, but it could help us if it's handled right. Eden, I've been confidentially talking with the federal prosecutor about getting a subpoena for the records to find out who hacked into your computer." She paused so Eden could process her words. Katheryn was not sure if Eden realized the packet she handed over had included possible evidence from her personal computer. Evidence the FBI might be able to use in a federal criminal case. Unfortunately, she was limited to only giving Eden information relevant to the injunction case right now.

"If we can get it," Katheryn continued, "and we find out the person who hacked into your computer is associated with the group who filed the injunction, we may be able to have them brought up on federal charges. Here's the thing," she hesitated, "once I hand this over to the feds, your anonymity will be compromised. They may talk to everyone you know, including Rafe." She waited to let her statement sink in for Eden.

Katheryn wanted Eden to be onboard with going to the FBI. It would be better for her if she went to them with the evidence represented by an attorney than if they somehow found out about it and just showed up at her house with warrants in order to obtain what they wanted. She had not, and would not, reveal Eden's name to the FBI until she agreed, but it didn't mean they wouldn't find out about her eventually. Through her research, she had found there were several ongoing federal investigations that seemed to be looking at the Stewards or a similar group. When one of her assistants reached out to the FBI for information on subpoenas for computer hacking, an astute agent put the inquiry and the case for the injunction together, and suddenly, Katheryn got a call from a special agent. Her call was what led her to this conversation with Eden.

"On the other hand," she continued, "if the hacker is arrested, and is found to be affiliated with them, we can file a motion to dismiss based upon the criminal act used to obtain information about you, and the adoption will be back on the docket. I need to know if you're willing to do this and if you'd like me to represent you."

Eden looked at Katheryn warily. She forgot the information Flynn had given her was in the envelope she gave to Katheryn. "I don't know. What if they do this, and they can't find the person? What if the person has nothing to do with the injunction? What if the search leads nowhere? I would be taking a risk for nothing."

"It's possible." She nodded because it was possible the hacker had nothing to do with the case.

"Is there any way to do this without the federal government?"

Katheryn sighed and shook her head in a definite no. "Not unless the hacker drops his computer off at my office and confesses."

"Katheryn, I have to think about this," said Eden with uncertainty. "Give me some time."

"Just don't take too much time," warned Katheryn. "Some opportunities only appear for a short time, and then they're gone."

30

EDEN KINGSLEY LOOKED at the time in the corner of her computer screen and saw it was already five o'clock. She closed out her programs and gathered the scripts she needed to read over the weekend and put them in her briefcase. As she walked to the door, she looked over at the artwork on the wall. It was Bronte's first painting, the one Rafe had framed and gave her for Christmas.

Rafe, she thought and sighed.

She had spent the week thinking about Rafe and everything going on, including her meeting with Katheryn about getting the Federal Government involved in their case. She still didn't know what she wanted to do. She had to tell Katheryn soon, but every time she thought she had made up her mind about what she wanted to do, and picked up the phone to call, an all-consuming dread came over her. She hefted her bag on her shoulder and made her way out of her office.

"Good night, Ms. Kingsley," said the receptionist.

"Night," replied Eden with a smile as she made her way out of the building.

She took the short walk through the studio parking lot anxious to be on her way to pick up Bronte from day school. She wanted to spend time with her before the nanny came so she could meet Abby and the others for dinner. She approached her car, and something didn't look right. As she got closer, she suddenly stopped. She took out her cell phone and dialed.

"Security? This is Ms. Kingsley. I'm in the south lot. I need someone to come right away. The tires on my car have been slashed." She paused to listen. "No, no, I'll be inside the building. Okay, hurry." She disconnected the call and threw her head back. "Cripes!"

Eden headed back to the building and dialed Flynn as she walked. "Flynn, are you home or at work?" she asked as she stepped inside the building. "I'm fine, but the tires on my car have been slashed. Can you come to the studio, south lot entrance, and help me? I'll need a ride home. No, I don't know who did it. I have a feeling you're right," she sighed. "See you when you get here. Bye."

The security guard sped up to the building entry in his security cart, and Eden stepped outside to meet him. "Ms. Kingsley?" he asked professionally.

"Yes," she confirmed and looked at his ID badge. Juan Mendez, it said in large block letters.

"Hop in," Juan ushered. "Let's take a look at the car."

They sped through the lot to her car. When they pulled up, a second security guard was walking around the car. He waved as they pulled up, and when the cart stopped, he leaned in, "Well, they got all four. They must really have something against you. They left a message," he said, and he thumbed in the direction of the car.

They got off the security cart and walked around to the driver's side of the car.

"Doing another movie the religious folk don't like?" asked Juan as he read the spray-painted message on the car. The word REPENT was in red letters in the middle of the car.

Trying to hide her fear, Eden swallowed and put on a brave face. "Something like that," she lied. She wondered if this meant Jake knew she had the information about him and his group. "How did this happen? How did some unauthorized person get in this lot? It's supposed to be secure."

The second guard, Derrick Muntz his badge indicated, stiffened defensively. "The lot is secure but mostly against people who drive onto the lot. If someone snuck in on foot," he shrugged, "well, pedestrians are harder to guard against."

Juan signaled Derrick to stand down and looked at Eden apologetically. "It had to have happened shortly before you came out because we patrolled this lot about a half an hour ago, and we didn't see anything wrong. We'll write our report and file one with the police. Do you want us to call a tow truck?"

"Yes," Eden nodded, and as she looked at the slashed tires and red paint, her phone rang. "Hello," she said into the phone. "Flynn, good you're here." She paused. "No, they're calling a tow truck. I'll be at the gate in a few minutes." She hung up and looked at Juan. "Can you help me get the car seat out and give me a ride to the gate? I called a friend to take me home."

"Sure, no problem." Juan smiled, and after they had removed the car seat, they got into the cart and drove to the gate.

"Thank you," Eden said to Juan and waved to Flynn.

"No problem. We'll have the car taken to a studio garage," said Juan. "I'll leave the information at your reception desk."

"I appreciate it," said Eden feeling sick.

They got out of the security cart and walked to Flynn's truck where he had opened the door to the cab section to load the car seat. They got it loaded, and Eden climbed into the passenger seat.

As Flynn put the truck in gear, Eden looked at him and could not hold back her tears. She took a deep breath and let it out to calm herself.

"I think I'm getting in over my head." She looked into Flynn's eyes and could see he was at a loss for what to do to help her feel better. She glanced at her phone then at Flynn again and dialed. "Is Katheryn still in? Katheryn, hi. I'm glad I caught you. Listen, something happened. My car tires were slashed, and the car was spray painted with the word 'repent' in red spray paint." She paused to listen. "Yes, a police report is being filed. I'm doing a walk-in report tomorrow." She closed her eyes and steeled herself. "Katheryn, I think we need to figure out a way to warn Rafe something like this could happen to her," she said quickly. "No, I still don't want her to know it came from me. Okay. Okay, thank you. Bye." She put the phone down and looked at Flynn as she fought another wave of sickness.

31

THE BAWDY TABLE was crowded but not as loud inside as the name of the place suggested. Abby Van Falkov had gathered everyone together to try out the new restaurant that had been getting rave reviews. She wanted to see for herself, and then she would write about it on her blog. She looked around the table at everyone talking and giving the waiter their orders as another waiter poured everyone a glass of wine, leaving the carafe. She looked at Rafe and saw a camera sitting on the table beside her. "So, Rafe, what's with the camera?"

Rafe picked up the camera and turned it in her hand. "I'm taking a photography class at the Conservatory. I got some good advice from a friend to find something to put my excess energy into," she said and smiled at the thought of Greer. "It's a lot of fun, and the teacher is brilliant."

"Another teacher?" Abby said insinuating Rafe was trying to date the teacher.

"No, Abby, she's just the teacher," Rafe said as she focused the camera. The flash went off as she took a picture of Abby.

"Whoa, I think I'm blinded," complained Jude as she blinked her eyes to focus.

"Sorry, I'll warn you next time." Rafe laughed. "Maybe I'll just turn the flash off." She looked down and began adjusting her camera settings.

Abby looked up and saw Flynn and Eden as they walked into the restaurant. She waved to them as they looked around the crowded restaurant. "Hey! Flynn, Eden, over here," she called.

Rafe turned and saw Eden coming toward the table. She looked at Abby with a half-smile. "Abby, you didn't tell me Eden was going to be here."

Abby looked back at Rafe who had what she considered a smirk on her face. "I said I was inviting everyone, which includes Eden," she said unsympathetically.

Rafe could see Abby was being defensive and shook her head. "No, you don't understand. I'm glad you did."

"You are?" Abby asked then she looked at Jude confused.

Julia walked into the restaurant right behind Eden and got to the table at the same time. She sat down and looked over at her. "Eden, come sit next to me. What was going on? I saw you get out of Flynn's truck. Where's your car?" she whispered as Eden sat next to her, and Flynn went to sit next to Jude.

"Oh, nothing's going on. We just decided to ride together tonight," Eden whispered back as Julia poured them some wine. Eden looked up and noticed she was sitting directly across from Rafe. "Hi," she said in surprise.

"Eden, how have you been?" Rafe smiled warmly.

Eden looked down at her placemat. "Fine," she said quietly, unnerved she had to face her right after her car being vandalized and talking with Katheryn.

Abby looked from Rafe to Eden and was frustrated at Rafe for looking at Eden like a cat about to pounce on a mouse. It was clear Rafe was making Eden feel uncomfortable, so Abby took it upon herself to try to change the mood of the table.

"Well, this is great," she announced to the table and held up her wine glass. "We're all here. Now let's toast to us!"

They all raised their glasses in salute and took a sip from their glasses. The group was enjoying their time together and their food. The restaurant had a five-star review in Food Magazine, and they all agreed it was well deserved.

Rafe openly watched Eden throughout dinner looking for those unspoken clues Letty said she was supposed to be leaving.

Eden averted her eyes but could feel Rafe looking at her. She was not sure what she had done wrong to be stared at so intently. Between Rafe staring at her, the guilt she was feeling, and the nervousness of not knowing what was wrong, she kept dropping things like her fork or her napkin. Once she almost spilled her wine, but Rafe reached out and caught the glass.

"Excuse me," Eden said softly when she finally couldn't take it anymore. She got up and headed for the restroom.

Abby glared at Rafe who was watching Eden walk away. "What the fuck," she hissed and threw down her napkin. She quickly followed Eden and found her leaning against the bathroom sink. "What's going on? Are you okay?"

"I'm fine."

"Well, then, what's wrong with Rafe?"

"I don't know. I think she may still be upset because of the New York thing." She sighed. "Maybe I shouldn't have come."

"You two have to be able to be in the same places together every once in a while," said Abby in frustration. "It's not like it's every day. When she said she was glad you were coming, I thought it was because you were getting along, not because she wanted to intimidate you."

Eden looked up at Abby warily. "She said she was glad I was coming?"

"Well, yeah," stammered Abby. "I thought it was why you sat across from her, but then she started doing her weird staring thing."

Leaning over the sink again, Eden groaned. "That's probably the problem. She's wondering why I'm sitting across from her. I just sat down and didn't realize she was there until I looked up." She groaned again. "I'm such a screw-up. I should have been paying attention."

"Well, there's nothing we can do about it now," said Abby. "Do you want me to talk to her and tell her to knock it off?"

"No," Eden said quickly, "don't say anything to her. You'll just make her mad and cause a scene. Besides, it's not her fault. I'm the one who sat across from her."

"Whatever." Abby rolled her eyes.

"Did she say why she was glad I was here?"

"Uh, no." Abby scoffed. "She's not a big sharer."

"Right." Eden sighed again. "Well, I guess we better go back. I just had to take a moment, you know?"

"Oh, I know," Abby assured her, "I know."

They made it back to the table, and Eden found it was easier to remain calm once she was able to enjoy another glass of wine. It was also helpful Rafe's chair was empty for a while because she had started focusing on taking pictures.

The group posed for the camera as Rafe took photos of everyone eating desert and having fun as they laughed and talked around the table. Abby insisted Rafe take some photos of her desert for the blog too. Rafe made her way around the table taking photos of her friends, the wait staff, and the food. At one time, she was even allowed to go back into the kitchen to meet the chef and take photos. Soon, she was back, and everyone had finished eating and were relaxing with a last glass of wine.

Rafe looked across the table thoughtfully at Eden over her glass of wine. "Eden," she said just loud enough for her to hear over the chatter around the table.

Surprised at hearing her name in with Italian pronunciation of *Adan*, she looked up at Rafe. It made her smile slightly Rafe had just enough wine to make her slip into her Italian accent. It meant she was comfortable because drinking wine when she was in a good mood made her very open and playful.

"Yes," she answered tentatively.

"Would it be okay if I hung out with you and Bronte at the park Saturday before her art class?" Rafe asked as she sat her wine glass on the table and picked up her camera. "I'd like to take some pictures of her in the park."

It was surprising Rafe wanted to spend time together for anything, and Eden hesitated for a moment. "Sure, it would be nice."

Rafe snapped a picture of Eden. "Great! See you tomorrow then."

When dinner was over, everyone said their goodbyes and went their separate ways. Julia and Rafe were walking together to their cars.

They stopped at Julia's car first, and she turned to look at Rafe. "You were awfully attentive to Eden tonight. What's going on?"

"Nothing is going on," she assured her and laughed seeing the old jealousy Julia was trying to hide. "I've just been given the same advice by a lot of different people lately. So I'm going to make an effort to follow it."

Julia raised her eyebrows wondering who got to Rafe to make her want to take their advice. "What advice? Stare so intently at her she can hardly function?"

"I wasn't staring at her," Rafe insisted. "I was just looking at her."

"You were staring." Julia laughed. "I'm surprised Abby didn't say anything. She looked at you a couple of times like she wanted to stab you with her fork."

"I can't believe this," said Rafe flailing her arms in frustration. "I'm being nice, and I still have everyone on my back."

"Rafe," Julia said evenly. "That look, well, it wasn't really nice," she paused, "it was unrelenting. It's no wonder she could barely look at you all night or hold on to her cutlery. What is it you're trying to do?"

"I'm not trying to do anything anymore," Rafe said calmly. "I'm just watching and waiting for *her* to do something." She looked up and sighed. "I'm just trying to figure myself out and if she's even what I want anymore." She flashed a sad smile then walked off into the night toward her car.

32

SATURDAY MORNING WAS perfect. Eden Kingsley could not believe what was happening. She was watching Rafe follow Bronte around the lush green park with her camera. They were finally doing something together as a family besides the art lessons. Eden hoped this meant they were starting to be in a place where they could do more things like this for Bronte.

She watched Rafe look at her camera with a frown and then let it down, so it was hanging from the strap around her neck. Bronte was running around with her pink and purple cape with a lightning bolt in glitter emblazoned on it flowing behind her. It had been a chore to get her to take it off since Rafe had brought it home to her. It was almost too long for her and dragged the ground a bit when she stopped, but it seemed like she never stopped for long. Rafe called to her, but she wanted to play, so Rafe chased and wrestled her down playfully then let her run again after detangling from the silky cape.

The next time Rafe caught Bronte, she grabbed her up and lifted her above her head and then brought her back down for a kiss. Next, she swung her down and put her under her arm where Bronte laughed and hung like a rag doll while Rafe carried her over to the bench.

"Look what I found," Rafe said as she laughed. "I think it's a Bronte. Do you think we should keep her?" she joked as she handed over a laughing Bronte, who was still hanging sideways under Rafe's arm, to Eden.

Taking Bronte and putting her to rights, Eden laughed with them and fixed the loose Velcro on the cape. "I definitely think we should keep her. Just look at this face." She smiled up at Rafe. "I've never seen you play with her like that before."

Rafe flopped down on the bench beside her and started looking through the images in her camera. She shrugged. "I play with her like that all the time."

"You toss her around and chase after her all the time?" Eden asked in disbelief. "How can you keep up with her?"

"I keep up with her fine," growled Rafe as she tickled Bronte. "She likes to play rough, don't cha? You should see our good night kiss routine. Her favorite part is crashing in for a kiss." Rafe laughed.

Eden shifted Bronte into a more comfortable position. "I'll have to see it sometime."

Switching her camera back to photo mode Rafe stood and faced Eden. "Okay, sit her forward on your lap, and I'll take some pictures of you together."

Eden looked down shyly and covered her face with her free hand. "Oh, no. I'm a mess today."

"The pictures are going in an album, not a museum. You look fine," said Rafe and smiled reassuringly. She knelt down and reached out to straighten out Bronte's clothes and cape. "There. Ready?" She took several shots. "Very nice," she praised and caught Bronte as she reached out to her. She put her down on the ground and let her look through the camera. "How about some of just Mommy? What do you think, B Girl?"

"No, it's okay," Eden said blushing.

Rafe smiled convincingly. "Come on. Bronte wants a picture of you."

"Okay," Eden relented because it was so good to see Rafe's smile.

"Come here, B Girl," Rafe said as she took Bronte's hand and brought her in front of her. "Okay, B Girl, look through here. Can you see Mommy? Let's see... there she is. Now just push this button. Good! We got a picture of Mommy! Let me do one more just in case." She put the camera to her face, looked through the lens at Eden, and focused the camera. "You look beautiful today, you know?" Eden smiled without realizing it, and Rafe snapped the picture.

Rafe picked up Bronte and kissed her several times then handed her to Eden. "Well, I have to get home. I need to help Annie get everything ready, and I promised Abby I'd send her pictures from last night. I'll see you two later." She snapped one more picture. "Bye."

"Bye, Rafe," said Eden. She watched Rafe as she walked away wondering what today meant for them... if anything at all. She sighed as those thoughts were interrupted by the fact she had to go to the police station to make the police report on the damage to her car before Bronte's art lesson.

33

RAFE SALVAGGIO WALKED briskly into her Tuesday afternoon appointment at Katheryn Hardam's Law Office. Katheryn had asked Rafe to come in for a meeting, and she was anxious to know what her attorney had to say. As usual, Rafe breezed into Katheryn's law office and walked toward her private office without waiting for Katheryn's assistant to announce her.

"Hi, Katheryn," said Rafe as she entered Katheryn's office. "Why did you want to see me? Is something happening with the injunction?" asked Rafe as she sat in one of the overstuffed leather chairs.

Katheryn looked up at Rafe, liking her down to business attitude. She closed a file on her desk and folded her hands together. "There are a couple of things I need to talk to you about, and yes, one is the injunction. But first, I want to talk to you about your will."

"My will?" asked Rafe with surprise.

Katheryn nodded. She had brought this topic up before, but Rafe had never done anything about it. "Rafe, you and Eden have been separated for a significant amount of time. I know you were hoping there would be reconciliation, but too much time has gone by. We both know there's no guarantee you'll reconcile. As your lawyer, I have to recommend, again, you think about changing your will. I should have insisted you make changes before now, especially in light of the sale of your companies and the significant increase in your personal net worth because of your inheritance."

Flustered, Rafe didn't know what to say for a moment. "I haven't even considered changing it, Katheryn."

"I know, or we wouldn't be here at this late date," said Katheryn. "You need to think about whether or not you still want to leave anything to Eden. Your current will has almost everything left to her in the event of your death. Maybe you should set up a trust for Bronte once the adoption goes through. Maybe set aside something for your cousin and consider leaving the bulk of your assets to a charitable trust or add more to the grant program for the Arts you started for the art studio you built in your neighbor's garage." Katheryn grimaced. She had no idea why Rafe did not just buy or rent a building somewhere rather than improve someone else's property. But it was not her money, so she kept her mouth shut.

As Rafe processed her words, Katheryn continued. "Also, you may want to divide up your artwork for donations to museums in your name now instead of leaving those things to Eden or whoever you make your executor." She watched as Rafe leaned back in her chair. She hesitated for a moment then went on. "In addition, right now you have Eden listed as your decision maker in your living will. Do you still want her to make those life and death decisions for you? Maybe you should think about changing your decision maker and power of attorney to your cousin Letty."

Feeling overwhelmed, Rafe ran her hand over her face. "I don't know what to say, to do. I always thought everything would go to Eden."

Katheryn could see it was difficult but also knew it was her job to put the hard facts in front of her client. She got up from her chair, walked around her desk and took the chair next to Rafe. "Listen, Rafe, you're dating other people, she's dating other people. Who knows who she'll end up with or who you might meet some day. You need to protect your assets for your family. Right now, it's you and Letty, and soon, Bronte. Hell, it's Bronte now if you want it to be. We can set up anything you want for her. You can even bequeath Eden something if you want," Katheryn said with a shrug. "Does Eden even know what you inherited?"

"No," Rafe said softly.

With an audible sigh, Katheryn shook her head. She didn't blame Rafe for not telling Eden or anyone else about the inheritance. Large amounts of money usually brought out the worst in people. But after almost a year, she felt she had given Rafe long enough to grieve over her relationship with Eden, too long in her personal opinion. "Unfortunately, Rafe, your situation has changed, and this is a serious issue you must address," insisted Katheryn. "Since your father's death, we're dealing with assets worth billions of dollars in four countries. Just last week, we found another partnership he formed with a man in London who bought a bunch of warehouses."

Rafe looked at her with a frown. She knew exactly what they were dealing with. She dealt with it all on almost a daily basis with all the emails and phone calls she had to handle. They had tapered off, but there were still a lot of things she had to oversee. "What the hell are my father's lawyers doing? Why are *you* finding things? He had teams of people who were supposed to be on top of this! If they can't, then fire them and find someone who can, but I'm not paying twice for the same fucking work," she said angrily because she was tired of dealing with them. It had been over two years since he died, and a lot of small things were still pending for one reason or another from probate to lawsuits, to waiting periods, to just fucking incompetence.

"We found it when we were setting up the new rent roll checklist for the trust transferred to you for the properties in England," Katheryn explained. "It was a note in a margin on a print out one of the clerks found and brought to Allan's attention. He made some calls and found out it was outside the trust. The lawyers there will get us a copy of the partnership agreement, so we'll know how to proceed."

"Fine," said Rafe still unhappy with the news and wondering if this meant she would have to have an independent audit done. "Maybe we should look into hiring and international REM company to cut down on the lawyers. It was different when my father was here because he was managing it all. I would consider his old company, but I don't like how they talked about him after he died."

Katheryn went back to her desk where she sat down and looked at her notepad in order to avoid Rafe's gaze. She remembered some of the things people said about Ettore

Salvaggio, and they did not remember him fondly. "I'll look into some options," she said as she wrote. She put her pen on the desk and looked up at Rafe to get to the next order of business. "I know we've discussed this, but we need to go over the cash inflow issue again for after the U.S. probate finalizes."

"I already told you what to do about it," said Rafe annoyed this was coming up again.

"I know," she said nodding her head, "but the more I look into the things your father's financial advisor, if that's what you want to call him, has him into, the more worried I am we should cash you out as soon as possible. If we do, where do you want the cash to go? Again, I'm not a financial adviser. Are you sure you don't want to consult with Ian Hawthorn about some of these investments or make him the agent on your behalf on the accounts?"

"Katheryn, I know you think the guy is shady," said Rafe in frustration. "Most of those accounts Papa probably had so he could cash out quick anyway in case he wanted to buy real estate. If you think I need to cash out, fine. Find a small firm, maybe a woman or lesbian-owned one and give them some business. It can't be too hard for you to find someone good with all your contacts."

"What about the—," Katheryn started.

"All of it," Rafe cut her off with a wave of her hand. "Whatever cash or payments are coming out of his accounts, open new ones at the new firm and reinvest for now. Just email me whatever I need to sign so we can get it done. Who knows what penalties I'll probably end up having to pay after all this time."

Katheryn looked at Rafe for a moment and, as her lawyer, she felt she had to try one last time. "Rafe, Ian has been your advisor for years. Are you sure you don't want to get advice from someone you know and trust?"

"Ian Hawthorn isn't the only fucking financial advisor on the planet," said Rafe hotly. "I already put my personal money at their company, and I transferred what I wanted to go to their company. I'm not giving them more reason to talk badly about my father and make money off him at the same time."

"Okay," Katheryn nodded and let out the breath she was holding in. "Well then, all of his personal holdings should be settled soon. What have you decided to do with the Salvaggio Family Trust?"

"I talked with Gabri, and we're leaving it where it is," said Rafe as she leaned back in her chair. "Moving it would be a headache, and it might hurt a lot of relationships in Italy."

"But you don't live in Italy anymore," said Katheryn not understanding because it made more sense to move it.

"But it is my home," said Rafe with a frown, "and my father's home. The trust holds Italian land, including the land of my father's grandfather who started the trust, and people would be upset if it was suddenly moved to America. There's a lot going on with it all the time, and moving it would make those things harder for Gabri and the lawyers to do. So it will stay."

"Fine," Katheryn conceded. "I'm going to send you with copies of everything for the will." She stood and gave Rafe a thick envelope. "You go over it and make any name or amount changes you feel are appropriate and bring it back. Now, there are no numbers or accounts listed in this copy to protect your privacy, but I trust you know what accounts you have. I'll go over it with you when you finish and add the new accounts when we get them. Then I'll make a new master list. After, we will need to contact your financial advisors and make appropriate changes needed there too."

"Okay, I'll start thinking about it," Rafe sighed, her anger gone to sadness.

"Rafe, don't put this off," Katheryn said firmly. "It takes time to change things, especially the things overseas."

"Katheryn, Eden and I are starting to get along better now. Maybe I should just leave it," Rafe said as she rolled the paperwork into a thick tube.

Katheryn tapped her pen on the desk. "It's good that you're getting along, but Rafe, you have to be realistic. You can't base your financial decisions on a fantasy. She isn't your life partner anymore."

Rafe looked down sorrowfully. *She was my life*, she thought. "I know, Katheryn. You're right. I'll look at it and get it back to you."

Katheryn took a deep breath and delved into her next topic, which was much more difficult. *Saving the best for last*, she thought. "Okay, the next issue is just as serious and even more immediate. I have a source who informed me the group filing the injunction might be planning to contact you or harass you in some way to force you to drop the adoption petition." She stopped and watched as Rafe went pale as the information sank in. "I strongly urge you to be aware of your surroundings at all times. Lock your doors and windows and take any other security measures you feel necessary."

Rafe stood outraged and paced the room. "Do the police know?" she demanded.

"It's been reported to the authorities, but it's only a threat right now, and a vague one. But I believe even a small threat should be taken seriously," Katheryn said calmly.

Rafe spun back toward her worried. "What about Eden and Bronte, have they threatened them?"

"It affects all of you, Rafe," Katheryn warned. "Anyone you're near or close to can be affected by threats like this."

"What do I tell them? My friends and family?" Rafe asked at a loss.

"We don't want people getting jumpy so just keep it to yourself for now, and I'll let you know when I find out more," Katheryn suggested.

"I have to tell Eden. I can't *not* tell her. If it means her or Bronte's life, I have to tell her what's going on. Their safety is important to me," declared Rafe

"I'll leave that decision to you," said Katheryn. "I just don't want undue worry where it isn't needed. Would you like me to tell her?"

"No," Rafe said as she paced fretfully. "I think I should be the one to do it. I'll call her as soon as I get back to the office."

Katheryn nodded her acceptance of her choice. "Call me when you've gone over your will."

Rafe made it back to her office, and she impatiently waited on hold for Eden to pick up on her end. She heard the click of her picking up the call. "Eden? Listen I have something important to talk to you about."

"What is it?" Eden asked evenly through the phone. She knew why Rafe was calling, and she had been preparing for it all day.

"I just got out of a meeting with Katheryn, and she received some information from one of her sources the people filing the injunction may be planning to threaten us physically if we don't drop the adoption petition," Rafe said quickly. "A police report was made, but it's all that can be done right now."

"I see," she said calmly. She knew more than a police report had been filed. Katheryn had just reported the vandalism incident to the FBI agent in case it had something to do with their investigation. Katheryn wanted to warn Rafe, and Eden had agreed. She didn't want anything to happen to Rafe if it was Jake and his group and they were going to target them both.

Perplexed at Eden's calmness, she spoke in a firm voice. "You need to be extra careful and aware of your surroundings. See if you can get someone to walk to your car with you after work, lock your doors and windows at home, be aware of your surroundings, and make sure Bronte is safe."

Eden took a deep breath to control her anxiety the call was causing her. "Okay, I will."

"It may be nothing but please... please, take it seriously," Rafe begged.

"Believe me I will, I will," Eden said trying to sound reassuring. She was already doing everything she could think of within her power to keep safe. She even had a difficult time letting Bronte go with her nanny Lydia. She was on edge every day until she could call and check to make sure they made it to Bronte's school, or they were safely home from whatever outing Lydia had planned. She was sure Lydia thought she had turned into an obsessive mother. Lydia knew about the kidnapping attempt so understood why Eden needed to check in so often. Rafe made a point to tell Lydia about Jake and how he came to the house to try to pick up Bronte. Rafe made it clear exactly who could pick up Bronte from her. She felt lucky Lydia was such a great nanny and was alert for any potential problems.

Still wondering why Eden was not more concerned, Rafe tried not to show her frustration. "Okay, that's all I guess," she said at a loss. "Just keep Bronte and yourself in safe situations."

"Thanks for calling," Eden said wanting to end the call because it was making her anxious. "I have to go. Bye."

"Bye," said Rafe. She looked at the phone realizing she was talking to a dial tone. She hung up the phone carefully, wondering if Eden was going to take this threat seriously.

34

THE REST OF the week had passed with no sign of any trouble, and Rafe Salvaggio and Eden Kingsley were both relieved, but for very different reasons. Rafe had been checking in with Eden every night, and it was sweet, but it wasn't helping Eden's anxiety. She couldn't tell Rafe just how worried she was, and her calls made it harder knowing she was keeping things from her.

Her saving grace was the Saturday art lessons. She was with Rafe, and Rafe was focused on Bronte, and it meant Eden could truly relax.

Eden watched as Rafe worked with Bronte to put her paints away. They were covered in matching green paint, and Eden smiled at their mess. She had managed to keep the paint only on her hands.

Rafe handed Annie their messy paint smocks. "Who knew making circles for an hour could be so much fun?" Rafe laughed.

"Well, circles are pretty important, you know." Annie smiled at the green-streaked Bronte.

"They all did such a good job today," said Jude who had been helping Annie with the lesson. "Rafe, did you get a picture of Bronte helping her friend?"

"I think so. I think I filled up the memory card. I can't believe I took so many pictures," Rafe said as she hung the camera back around her neck. "I hope they're decent."

"I'm sure they'll be fine." Eden laughed as she tried to wipe some paint off Bronte. "Okay, we're ready to go get cleaned up now."

"See you later, Annie," said Rafe and waved as she followed Eden into the house carrying Bronte. "This was a great day."

"Yes, it was," Eden agreed.

Rafe looked at Eden and smiled warmly. "Eden, I was just wondering if you had dinner plans for tonight."

"No, I don't have any dinner plans," she said as she looked at Rafe smiling at her.

"So, you don't have birthday plans?" she asked tentatively. "If you do, it's okay."

"No," Eden said as she looked away. She didn't really feel like celebrating this year. She wasn't surprised Rafe remembered her birthday was Monday. Rafe seemed to always remember those kind of things. "I don't have any plans."

"Would you and Bronte like to stay and have lunch with me? I don't have anything fancy, just some chicken strips and macaroni." She shrugged and smiled because she had actually gone to the store just to have food to invite Eden for lunch. "I just thought it would be nice. You know, all of us having a meal together."

Eden looked at the matching pair and nodded. "I think it would be nice too."

"Okay," said Rafe excited and pleased they would be staying. "I'll get Bronte and myself cleaned up. Then I can start lunch. You just sit down and relax, and we'll be right back."

Rafe went to her room with Bronte and closed the door behind her.

Eden watched Rafe go and looked around the house at a loss for what to do. She went up to Rafe's door and knocked. She then tried to talk to her through the door. "Rafe, I can start cooking if you want." There was no answer. "Rafe?" she tried again. She shrugged and went into the once familiar kitchen and started getting things out to cook for lunch. She laughed to herself because practically the only food in the refrigerator was what they would have today. Rafe was still a 'buy as she needed it' shopper when it came to food.

Rafe and Bronte were fresh from their shower and getting hungry, despite all the paint ingested by Bronte. Rafe carried the baby out of the bedroom and found Eden in the kitchen.

"Okay, we're sparkling now," she said then noticed Eden had started cooking. "You didn't have to do this."

Eden smiled at Rafe and kissed Bronte. "I know. I wanted to do it. I enjoy cooking, and I wanted to help out."

"Thank you. It'll definitely taste better if you cook it anyway," Rafe confessed. "I'll make the salad."

When Rafe and Eden finished making lunch, they sat down with Bronte between them to eat. As Rafe ate a chicken strip, she watched as Eden helped Bronte. The meal brought back memories of coming home to Eden for dinner and just being together. She missed the familiarity and comfort and wondered if she would ever have it in her life again with anyone.

When they were finished, Rafe picked up Bronte and took her into the living room as Eden started to clear the dishes.

"Don't worry about it," said Rafe. "We can let the maid get it later. Come into the living room with us."

"Are you sure? It'll only take a minute, and I don't mind," said Eden as she shook her head at the thought of Rafe allowing a maid in her house. She knew Rafe hired one after she moved out, and she must be really good to be able to put up with Rafe's organizational demands.

"No, just leave it," insisted Rafe. "Come on. I know you guys need to leave soon, and Bronte and I want to show you something."

"Okay," shrugged Eden curious about what Rafe wanted to show her. She followed Rafe into the living room.

"B Girl, let's show Mommy what we have to do every night before we go to bed, okay?" Rafe sat on the living room floor in front of the fireplace in her meditation position and closed her eyes.

Eden was bemused.

Bronte went up behind Rafe and put her small arms around Rafe's neck. "I feel something on my back. What is it?" asked Rafe in a funny voice and Bronte laughed. Rafe leaned forward with Bronte on her back. "It is so heavy, what is it? I think I'll shake it off."

She shook herself, and Bronte slid off her back and landed next to Rafe. She sat up, opened her eyes, and acted surprised. "Look! It's a B Girl! I think she's looking for her bed! Come here, little girl, and I'll help you."

Rafe pulled her legs up and sat with her knees up in front of her chin. Bronte ran up to her and put her arms around

Rafe's knees. "Should we fly around until we find a goodnight kiss?" Rafe asked, and Bronte laughed. "Okay, put your arms out." Bronte leaned against Rafe's legs and put her arms out from her sides, and Rafe held her under her arms. "Are you ready? Here we go!"

Rafe fell back lifting Bronte off the floor with her legs, so she was parallel to her. "We have a lift off! Here we go!" Rafe moved her legs from side to side making Bronte 'fly' through the air.

"Look, over there," Rafe whispered to Bronte. "It's the good-night kiss! Can we make it?"

Bronte was laughing and swaying with Rafe's legs.

"Oh no, Captain, we have a problem! I think we're running out of fuel!"

She started jiggling Bronte whose laughter got harder.

"Oh, no! We have to make it to the good-night kiss! Must... make... it!"

Rafe, still jiggling Bronte, slowly lifted her legs so Bronte's head lowered and she started sliding down them. "Captain, we're going down! Will we make it?"

She brought Bronte's face to hers and Bronte took hold of Rafe's face and gave her a kiss. "She did it! We're saved! B Girl got the good-night kiss!"

She hugged Bronte tight then sat up with her. "One more?" Rafe asked, and Bronte kissed her again. "*Mmm, ti voglio bene!*"[8] Rafe said and then looked at Eden with a smile. "Now you know about the good-night kiss."

---

[8] Mmm, I love you!

Eden smiled as she looked at the two of them together. Bronte was crawling over her and Rafe's curly hair was disheveled. "No wonder she's always so worn out when I take her home from your house," she said amused.

"I think we help each other burn off all the energy we have." Rafe laughed. Bronte ran and jumped into Rafe's arms, and Rafe rocked back, lowering Bronte slowly to the floor and tussling with her. "Okay, I think we've played enough." She got up and fixed her clothes. "I think it's getting close to your nap time, little girl, and your mommy needs to get you home."

Eden's heart jumped as she remembered she would have to leave. "Yep," she said recovering. "Let's get all our things." After they had gathered everything, she turned to Rafe. "Thank you for inviting us to dinner."

Rafe smiled warmly and was glad she'd had a nice time. "Thank you for accepting. Here, let me help you get this stuff to your car." They walked out to the car and started loading Bronte and her things. "Did you get a new car?"

"Oh, no, this is a rental," said Eden. "My car has been in the shop for a week," she said while buckling Bronte into her car seat.

"What's wrong with it?" Rafe asked as she handed her Bronte's bag. "I think it's still under warranty. Did you take it to Park Motors?"

"Uh, well..." She paused anxiously not wanting to tell her about the vandalism to her car. "I'm just getting a new paint job. There was some paint overspray at the studio lot. I should have it back in a few days. The studio is taking care of it."

"Oh, okay," she said glad everything was good. She waited until Eden turned around and held the driver's door open. "Eden," she said looking openly into her eyes. "It really was a very good day."

Eden reached out and touched Rafe's hand resting on the door. "It was a good day."

"Happy birthday," she said softly.

"Thank you," said Eden and looked away feeling guilty because she never wished Rafe a happy birthday back in October. She got into the car, and Rafe closed the door for her.

"Bye." Rafe gave a wave as Eden backed out of the driveway and watched them move down the street.

Rafe went back into the house and looked at the dishes on the table. She went to get her camera and took some shots of the table. *Lunch for a family of three*, she smiled at the thought. *But is it meant to be?* She shook her head at the rhyme. Maybe it will just be lunch for three every once in a while.

35

THE CALIFORNIA CHILDREN and Family Services Department opened at eight a.m. on Monday morning, and Jake Thomson had been there when they unlocked the door. He had to find something to help stop, or at least delay, the adoption of Eden's baby to Rafe and save his own skin at the same time. He was getting desperate because Daniel's idiotic stunt of vandalizing Eden's car to scare her back into the fold almost got them pulled out of the state. Jake was angry at the possibility the vandalism could be traced back to them, especially since Daniel had to spray paint a message on the car. The message was blatantly religious and was a huge blunder. The reverend was already so angry he had decided to file an injunction, and if it went in front of a judge, it would take the mission out of Jake's hands. Unless he did more, it meant this mission could be deemed a failure on his end, and Jake could not allow that to happen.

"Here's my statement," he said handing the caseworker the form. "I really hate to do this, but I just can't sit by and do nothing," he explained earnestly.

"You're doing the right thing, sir," said the middle-aged caseworker. "A lot of people just ignore these kinds of situations, and that's when kids end up hurt or dead."

"I couldn't live with myself if something happened and I hadn't done anything," Jake said sounding distraught and nervous. "I just hope I'm wrong about the situation. This is why it's so important to me that I remain anonymous."

"Sir, when people have suspicions like this, it usually turns out to be true," stated the caseworker.

"So, what will happen?" he asked as if he didn't have any idea how the department worked.

"Well, the case will be assigned, and then someone will go out to make a home visit to assess the situation," she informed him.

"I just hope the case is assigned to a caseworker who can see through her innocent act." He sighed audibly so he would look more sympathetic.

"We all know what to look for, sir. We get all kinds in here," she assured him. "If something's going on, we'll get to the bottom of it. Our main function is to keep families together, but if there's abuse, we can take the child and put her where she'll be safe until the parent can get help or the child can be placed in a safe home."

Jake smiled at the caseworker. "I know the department will help. I mean, it's why you're here, right? I trust your judgment. I just hope you don't get there too late," he said re-expressing his concern. "I'm afraid of what might happen if no one acts fast."

He left the office and knew, even if they didn't take the child, just the fact California Children and Family Services Department was looking at them and had opened a case file, it would delay the adoption. More importantly, it would give him more time to fix things so he didn't fail his mission for the Stewards and rescue the child. He smiled to himself. "Happy birthday, Eden." He chuckled. He hoped Eden liked her Birthday present.

36

EDEN KINGSLEY WAS coming to love her Saturdays with Rafe and Bronte and did not want anything bad to happen that might stop them. She was relieved two weeks had passed since her car had been vandalized and they had been without any problems from Jake or his group. She was hoping the event with her car was just a one-time thing and had more to do with the studio than the Stewards.

They were finished with the art lesson, and Eden followed Rafe and Bronte into the house. Bronte was babbling and still sucking some of the edible paint from her fingers while Rafe talked to her in Italian. Sometimes, it was hard for Eden to leave. She fought the feeling because it conflicted with all the other feelings she was still trying to figure out. She didn't want to do anything to make Rafe stop letting her come over for the art lessons.

"I don't think she'll be hungry for a while," said Rafe as they entered the house. "She ate a lot of paint today," Rafe said as she laughed.

Eden smiled and nodded as she used the towel she was holding to wipe a spot of paint off Bronte's cheek. "What are you guys doing today?" she asked because she couldn't help herself.

Rafe shrugged. "Not much. I think we'll swim for a while since she's not hungry right now, then see about dinner after her nap—if she takes one."

"Sounds like you're gonna have some fun," she cooed to Bronte.

Rafe looked sideways at Eden. "Do you want to stay and swim with us?"

Eden felt her heart thud in her chest and then shook her head not wanting to wear out her welcome. "No, it's okay."

"You can," said Rafe earnestly. "You can use one of the spare swimsuits. Maybe we can talk."

Eden looked into Rafe's beautiful glowing gray-blue eyes and swallowed. She wanted to stay, but it was so hard. She had to keep herself from talking about everything going on. She wanted to be close to her, but she knew she couldn't hurt her again. She sighed and looked away. Then she heard herself saying the opposite of what she probably should have said. "Okay."

"Great, I'll get her swimming suit, and you can get one from the guest room," Rafe said happily. "Then why don't you fix us some drinks and meet us by the pool," she said and went into her bedroom.

Eden frantically searched through the swimsuits until she found a one piece she thought would work. She couldn't believe she agreed to stay and swim. She was still a bit self-conscious about her body around Rafe. She was back in shape, but she did not think she would look as good as she used too in a bikini after her C-Section. *What am I thinking*, she thought. She didn't know why she was so nervous. She kept picturing Greer and all the other beautiful women she had seen Rafe with. She just didn't think she measured up anymore. She looked in the mirror and sighed. *It doesn't matter anymore,* she reminded herself. *We're doing good just to get along now.*

When she was dressed in her swimming suit, she entered the kitchen and began to fix their drinks. She decided on a glass of wine for Rafe and one for herself, and juice for Bronte. She opened the cabinet to get a couple of wine glasses, and as she took them out, she noticed a notepad filled with Rafe's crisp handwriting and a stack of papers lying on the counter. One of the papers said 'Last Will and Testament of Rafaella E. Salvaggio.' Eden hesitated then moved the pad off so she could see the will.

37

BRONTE LOVED SWIMMING and was laughing and splashing as Rafe Salvaggio played with her in the perfectly heated water. Rafe was pulling her around in a swim ring when Eden came out with their drinks and sat down on the side of the pool, putting her legs in the water. She watched them play and got lost in her thoughts.

Rafe broke the silence between them. "How's your work going?"

Surprised at Rafe's interest, she hesitated. "It's going good. Good," she repeated.

"Julia said you told her you were working on a project that could sweep the awards next year," Rafe said as she pulled Bronte back and forth through the water.

Eden flushed with embarrassment at the compliment. "I don't know about sweeping them, but we hope to get several in its genre. It's kind of an autobiography slash horror slash mind trip about Edgar Allen Poe and his work."

Rafe smiled because she knew Poe well. In her best Vincent Price voice, she quoted Poe. "Ah, 'Once upon a midnight dreary while I pondered weak and weary, over many a quaint and curious volume of forgotten lore.'"

"Yeah." Eden laughed.

"One of my favorite Poe poems is the one titled *Alone,*" Rafe admitted. She thought this would be a good time to try to be open and ask some questions. She thought about the poem for a moment then began to quote.

"From childhood's hour I have not been as others were—I have not seen as others saw—I could not bring my passions from a common spring. From the same source I have not taken my sorrow; I could not awaken my heart to joy at the same tone; and all that I loved, I loved alone."

Rafe stopped, though there was much more to the poem. She took a breath and swept away the feelings it invoked in her because of her childhood and all the things she experianced. The poem was all she was prepared to share.

"I carried a copy of the poem around with me for a while when I was younger. I felt the same way about my life. I haven't thought about it in a while," she said. "I hope I can show Bronte she's never alone." She spun Bronte in her ring again and changed the subject. "So, tell me about the script."

Eden hesitated for a moment wondering why Rafe would carry such a sad poem around. She shrugged it off thinking it must have been teenage angst.

The thought of how well work was going caused her to beam proudly. She was happy to just talk about work and keep things simple. "The script is incredible and very ambitious," she began. "I've been able to help more than usual by making suggestions to the producer on putting together a crew rivaling some of the really big budget films just because everyone is so into Poe. Several main people on our costume and set crew did Chicago, and we've got an amazing special effects company coming in, not to mention we're talking to Johnny Depp about playing Poe since he's worked with the director in the past. If everything works out, it could cross genres."

"Wow," said Rafe as she wiped water from Bronte's face. "It really sounds remarkable." She smiled up at Eden. "You're amazing at your job. I'm glad you're doing what you love again."

Eden smiled and took a drink of her wine taking the compliment with grace. "What about you? Annie said you were giving a lecture sometime soon."

Rafe gave a short laugh. "It's nothing. I haven't even decided on a topic yet."

"Annie says every student she's talked to is going to hear you," Eden revealed. "She says you have a big student body following. Half are in love with you and the other half wants to be you."

Rafe smiled and shook her head. "She told me I could talk about the history of the mobile and the room would still be packed. I told her it might be a good subject to cover, and actually, the history of the mobile was quite interesting."

"You didn't! The mobile!" She laughed at the thought.

"Yeah, she thought it was funny too, but I was serious." She took Bronte out of her ring. "Wanna go under? Ready? One, two, three!" She dunked herself and Bronte under the water and came back up quickly. "Whoa, that was fun, wasn't it?" she said as water ran down their faces." Bronte wiped her eyes. "Here, let's get the towel." She went to the edge of the pool, got the towel, and wiped her eyes. "There you go. Now let's do some kicks. Can you kick? Good!" She picked Bronte up and held her as she bounced around the pool with her.

"Rafe," Eden started cautiously. "I didn't mean to but, I saw your will on the counter when I was getting our drinks."

Rafe looked at Eden then looked away. "It's okay. It's become a hard thing for me to sort out."

"I think it's great what you're thinking about doing for Bronte," she said appreciatively. "I didn't know you had planned to leave everything to me. We never talked about it."

"Well," said Rafe trying to hide her sadness, "I just wanted to make sure you would always be taken care of no matter what." She took a deep breath and let it out. "But now I want to make sure Bronte will be set." She looked at Bronte. "Because you, my girl, are going to do great things."

"She will," agreed Eden as she looked kindly at Rafe.

Rafe looked up at Eden intently, studying her. She had so many unanswered questions for herones she had not even told Greer about. She debated with herself whether or not it was worth the risk to ask them now. Like Greer said, there would be no way to figure things out between them unless she knew some of the answers. Even if she didn't like the answers Eden had given her, at least she wouldn't be living in the dark anymore, and it might help her move on.

"Eden, with the risk of you running out of here as fast as you can, I'd like to ask you something, and it's probably a very hard and personal question."

Eden looked around nervously everywhere except at Rafe. "Sure. Okay."

"Have you figured out yet why," she hesitated, "why your feelings changed the way they did?"

Eden closed her eyes so she couldn't see Rafe's. "No, not really." She paused. "I guess it's just, I thought things would be different when I started a family."

Careful and not wanting to push too hard Rafe pressed on. "Different?"

Eden sighed heavily. "Rafe, my dream before I met you was to find a husband and live in a house with the white picket fence, probably on a farm somewhere, have two point five children, a dog, a cat, a goldfish and maybe some other animals. I thought my life would be a lot like my parents. You know, not every little girl's dream is to grow up and become a lesbian, become estranged from her family, and kicked out of the church she had gone to since birth."

"True," Rafe mused, wishing she knew this back when they were talking about having a family. "But I thought you wanted to have a family with me," she said not understanding what things before they met had to do with why her feelings changed.

Eden could feel herself flush and knew her face was red. She looked down and swallowed back her guilt. "I did," she said softly. "We have a family. Just not the way either of us planned it." She hesitated and looked at Rafe. "I guess the way I was raised just made things hard for me."

"I thought you moved here because you wanted to be in the movie business. It's what you told me. I didn't know you wanted to go back there someday."

"I did move here for the movie business," Eden confirmed softly. "I guess I still felt like someday I would go back when I started my family. But now..." she trailed off with a shrug. Rafe knew everything she went through with her family when they were told about the way she wanted to live her life and her new relationship.

Rafe thought about Eden's words and still didn't really understand. "I guess I was lucky my papa was accepting," she said. Sometimes she thought it was more like he didn't care about her being gay. He kept his private life to himself, and so did she. It was an understanding they had. Rafe wondered if maybe the change in Eden was about her parents. "I can't say becoming a lesbian was any kind of a dream. It's not something I became." She shrugged and continued, "It's more like a trait I was born with like the color of my eyes. Being a lesbian is just an intrinsic part of who I am." Rafe considered Eden's answer. "I don't think I ever dreamed of a white picket fence, either. Look at my papa and how I was raised, traveling everywhere, never staying long enough to make friends. School was really the only stable place for me, and I didn't really like it until I found a purpose for going. I dreamed of art and architecture, new exciting places, adventure and taking what the world had to offer to me and making it my own. I guess I dreamed of being a lot like my papa." She knew no one understood their relationship, but as strange and different as it was, they did love each other under it all.

It made Eden smile that Rafe couldn't see what she saw. She remembered the big tour Rafe gave her of her company *Eroina Conservazione e Design*. Rafe was so excited to show her all the equipment they had in the workshop, introduce her to her employees, and talk about all the projects she had going. She did some amazing things on her own and with her father.

"I think you got your dream."

"Possibly," Rafe conceded and brought Bronte over to her. "So," she asked cautiously, "do you think your feelings changed because you thought you were losing your dream of a white picket fence and all the other stuff?"

"I don't know," said Eden shaking her head as she slipped into the warm pool and held Bronte as she played with a pool toy.

"I could have painted our fence white," Rafe joked wanting to ease the tension.

"I think it was more than a fence." Eden smiled as a picture of Rafe out painting the fence in her work clothes, sporting her tool belt and hardhat, popped into her mind. She knew Rafe was joking, but Eden did not doubt she would have done it. Eden knew she needed to try to explain herself. She wanted to tell her why. It was just hard to say the words while looking in her eyes. She looked down at the pool water. "I think it was more because all of the images and ideas I'd been exposed to defining love and family and happiness and security had a man in them. I guess all of those images and ideas are too hard to undo." She stroked Bronte's head absently. "You've been sure of yourself your whole life and comfortable being a lesbian for more than half of it." She hesitated. "I've never been sure of myself. I guess, at that moment, the four and a half years I was with you just couldn't compete with all of the years before I met you."

Sad and not really understanding, Rafe tried to lighten the mood as she took Bronte again and dipped down into the pool with her. "I could have never given you two point five kids. I'm terrible with fractions." She smiled at Eden and spun around in the water with Bronte.

Eden gave a short laugh. "Funny."

"It was, wasn't it?" Rafe cooed to Bronte who laughed. She looked up at Eden with a slight smile. "So, I never got to ask you, did you tell your mother about Bronte?"

Looking down at her hands, Eden's emotions swung from guilt to anger at her mother. Since her father's death, she had only been in contact with her mother once and was unceremoniously rejected. Eden knew it mostly had to do with her father and his views, but the church community had a big influence too. Small towns were brutal.

"No," she said feeling the pain of their rejection in her heart. She looked up just in time to see Rafe kiss Bronte sweetly.

Eden debated with herself about telling Rafe what Jake's plan was for them. He wanted to contact her mother and make her part of the wedding and her life again. The problem was the plan included excluding Rafe and moving far away. She decided Rafe was better off not knowing any of those plans.

"Do you want to tell her?" asked Rafe as she dried Bronte's face again.

"No. I don't know. Maybe," Eden stammered. "I just don't want to do anything that might hurt Bronte." Or herself or Rafe, but she kept it to herself. "I don't know if I can take more rejection, and I know it would be very hard for me to know my mother rejected my child."

"It's okay," said Rafe seeing the conversation was upsetting to Eden. "I just asked because we talked about it. I never knew if you and Jake took her to see your mother or not." She had wondered back then if the problem with Eden's parents was one of the reasons Eden left to be with Jake. So she could go home and be with her family and the community she knew as a child. Rafe understood loss but could not imagine what it was like to have a mother who was alive she could never see.

Rafe looked at Bronte's crinkled hands. "I think it's time to get out for a while. Look at your fingers. Here, you go to

Mommy." She gave Bronte to Eden who took her up the pool steps then wrapped her in a towel. Rafe pushed herself up over the edge and out of the pool in one swift movement. She dried off quickly, sat on a lounger, and picked up her glass of wine.

Eden finished drying off Bronte and sat down with her in her lap in the lounger next to Rafe. She gave Bronte her drink. "Here you go, baby."

"So, why Jake?" Rafe asked the question she had been burning to be asked for months. Cautiously, she explained her question. "I just mean he's not very good looking, you could do better. You're beautiful so you could have some rich movie executive or something." She watched as Eden blushed at the compliment. "If I were going to be with a man or anyone for that matter, it would have to be someone who could at least share my interests in some way—even a small one. Jake doesn't seem to know Dr. Zhivago from Animal House. Does he know *anything* about any kind of real art including cinematic arts?" She paused and took a sip of wine. "Plus, there's the fact he's just a real fucking bastard who was trying to ruin my life," she added with a small amount of venom.

"Rafe," Eden said sternly and nodded toward Bronte.

Rafe cringed at being chastised. "Sorry," she said. She needed to do a better job watching her language around Bronte.

Eden thought about Rafe's question for a moment. She didn't want to think about Jake but knew Rafe would not let the question go. "I don't know," she said hesitantly. "He fit the caring male image I was brought up with, and he had strength, and I felt protected."

"So, he made you feel safe?" Rafe asked softly trying to understand and remembering what Greer had told her.

"Yes, for a while," she admitted softly while hating the truth of the statement and not wanting to talk about him anymore. Jake had turned out to be a lot like her father, and he was definitely not the kind of man she wanted.

"So now," Rafe started pensively, "for you—love is safety?"

Eden sat Bronte down on a towel and let her play with the water toys Rafe had out for her. She thought about how to best answer the question. "I never thought about it like that, but yeah, I guess. Isn't it for you?"

Rafe laughed and shook her head. "No. My definition of love has never changed," she said. "Love is always pushing me, making me question myself, driving me to the edge and burning me up inside. It's anything but safe—it's terrifying. It's like," she paused, "stepping off the edge of the world into chaos. Then, once I take the chance and jump off the edge, it's either the most painful or the most glorious feeling imaginable. Depending on whether or not the person I'm jumping for jumps in with me, of course. It's why I don't jump much."

Eden smiled as she pushed a loose strand of her golden blond hair behind her ear. "It seems to me like you jump a lot."

Rafe looked at Eden with a churlish grin. "No, that's not love. That's pure passion," she declared.

"There's a difference?" Eden asked as she raised her eyebrows.

"Absolutely," Rafe confirmed earnestly. "Love is supposed to last like a big fire you can't be put out, and even when there's no flame, there is still heat, and any little thing can ignite it again. Passion is like a spark that flashes and then is gone."

"Whoa," Eden blurted. "I guess I never thought of it like that before." She looked at Rafe wondering where all this was coming from. Rafe had never talked like this to her before, about what was going on inside her. Rafe tended to be on the more rational side of everything when she talked. She was emotional and passionate but never really spoke about her feelings.

"Mixing them feels dangerous to me, so I've learned over the years to keep them separate and stay in control. I don't always win that battle," Rafe admitted but stopped short of confessing the fight for control mostly happened when she was around Eden. It took everything in her sometimes not to just walk up to her and touch her or kiss her like she used to when she saw her.

"I knew you were passionate, but I never knew there was so much more going on inside you," Eden said bemusedly.

Rafe shrugged and took a sip of her wine. She didn't know if she could have talked to Eden this way if it weren't for Greer's help and was glad she had the chance to now. "I guess the chaos inside me was why I said and did some of the things I did after you told me you were having feelings for men."

"What?" Eden asked not sure if this was going to lead to Rafe raining her anger down on her for leaving without a word. "What do you mean?"

Rafe hesitated as she saw Eden's face had flushed red again. "Well, when you told me," she paused to make sure she said her words right, "I just wanted to prove you didn't need some man. When we lay in bed, I wanted to touch you and kiss you and make you want me again." She put her head back on the lounger. "But I knew you could, and would, refuse me. So I had to get you out of my bed." She breathed deeply remembering the pain and confusion she felt. "Just knowing you were laying there wanting someone else was too much for me," she confessed with a shrug. "So, I told you to explore the feelings and figure things out. By doing that, I gave you something you couldn't refuse because I didn't know if you could see I had given it to you."

Eden looked at Rafe with a slight frown. "What did you give me?"

Rafe looked up into Eden's eyes. "Trust."

There was a long silence as Rafe tried to see if she had opened up too much. Eden was looking away now and had picked up Bronte to rock her.

Rafe decided to continue quickly, and hopefully, nonchalantly. "But I even messed that up by qualifying it and saying I may not be there when you figured it out." She waited to see if Eden would respond. "I should have just tried to make you want me again. I think your refusal of me then would have been less painful."

Eden, still looking away from Rafe, was overcome with her openness. "I'm sorry it caused you so much pain," she said softly.

Rafe smiled appreciatively, though Eden would never see it because she was looking away. She geared herself up to ask another hard question. "Do you think your experience with Jake verified your feelings?"

Eden was filled with trepidation by the question. "If you're asking me if I still have feelings just for men, I can't answer you. I don't know anymore. So much has happened so fast." She sighed and pushed her hair back. "I'm still figuring things out."

"So, is that why you broke off your engagement?"

Eden looked down at Bronte and ran her hand through her soft dark curls, hesitant about answering Rafe's question. She might still be engaged to Jake if she hadn't received the anonymous envelope. Even though she had tried to give him his ring back, and was having doubts before the package came, the thought still made her feel sick.

"I think things were just going too fast," she said hesitantly. She decided to tell Rafe about her feelings before she received the envelope so she could tell her most of the truth. "When I slowed down, and really looked at my situation, I realized I was about to become some heterosexual archetype who marries first and thinks later, and I couldn't do it. I thought about my mother, how she blindly followed my father just because he was her husband, and never really had a say in anything. I guess I just felt like, even though I have feelings for men, I didn't want to become a conformist or give up being in control of my life."

Rafe looked at Eden a little confused by her rambling answer. She knew not all men were like Eden's father so Eden didn't have to marry anyone like him. "So," she started slowly, "you're just saying Jake was the wrong man? Did he not want to live on a farm? He seems like the type who might," she joked.

A wave of anxiety flowed over Eden at how right Rafe was about Jake. He was the wrong man but not the way she thought. "I think he would have moved to a farm," she revealed cautiously. She didn't want to remind her of Jake's announcement of their engagement and his revelation they would be moving away. But Jake wanted more than to move away. The thought of what Rafe's reaction might be toward her if she ever found out the truth about how she got involved with Jake and his group terrified Eden. "I just think I wasn't ready to move away and give up my life here yet." She looked up and saw Rafe looking at her expectantly. "He was definitely the wrong man."

Rafe wondered if the hesitation in her answer was because there was another reason Eden left Jake. She also could not understand how, after all their years together, and the rally's for equality they had participated in, Eden could ever go into marriage without thought. Rafe never thought marriage would even be an option in her lifetime, so knowing now it was a possibility made her think more seriously about the responsibility and commitment it implied. It would never be anything she would just do on a whim.

"For me, with everything we were involved in the fight for equality, I don't think marriage is something I could just go into without thinking," Rafe said as she shook her head.

"I don't know," said Eden softly as she too remembered all the stories she had heard and the rallies they had attended. "Maybe marriage just isn't for me."

"Well," Rafe responded solemnly, not knowing what else to say, "I hope you find whatever makes you happy."

"Thank you," Eden said quietly. She didn't think she could talk about this anymore. "Please, I just don't know what else to say or tell you about it."

"You don't have to say anything more," Rafe said then lifted her head and looked at Eden with a playful smile and a wicked glint in her eyes. "Was the sex better?"

Eden scoffed, rolled her eyes, and shook her head. "It was different."

"But not better," Rafe grinned feeling a little triumphant and took a drink. "So, since you've dropped Jake, have you been dating?"

Eden smiled, relieved at the subject change, so she didn't have to think about Jake—or sex. "No. I just haven't had time with work and Bronte."

"Why don't you bring her over Friday night and go out, have some fun, and maybe meet someone?" Rafe looked at Eden and saw she looked tired. "It sounds like you need a break."

"Really?" Eden said, surprised. "I don't know." She shook her head.

"Sure," said Rafe and looked at Bronte in Eden's arms. "I'd like to take some more pictures of her, and I bought a new art book to show her."

"Okay," Eden nodded wondering what just happened. "I'll bring her over, and I'll think about going out." She looked down at Bronte. "She's asleep."

"We bored her." Rafe chuckled. She got up and lifted Bronte out of Eden's arms. "Come on, sleepy head."

"Let me get the door," offered Eden as they walked toward the house. They went inside and changed Bronte out if her swimsuit then put her in her crib. Eden looked at Bronte sleeping and then at Rafe who was putting on her robe. *She's so beautiful,* she thought. "I better get going," Eden said and turned quickly to leave the room and change back into her clothes.

When Eden had changed her clothes and came out of the guest room, Rafe followed her through the living room and opened the front door for her. She stepped out and walked down the steps after Eden.

"*Ede,*"[9] Rafe called softly, but Eden didn't hear the intimate name she had once called her. She grimaced to herself for being careless then cleared her throat. "Eden," she called again, and Eden turned to look at her. "I'm sorry I wasn't the one who made you feel safe." She watched as Eden tried to think of a response then lowered her eyes and awkwardly turned to leave. Rafe watched Eden walk away hoping Eden could believe her.

---

[9] ādā (Italian e's sound like long a's or like the e's in eggs)

38

AFTER A BUSY first part of the week Rafe Salvaggio was happy she finally made it to Thursday and had a relaxing dinner scheduled with Julia. She thought after Julia moved out, she would go back to seeing her only occasionally, but Julia kept calling, so she finally relented, and they continued to hang out whenever Julia was not going out with the girls. They alternated whose place they used depending on whether or not it was a night Rafe would have Bronte. Tonight dinner was at Rafe's house.

Rafe thought when Julia moved in she would be all about talking about her job and brokerage investments, but she soon found Julia wanted to talk about anything but her job when she was off work. It turned out she could actually still be very good company, and it was sometimes like they were back in school. That and she was a great cook.

Rafe knew she would have to make an appointment with Julia soon regarding changing beneficiaries in her financial accounts when she made changes to her will, but she still had not gotten through everything. It was difficult when you had everything so planned, and now it was all up in the air. She knew Julia would be angry when she found out she was not giving her any more accounts from her father's estate, but she would have to get over it.

Julia made a very comforting Italian dinner using Rafe's gourmet kitchen. Rafe was full and happy. She remembered going out with her mother and father in Italy to the family style dinners they were invited to for weddings, birthdays, and all kinds of special occasions. There was always great food and interesting conversation as well as other children she could run with and feel part of something exciting for a while.

They took their wine to the living room to relax after their delicious meal, and Julia looked over at Rafe musingly. "Rafe, how long has it been?" she asked suddenly. "It seems like months since you have been out? Come on. Come out to the Candy Club or The Kiki Bistro or anywhere with me," she pleaded. "You can make it so much more interesting."

"I can't," said Rafe as she stretched out her legs and shook her head. "Remember, I'm trying to be good and figure out what I am doing."

Julia looked at Rafe over her wine glass and bit her top lip. "So," she dragged out the word, "are you really trying to get Eden back? She said you guys had a long talk. She didn't say about what, though."

Rafe looked at the ceiling and sighed. "I don't know. I'm just trying to make a calm place in my life so I can see things clearly. I really surprised myself at how calm I stayed while we talked." She looked over at Julia, and by the expression on her face, she could see she was anticipating more information. "Don't look at me like that. If she didn't tell you what we talked about, I'm not going to either."

Clearly disappointed Julia took a drink and changed the subject. "Abby told me the reason you took up photography was to use up your excess energy." She picked up the loose photos on the coffee table and looked at them. "She said a friend advised it. Was it Greer?"

Rafe smiled and winked. "Yes, as a matter of fact, it was."

Julia nodded, proud of herself for getting it right. "Just a little ratiocination," she quipped. "You did take it up right after you got back from seeing her." She shuffled through the photos on the coffee table. "These really are quite remarkable."

Rafe leaned forward and looked at her intently. "Can I trust you to keep something to yourself?"

"Not if it is too juicy," Julia admitted excitedly.

"Never mind then," Rafe said dryly and sat back.

Julia tossed the photos onto the table and sat back in disappointment. "Oh, why didn't I just say yes?" She leaned forward again and smiled at Rafe. "Please tell me. I promise I won't tell," she said as she tried to look at Rafe somberly. "*Lo giuro,*" she said like she used to in school hoping it would get her to tell.

Rafe looked at Julia slyly and then smiled because she remembered how to say 'I swear' in Italian then decided she could trust her enough. She knew Abby would probably crack her eventually. She took a sip of wine and then sat the glass on the table. "When I went to see Greer, I told her I wasn't there to check to see if I loved her. I told her I went because she made me feel calm."

Julia deflated with disappointment. "So why are you making it out like some big secret?"

"Because," Rafe said cautiously, "what I told her was true. I didn't have to check. I already knew when I left I loved her," she explained. "While I was there, I even went to talk with a contact at the Historical Society Museum about job possibilities and restoration projects."

Shocked, Julia held her hand out like she was expecting an offering. "Well, what about Eden?"

Rafe swayed her head from side to side and grimaced. "Well," she paused, "I love her too," she admitted. She had thought a lot about what Greer had said and realized she was right about her feelings for Eden. She also knew Eden didn't want to be with her and there was a chance the adoption wouldn't go through. If she lost Bronte again, she didn't think she could stay around Eden. It would be too much to face every day so she would have to move away. Right now, the options were Italy, New York, or Baltimore.

Julia scoffed then laughed. "Rafe, you have a big problem."

"I know!" Rafe grinned. "I guess I could marry them both, but then I'd be a bigamist." She looked down then looked back up soberly. "What do you do when you love two very different people for totally different reasons—but so much so it hurts?"

Julia let her breath out slowly as she considered everything Rafe had said. She knew now, with this revelation, her hopes for anything between them were dashed to bits. She resigned herself once again to the friend zone and then threw her hands up and shook her head.

"You have to choose one."

Rafe took another sip of her wine. "That won't be a hard decision," she said confidently.

"But," Julia said confused, "you just said," she stopped and shook her head.

"I know what I said. I don't think Greer loves me." Rafe sighed. "After we made love, well," she grinned and corrected herself, "had incredible sex, anyway. She said it wasn't love. And you know what I did?" Julia shook her head no. "I agreed with her."

"Why didn't you tell her the truth?" said Julia exasperated she had given up hope when Rafe was just spinning in emotional circles.

"Because, just two days before, I used her as a sounding board about Eden. I think," she paused, "no, I know she believes I'm still in love with Eden. Which I may be." She swallowed the last of wine from her glass. "You see how fucked up this is?"

"So what are you going to do?" asked Julia at a loss.

"I don't know," said Rafe frustrated. "I feel so much tension when I'm around Eden I feel like I'm losing control. But I don't think she loves me, either. She sends so many mixed signals." Rafe groaned at her dilemma. "I love two women, and neither one loves me. Feel sorry for me and pour me some more wine." She held her glass out, and Julia poured more wine.

Julia sat the wine bottle down carefully and looked at Rafe thoughtfully. She wanted to tell Rafe she loved her but knew it would not be well received at the moment. "So, you want her? Eden, I mean."

"No, Julia," Rafe said with her gray-blue eyes blazing. "I don't just want her—I fucking crave her."

Julia looked at Rafe in surprise. "So that's the look."

"The look?"

"Yeah, the look Abby calls the 'crazed wildling' look," Julia explained.

Rafe scoffed. "Abby."

"She's obsessed with the idea, you know," Julia declared then got back to the juicy subject. "How are you going to handle the Eden situation?"

"You're not going to believe what I did."

"What?"

"I told Eden I'd watch Bronte Friday night, and she should go out and find someone to take home," Rafe confessed.

Julia looked at Rafe as if she were crazy, which she was beginning to believe she really was. "Why would you do such a thing?"

Rafe laughed at her reaction. "I don't know. She's still on the fence, and I guess I just thought if she takes home a girl, maybe I have a chance, and if she picks up a guy, I can move on."

"Is she going to do it?"

"I know she's bringing Bronte over, but I don't know if she's going out." Rafe shrugged then looked at Julia and smiled. "Why don't you see if you can go with her?"

Julia thought about it and decided she would like to know what Eden would do too, but for different reasons than Rafe's. "I'll talk to her tomorrow."

"Remember," Rafe said firmly, "you can't say anything about our conversation, especially if Abby is anywhere around. I don't want to become the next subject of her blog or some webcast again."

"Okay," Julia agreed. "What if Eden doesn't go out or pick anyone up?"

"Then I think I'll have to try and have another serious conversation with her somehow," said Rafe as she put her empty glass down. "I can't go on like this forever."

Hopefully, figuring out all of her wants will get me what I want, Rafe thought.

39

EDEN KINGSLEY HAD a rare Friday off and was enjoying a delicious lunch at The Kiki Bistro with Abby. She had been thinking all week about her conversation with Rafe and all the things she did with Bronte. She was feeling even more positive her decision to keep her promise to Rafe about Bronte was the right one and was glad she was out from under Jake's pressuring influence. She was feeling like her hope for them to get along now was going to work out.

As she and Abby ate, they looked at the photographs Rafe had given to Eden of her and Bronte in the park.

"Wow," exclaimed Abby. "I should have known Rafe would be good at photography. Her being sensitive and artsy and all.

These photographs are so beautiful. She was just shooting these in the park?"

"Yeah," confirmed Eden, "while she was chasing Bronte around. I don't know how she did it."

"This one of you is amazing," declared Abby as she looked at the photo of Eden. "How did she get the light like that?"

Eden laughed. "I was there, but I couldn't tell you. All I know is she snapped a picture, and then I get this." She thought about her talk with Rafe and sighed. "You know, Abby, I'm finding out a lot of things about Rafe I didn't know. You would think, after almost five years together, I should know everything about her, right? But she just keeps surprising me."

"She did change a lot when she met you, for the better in my opinion," Abby said through her mouth full of food.

"You should see her with Bronte," she said as she looked at one of the photos of Bronte playing in the park. "I really hadn't been around them when they were together before, except to drop off, pick up, and go to the art lesson."

She laughed at her memory. "The first time I saw them playing in the park, I didn't know what to think of them. They were running around, and Rafe was wrestling her to the ground and picking her up over her head. It looked really rough, but Bronte was laughing the whole time. It's no wonder every time I pick Bronte up she's so tired. Rafe wears her out. Then the other day, they were so cute doing their good-night kiss." She sadly shook her head at what might have been with them if they were still together.

"So, she's a real mom, huh?" Abby said in surprise and shook her head. "I can't picture it."

"She is," Eden said with a smile. "She's so confident and sure with her. I gave birth to her, and I don't think I would have the nerve to do what Rafe does. I'd be too afraid of dropping her or something. I'm really regretting not letting her take Bronte to New York," she said. "She's even started potty training her!" She laughed.

Abby laughed with Eden. "Now that, I just can't picture!"

Eden took a bite of food and thought about the time she had been spending together with Rafe and Bronte as she chewed. "These last few weeks have been really unbelievable."

Abby thought about the fact she really had not seen Rafe for a while and thought it was odd. "Yeah, she has been kind of quiet."

Eden took a sip of her iced tea. "She told me I should let her watch Bronte tonight and said I should go out. Julia invited me to go with her. Do you want to go?"

"She told you to go out, and you're going to do it?" Abby looked at Eden in disbelief. "Why did she tell you to do that?" she asked suspiciously. If after talking this is what they decided Abby was not sure what more she could do.

Eden shrugged. "I guess she thinks I need a break. I don't know."

Abby nodded. It seemed reasonable to her. Eden did look like she needed a break and getting out there couldn't hurt if they really had decided to just be good co-parents. "Okay, where are you going?" she asked excitedly glad to have another friend to hit the clubs with. "I mean are you going guy or girl tonight? I know some good places for picking up guys—and girls—or both."

Eden laughed and used her napkin. "I'm just going to have fun and relax. I'm not going to pick up anyone. I'm not like Rafe in that area."

"Well, maybe someone will pick you up," Abby said helpfully.

40

WITH BRONTE IN her arms, Eden Kingsley knocked on Rafe's door. She was surprised she was excited about going out tonight. She thought initially she would just stay home and read a few script outlines then relax the rest of the night, but after talking with Julia, she made the decision to go out with the girls. It was easier to do things like going to a bar at night when she was with people she was comfortable around. She had just dressed casually in nice jeans and a blouse and decided not to go into anything with too much expectation. She decided she would ask Rafe what she thought about her outfit since this was her idea.

She shifted as she waited and was surprised there was no answer. She knocked again then tested the door and found it unlocked. She put her head inside and called out. "Rafe? Are you here?"

Transferring Bronte to her other hip, Eden walked into the house. When she entered the dining room, she saw Rafe sitting on the floor in front of a large painting. It was a large nude done all in blues with lip marks in red on the body.

She walked up and saw Rafe staring at the painting with tears running down her cheeks. "Rafe?" she said quietly. She put Bronte down, and the little girl walked up to Rafe and sat down in her lap.

Rafe felt a slight shift in the air around her then felt the warm body of Bronte in her lap. She looked down at her. "Hi, B Girl." Bronte smiled and made the sign for blue. Rafe gave a small laugh. "Yes, blue."

"Rafe?" Eden whispered again softly.

Rafe looked up at Eden and spoke softly. "Hi. It just came today. Isn't it beautiful?"

"It's nice." Eden nodded hesitantly. "Are you going to be okay?"

"We'll be fine." Rafe smiled through her tears. "See you in the morning." She turned back to Bronte and spoke gently to her. "Let's look at this work for just a minute more and then we'll put it away."

Eden put down Bronte's backpack and looked at the two of them staring at the painting, not sure what to say or what to think. She decided not to disturb them with a good-bye, so she turned and walked out the door.

41

JULIA HAWTHORN WAS excited about finding out the answers to the questions Rafe was trying to address about Eden. She hoped tonight she could help find the answers and help her friend while trying to push away the disappointment, once again, Rafe would always just be a friend. Maybe, once she knew the answers about Eden, she would consider telling Rafe how she felt again. She didn't know, after all these years, why she just could not give up. As selfish as it may seem, she knew even if she couldn't have Rafe as a girlfriend, she wanted to keep her as a friend. Rafe just made life interesting.

She looked at the clock on her phone, and Eden was late. She had been sitting at The Kiki Bistro nursing a drink with Abby for an hour, and there was no sign of her. She started to wonder if Eden had changed her mind and was about to phone her when she walked through the door.

"You finally made it," said Julia relieved. She waved down a waitress to order more drinks.

"I know, I'm running late," said Eden apologetically. "I had to stop by the office because I left some paperwork there I was supposed to have taken with me. Then I had to drop off Bronte." She looked at Abby and Julia and cleared her throat. "Rafe got a new painting today. There must be something really great about it."

"Why?" Abby asked, inquisitively.

"When I walked in, she was just staring at it and crying," Eden said and took a sip of the drink delivered to the table by a busy server. "When we went to museums, it was something that hit her when she saw really moving art. It had only happened a couple times, but it was the only time I actually saw her really cry. It was kind of a strange experience to have with her, and all I knew to do was to just leave her alone when it happened."

Letty appeared at their table to check on the group. "Hi, girls. Having fun?"

"Hey, Letty. We were just talking about Rafe," Abby confessed. "Eden says she just got a new painting and is home crying over it."

Julia rolled her eyes at Abby blurting it out. "Abby!"

"Oh, is it the one Greer did of her?" Letty asked not knowing Rafe had not talked to any of them about Greer sending her a painting.

Eden looked up and tried to hide her surprise. "Greer?"

"Yeah," Letty said looking at Eden and then the others. She could see they were all surprised. "When Rafe got back in town, she told me Greer was sending her a painting. I asked her what the subject was, and she said it was her," she said with a wink.

Eden was rattled by the news, and when she thought about the primal, carnal image in the painting, she felt her stomach knot.

"Then," Eden stammered, "then, I guess it is."

"She painted her portrait?" Abby asked, impressed.

"It wasn't a portrait, exactly," revealed Eden.

"What was it then?" Julia asked, frowning.

Eden hesitated and took another drink before answering. "It was a blue nude."

Abby laughed. "She's crying over a blue nude?" She took a sudden quick breath in realization. "Do you think Rafe posed nude for it."

"I wouldn't know," said Eden as she swallowed back her emotions and looked away.

"I'll have to go over and see it. Is it any good?" Letty asked Eden.

"I don't know," Eden admitted. "I didn't really look at it long. Rafe was," she paused as the image of Rafe just staring at the painting with tears on her face appeared in front of her, "she was just staring at it."

"And crying," blurted Abby.

Letty smiled and nodded. "'It must be good. Rafe knows her art," she said as she left to go do her rounds through the crowd.

"Maybe she was crying because she misses Greer," said Abby thoughtlessly. She noticed Eden's anxious look and bit her lip. "Oh, sorry, Eden."

Julia watched Eden's reaction with interest. "Why are you sorry, Abby? Eden doesn't care what Rafe does or who she misses."

"Well," Abby hesitated, "she might." She looked pointedly at Eden. "Do you care?"

Julia interrupted and waved Abby back. "Abby, Eden is here to pick someone up and have fun, remember? Rafe doesn't mean anything to her anymore." She smiled at Eden. "Right, Eden?"

Eden looked down at the table with apprehension. "I don't know," she said hesitantly. "I guess."

"I'd like to see this blue nude," proclaimed Julia. "I think I'll pop in on Rafe in the morning." She winked at Abby. "I want to check out just how much those two liked each other."

"They must still really like each other." Abby laughed with Julia.

Eden didn't join in the laughter. She just smiled sadly and took another drink not really tasting anything.

42

IN THE EARLY morning hours of Saturday, Rafe Salvaggio was in the dining room while Bronte was still sleeping. She looked up at the large painting on the wall of the beautiful and erotic scantily clad woman with golden blond hair, and a face blushed with pink holding an apple. The beautiful woman was standing in an overgrown garden setting complete with apple tree and a mysterious vine-covered marble structure with Greek columns in the background. It was painted in a high Renaissance style. It had been a favorite of her personal work for a long time. It was the painting she had done of Eden when they first met. She had titled the painting, *Il Paradiso Terrestre, l'Eden.*[10]

She sighed at the memory then reached up and took the painting down from the wall. She put it on the dining room table and wrapped it well in crescent board and acid-free paper for delivery to her storage company. When she finished labeling and recording what she was sending, Rafe placed it in the living room to store it until she could take it to her art storage unit.

Rafe returned to the dining room and picked up the painting by Greer Noble, placing it in the empty space on the wall. She stood back and looked at the painting in its new home and smiled, pleased with what she saw. She turned as she heard a knock at the door and went to answer it.

"Good morning," announced Julia as Rafe opened the door.

Rafe shook her head annoyed. "What are you doing here so early?"

Julia smiled and walked into the house past Rafe. "I have some plans in a little while, and last night, Eden said you had an amazing new painting. I thought I would pop by and have a look."

"I'm glad she liked it." Rafe smiled, excited to show off the painting. "Come in. I just put it up in the dining room."

"I wouldn't say she liked it," said Julia bemused. "She just said you must really like it."

Rafe gave Julia a big smile. "I do. Come look."

---

[10] Paradise on Earth, Eden

Julia followed Rafe into the dining room and stood in front of the large painting on prominent display. "My god, Rafe! Letty said this was of you!" She looked at Rafe in shock.

"It is," said Rafe unable to stop smiling.

"I guess you're immortal now," Julia declared astounded.

"Well," said Rafe with a small laugh, "at least some part of me is anyway."

Julia looked at Rafe and back at the painting. "You're going to keep this here, in your dining room?"

"Sure, why not?" Rafe said confused.

"It's just so... primal and sexual." Julia looked around the room concerned. "Rafe, what happened to the other painting?"

"I'm putting it in storage," Rafe answered. "I don't have anywhere else to hang something this size unless I redo all of the walls."

Julia bit her lip and sighed. "Wasn't that painting special to you and Eden?"

"It was special to me. It's one I painted for Eden," Rafe said with a short nod. "I don't think she really cares about it one way or the other. She didn't take it when she moved out."

"I'm just taking a shot in the dark here, but I was under the impression the painting was of Eden since it is her portrait," Julia said with a raised eyebrow.

"It is," confirmed Rafe. "That's usually the definition of a portrait," she said sarcastically shaking her head at Julia.

Julia put her hands on Rafe's shoulders and looked into her eyes. "Rafe, don't you think by taking it down, you'll send a message to Eden you really have stopped caring?"

Rafe took Julia's hands off her shoulders. "Julia, if you have something to say, just say it."

Julia scratched her neck and shifted uncomfortably. "It's just," she started reluctantly, "last night, when Letty told us your new painting was of you," she paused, "and it was from Greer, well, Eden seemed like she cared about who it came from too much for someone who doesn't maybe..." she hesitated, "possibly have feelings for you," she finished weakly.

Rafe lifted her head and looked at Julia through narrowed eyes. "So, what are you saying? Eden was jealous?"

"Maybe," said Julia apprehensively. "But I could be wrong," she said quickly and looked at Rafe. "Rafe, stop smiling."

"I can't," said Rafe as she smiled. "This is the best news I've heard in a long time. If she's really jealous," Rafe pointed out, "it's not a mixed signal."

"Rafe, I mean it," Julia insisted. "I could be wrong, and you just can't keep this painting in here! You can't let Abby or Eden see it in the light of day. Maybe you should put the other one back up."

"Julia, this painting is who I am," explained Rafe. "Why wouldn't I let them see it?"

"It's who you are?" she hissed scandalized.

"It's who I am," Rafe confirmed with a nod and a shrug.

"Since when?"

"Since always," claimed Rafe. "It's just been locked away. Greer saw it, and she captured it."

Julia shook her head with worry. "Abby isn't going to like this."

Rafe looked at Julia and then at the painting with sparkling eyes. "Abby doesn't have to like this."

Finally, Julia had to leave to run her errands, leaving Rafe alone to think about all the things she had recounted. Rafe went into the kitchen and poured herself a cup of coffee then sat down at the island.

Eden was jealous, she thought. *It had to mean something.* It might be a small hope, but it was one she would take.

She put her cup down and walked into the living room where she began taking down the art over the fireplace. When she was finished, she went to another art-filled wall and began taking everything off so she could rearrange things to make space to hang both of the paintings in the house. She worked quickly so she could get most of it finished before Bronte woke.

Things were looking better today.

Eden was jealous.

43

THURSDAY NIGHT HAD come around again, and Julia Hawthorn was very happy there was another exciting event at The Kiki Bistro going on. Her workweek had been filled with meetings and a big stressful corporate event. She had talked to her father and told him she wanted to go back into sales because she was so bored in the office. So now, she needed a real break from all the stress and being 'on' all week.

Abby and Eden were sharing her table, and the place was jammed full. Julia looked around the room, and Abby nudged her.

"So, see anyone you like?" asked Abby as she scanned the room for someone herself.

"Not yet," Julia complained. "I wish Rafe would have come with us. She makes things so much more interesting. No offense Eden, but you're just not the same."

Eden laughed at Julia's complaint. "None taken. I'm sure you're right." She stood up and looked at the bar. "I'm going to get another drink. Can I get you guys anything?"

"I'm fine." Julia waved her off.

"I'll take another one of these," said Abby and held up her glass. "I'm not sure what it is, but it's good." Eden took Abby's glass and headed for the bar. "Julia, why exactly is Rafe convincing her to go out again?" Abby asked curiously.

Julia hesitated because she promised Rafe she would not talk to Abby about the situation, but as long as she didn't give Abby anything she would go crazy over, she figured it was safe. "I think her words were she wants her to 'get off the fence.' She thinks if Eden has time to go out, maybe she can figure out what she wants."

"It's just weird," Abby concluded. "I would have never thought Rafe could have this much patience. Is she up to something?"

"Abby, what are you talking about?" Julia shook her head. "I don't know why she doesn't just seduce Eden. I don't think Eden has had any for months. She'd probably appreciate it."

Abby looked at Julia as if she had just committed a felony. "Julia, Rafe can't do that to Eden! She's not just one of her conquests. She has to want more than sex from her."

"Of course, Eden is one of her conquests!" Julia laughed. "Don't you remember when she first introduced us all at the party at the mansion in the hills?" Julia tilted her head and gave her best Rafe Salvaggio imitation and Italian accent. "*Adan*, come away. I will show you the stained glass. It is beautiful, but it does not shine like your eyes. *Adan*, will you let me take you away for a small while? I want to show you a painting from Paris. *Adan*, follow me, and we will find the wine together." Julia laughed. "She kept taking her off places alone and pronouncing her name funny. She still does half the time, and when she calls her Ede."[11] She shook her head at Abby's frown. "But they turned into more, eventually. I'm just saying maybe they need a little of what they had back then back," Julia said and sipped her drink.

"Maybe," Abby said suspiciously, "but she wasn't that crazy wild Rafe we had known for months. Remember, you were the one complaining she had dropped off the planet again. Then she showed up with Eden. I think she changed because she met her." She looked at Julia a moment and wondered if she was up to something. "She calls her Edy, not Ede," she said annoyed. "I call her Edy sometimes too."

---

[11] ādā (Italian e's sound like long a's or like the e's in eggs)

Julia laughed at the odd things Abby's mind got stuck on. "Well, I'll bet she prefers Ede." She chuckled. "Think about it, her name is Eden, so would she like hearing someone screeching Edy in her ear, or someone whispering Ede in a sexy Italian accent?"

Abby rolled her eyes at Julia then looked up and saw Eden making her way back to the table. "If Eden would just figure out if she wants a man or a woman, it would help."

Julia nodded her agreement enthusiastically. "You're right. Besides, what if Rafe did seduce her, and Eden still doesn't want to be with her. She would just be hurting herself. Why does love have to be so hard?" She looked around the room again. "I'm glad I'm just here for the sex," she lied smoothly.

Eden put a drink in front of Abby and took her seat at the table. "What are you saying about sex?"

Abby took a sip of her drink and looked at Julia from the corner of her eye. "Oh, well, it's different with someone you love."

"Oh, yeah, I guess it is," agreed Eden, sipping her drink.

"So, Eden, want to go out again with me Friday?" asked Abby.

"I can't," Eden said as she stirred her drink." I'm going to a studio event, and I've invited Julia as my plus one. But thanks." She looked over at Julia. "You'll have a great time, Julia. You'll see."

"Sounds like fun," Abby said sarcastically, upset Eden didn't invite her over Julia. "So, Eden," she began and glanced at Julia knowingly, "how have you and Rafe been getting along?"

Eden swallowed and sat her drink down. "Good," she nodded. "She's been great. She's watching Bronte again tonight. I'm so glad we're getting along better now."

"Well," announced Julia, "I'm going to go ask that girl to dance. Eden, do you want me to see if she has a friend for you?"

Eden looked at the girl Julia was talking about. "No, it's okay, I'm fine," she said shyly.

"Hey," whined Abby. "What about me? You know Eden probably wants a man, and I'm not picky."

"All right, come on," Julia conceded. "Eden, if we aren't back in half an hour, we aren't coming back."

Eden laughed. "I got it," she said and held her drink out to them in salute. "Good luck, guys!"

44

THE STUDIO LOT at *Ascesis Studios,* where Eden Kingsley worked, had been transformed into a Grecian fantasy. Large tents were set up and each decorated so they represented different Greek myths. The main tent represented the set for the movie the studio was producing. Eden and Julia walked through the lot and made their way through the crowd to the main tent.

Eden was confident and in her element there, because it was her job and she knew most of the people. It helped, as an executive, she had a small amount of distance between herself and lower ranking employees, and a larger distance with her bosses. It gave her a small sense of control over her choice to decrease the distance or not. It was also easier to meet new people because she knew there were business boundaries. She knew people crossed them all the time at events like this, but it was always something she only heard about afterward.

Eden was excited to bring Julia along and share the experience of an industry party. She had taken Rafe to events at her former job, but since she started this one after they broke up, the only other person she had gone to events with had been Jake. All Jake saw were things and people to complain about all night. He would go on about how the movie industry was ruining the youth of America. It was nice to show someone around again who might actually be impressed with what she was a part of and did for a living.

Julia walked through the tents in awe of the extravagance. "See now, why can't brokerage firms have parties like this? I could even dress up like Helen of Troy."

Eden laughed. "Julia, you're thinking of the wrong story. This movie isn't about Troy. It's called *Media*. It's about a woman scorned. You really should read the script."

"I think I read the play in school," she said trying to remember, but then she gave up. "Send me a copy, and maybe I can use it for ideas. Do you think they would rent out these props," Julia asked admiring the scenery.

"Oh, I don't know. I think they may need some to actually use in the movie." Eden laughed. "I wish I was working on something like this. It's much better than the zombie scripts I've been stuck with lately. I never knew killing zombies could have so many scenarios. It's just mind-numbing."

Julia looked at Eden and leaned in close. "Who's that?" She pointed with her chin to a tall man who was looking at Eden. "He's checking you out."

Eden looked where Julia was subtly pointing. "I've seen him around. I think he's Michael Archer."

"He's coming this way," whispered Julia. "I need a drink, I'll see you later. Good luck," she said and walked toward the bar. She wondered if this would be the proof Rafe needed to move on from Eden. She held back the hope threatening to surface.

Eden watched as the tall, handsome dark-haired man swaggered toward her. He looked very nice in his Armani suit and tie. He stopped in front of her and smiled.

"Hello," he said smoothly his dark brown eyes sparkling.

"Hi," Eden said shyly.

"Looks like your friend abandoned you." He held out his hand to her. "I'm Michael Archer."

Eden took his large hand and smiled up at him. "Eden Kingsley. It's nice to meet you."

"So, are you here for the film or the food?" he joked and gave her another charming smile showing off the dimple in his cheek.

"Both, I guess." Eden laughed. "I work for the studio, and I haven't had dinner yet."

"In that case, let me escort you to the dining area," offered Michael and held out his elbow for her to take.

Eden looked at him and hesitated for a second then took his arm. She needed to network, and he could be a good contact for her writers. "Thank you."

Michael smiled down at her. "No, I should thank you. Having a beautiful woman on my arm makes me look better."

Michael and Eden sat at a dining table where they were served their dinner along with eight other people who were sitting with them. After dinner, when most of the people had left the table, Michael poured Eden another glass of wine. "So, tell me more about yourself. I know you work at the studio in script development. What else?"

"There's not much more to tell really," she said trying to keep the conversation about work. "Just boring contracts and a lot of bad scripts to be fixed mostly. Don't get me wrong—I love my work. It can be very exciting, but it can also get tedious. Parties like this make up for it though."

"So, do you have a significant other?" asked Michael. "Boyfriend?"

"No, no. I don't have a boyfriend or a significant other right now," answered Eden shyly because the conversation was turning personal. "I've just been too busy with work and my daughter. I'm a single mom," she said and took a drink wondering if it would put him off.

"Wow. I admire the fact you're working and raising a child alone," Michael said impressed. "Doesn't the father help you out?"

Eden hesitated not sure how much she wanted to share with this man. She took a breath. She had to start trusting people again sometime. He seemed nice, and he had something in common with her like Rafe mentioned. "No," she started, "well, she doesn't really have a father." She shook her head. "No, what I mean is she has a father, but he is just a donor."

Michael raised his eyebrows in surprise. "So you're a power mom. A woman who wants it all but can't be bothered with a relationship."

"No, no. I'm not a power mom or anything." Eden smiled nervously. "I was in a relationship when I got pregnant, but it didn't work out."

"Don't tell me, your boyfriend was sterile and so you had to get a donor," Michael guessed.

"Not exactly." Eden took a deep breath preparing herself for his reaction to the truth. "Michael, I was in a relationship with another woman, and we decide to have a baby together," she paused, "but things didn't work out between us."

Michael's eyes opened wide in surprise. "Another woman? Really?" He nodded as he took in the information. "So she left you? She must have been crazy."

"No," Eden said tentatively, "she didn't leave me. I left her. But really, it was more complicated."

"I see." Michael nodded again. "Well, I guess I should be asking if you have a girlfriend then," he said and smiled kindly.

Eden bit her lip and shook her head glad he was not angry or asking about two-woman hookups. "No, I don't have a girlfriend." She looked up into his dark eyes looked very soft and calm. "I don't date women anymore."

Michael smiled and took a slow sip of his wine. "Eden, you are so beautiful and surprising. I don't think I've ever met anyone quite like you." He leaned forward and kissed her lightly. "I hope you don't mind I kissed you," he whispered.

Eden looked at him in surprise, unsure if she minded or not. It was very presumptuous and forward of him, but he had a nice smile to go with his eyes, and he seemed kind. He even didn't mind if she had a child with another woman. Maybe Rafe was right about looking for someone who had the same interests in life. Maybe she should have been more open to looking for someone related closer to her career. She smiled invitingly at him. "I don't," she whispered back noting the soft smell of his cologne. "I don't mind at all." She reached out and put her hand on his.

Michael stood up taking Eden's hand with him. "Let's go for a walk outside the studio. It's getting too noisy in here for good conversation."

Eden couldn't help but notice how warm his hand was as she rose to follow him. "A walk sounds nice."

As they strolled through the studio lot, Michael and Eden, passed in front of a studio building then walked just outside the beam of light from a streetlamp. Michael stopped and turned to face Eden and then kissed her.

Moving his kisses to her neck, he pulled her to him. "You are so sexy," he murmured. Eden's eyes were closed, and she was willing her body to react to Michael's kisses and caresses.

She held onto his neck as he pushed himself against her. He kissed her on the mouth again and moved to her ear, and whispered. "Have you seen the set for *Media*?"

"No," she said breathing heavily onto his neck.

Michael backed up and took Eden by the hands. "I just happen to have the key to the set." He went to the door and unlocked it. Then he turned and held out his hand to her. "You have to see it."

Eden felt the warmth and strength in his hands. "Are you sure it's okay?"

Michael just smiled and pulled her along so she would follow. Inside the *Media* set, Michael turned on a couple of small spots and led Eden to the *Media* bedroom set. "What do you think?" he asked smiling.

"It's beautiful. I love all of the pillows and curtains," Eden told him as she felt the soft material.

Michael took off his jacket and then pulled Eden toward him, kissing her. "I want you," he whispered and began slowly pushing the straps of her dress off her shoulders.

Eden looked up at him and the hunger in his eyes. The memory of Rafe's gray-blue eyes with the sparkle they had when she wanted her flashed through her mind. She felt a charge run through her body, and a soft tone left her throat. She closed her eyes as he kissed her neck and tried to make the image of Rafe's eyes go away. Guilt shook her because the memory made her so wet, and she was supposed to be figuring out her feelings for men and focusing on Michael.

Kissing her neck and shoulder, Michael pushed her gently toward the bedroom set. "Will you let me have you?"

She took a breath and looked up at Michael pushing the thought of Rafe out of her mind. She could feel the need building up inside her for an intimate connection. Maybe he could be the one if she gave him a chance. Maybe their connection would be right, and she just needed to let go of the guilt of thinking about Rafe.

She started unbuttoning his shirt and took it off him, along with his tie. "Yes," she whispered. She looked down his body and moved her hands down his bare chest to undo his belt and pants. At the same time, she felt his warm hands loosen the hooks on her dress and felt it slide down off her body.

45

ON MONDAY MORNING, Eden Kingsley was running late. She rushed past the receptionist and into her office where the first thing she saw when she walked in was a large vase of beautiful red roses on her desk. She read the card and saw they were from Michael. *'Thank you for a wonderful weekend—Michael.'* She smiled and smelled their sweet scent before setting them on the credenza behind her desk. She sat down, looked at the flowers, and thought about the weekend she had just spent with Michael. He was so sweet and kind—maybe he really was the one this time. Maybe she had finally found the one she needed, the one who could confirm her feelings.

They spent the weekend at Michael's beach house together. They went for walks on the beach at night, ate great food, and talked about everything. It seemed like most of the things they talked about led to sex. She even told him about her feelings of how she should be in a long-term relationship with a man.

Maybe now she could finally move on, and so could Rafe. She hardly thought about Rafe the whole weekend. The only times she did were when she thought or talked about Bronte, and once when they were talking about old movies and Michael showed her a movie poster with Rafe's cousin Letty Carver he had hanging in the house. She smiled at the thought, and hoped someday, they could invite Letty out so she could autograph it for him. She thought even Abby would like Michael and hoped all the others would stay in her life if things worked out with him. Michael was a lot different from Jake. Good different.

She turned to face her desk as Jan from accounting entered. "Morning, Eden," Jan said all business. "Do you have the contract ready so I can finish the budget for the Zombornado project?" She stopped when she saw the roses behind Eden. "Wow. Roses. Who sent them?"

"Oh," she said blushing a bit from embarrassment. "Michael Archer, the director. We had dinner together at the party Friday night. He's nice."

"Michael Archer," Jan thought for a moment trying to recall who he was. "Oh, yes, I remember him now. He's going to be the director for the movie based on a popular young adult book. What was it? Oh yes, *The Girl Called Spark*. I think they're changing the title for the movie, though. I heard his daughter loved it so much he convinced Galen to write a screenplay, and he's trying to get our studio to produce it."

Eden looked up in surprise. "He has a daughter? He didn't mention her."

Jan nodded. "He has a daughter and two sons. One son from his previous marriage and he has a girl and boy with his current wife."

Eden was stunned speechless for a moment because they had talked about family and children over the weekend, and he mentioned nothing about having either. "He's married?"

"Yeah" she confirmed. "So, why is he sending you roses? Does he want something?"

Frowning, Eden tried to hide her disillusionment. "I guess you could say he does." Eden changed the subject and started pulling the contract Jan needed for her budget report.

46

EDEN KINGSLEY DROVE Bronte to Long Beach to look at the ocean. They were taking an evening walk along the waterfront and enjoying the mild weather. She pushed Bronte along in her stroller recalling the conversation with Jan this morning still weighing heavily on her mind about Michael.

She berated herself for not asking him questions about his life the night of the party. She felt so stupid. If she had asked around about Michael before going away with him, she would have known not to go. It felt like she was running from one bad situation to another. She had done it again. She just followed her emotions and got into a situation without thinking it through. It seemed liked she couldn't get it right with anyone.

She looked down the beach and thought she saw a familiar form. She got closer and saw she was right. *There really was no mistaking who that beautiful woman was*, she thought to herself as she watched Rafe take pictures of people on the beach. She approached her and waved. "Hey, how are you?" called Eden when she was close enough for her to hear.

Rafe was surprised to see Eden out at the beach and walked to meet her. "Hi, I'm fine," she said as she leaned down and smiled at Bronte. "What are you two up to?"

"We're just out taking a walk," said Eden and tried to hide the guilt she was feeling over what had happened with Michael and the fact she had not told Rafe the truth about why she was so willing to let her take Bronte for the weekend. Fortunately, Rafe did not question her vague excuse about doing something with work colleagues. It was not a complete lie because Michael was someone she met through work. But deep down she knew it was another secret she now had to keep form Rafe because of how badly things had worked out. "What are you doing?"

Rafe looked down at her camera then up at Eden and smiled. "I'm capturing life. Through the lens, life is framed so emotion can be captured and studied at leisure," she said grandly and laughed.

"That's nice. Did you make it up?" Eden asked as she noticed how beautiful she was with her windblown hair. Then she looked away berating herself again for going down a path she should not be going.

"As far as I know no one else has said it." She bent down to talk with Bronte. "Are you having fun out here with Mommy? This is a great time for a walk." She looked up at Eden. "Can I walk with you for a while? I need to go further down the beach anyway."

"Sure. We'd like you to join us." Eden smiled as they started walking down the beach together. "How's work going for you?"

"Good. I'm getting things ready for my presentation and working on more fundraising projects. What about you?" Rafe asked casually.

Eden shrugged halfheartedly. "It's fine."

Rafe looked at Eden and could see something was wrong. "You want to talk about it?"

Surprised, Eden laughed. "You want to hear me talk about my day? Usually, it's the other way around. Thanks, but it's fine."

"Okay, let's get a drink," said Rafe deciding it was probably best not to push. She didn't want to get into the old argument about who got to vent and who didn't. She just wanted to do what everyone had been telling her to do and try to listen. "Oh, I almost forgot. I told Stacey I'd ask you about calling her about getting a contact for her make-up work for the zombie movies your studio is doing. Apparently, Julia said something about them to her, and she needs some work if there's any for her."

"Oh," Eden sighed about the other trouble in her life. She didn't mind the premise of the zombie movies. It was the terrible scripts she was given, and the quantities. The writers must never sleep, and they obviously spent little time thinking through plot lines. "I have no idea why those things are so popular right now. With the amount we're doing, there should be plenty of work. I'll call her tomorrow."

"According to Stacey, zombies represent the forgotten and downtrodden in society," said Rafe with a laugh, "or something similar. I'm sure she can fill you in on everything about zombie theory."

Eden looked at Rafe with amusement. "When did she tell you about zombies?"

"I let her use the theater room upstairs for a zombie movie night. So I got schooled on all things zombie every time I saw her for about a month." Rafe winked and gave her a smile.

"Oh," she said softly remembering their movie nights. "Well, I guess I'm just out of the loop on zombie stuff," Eden said, laughing as she walked beside Rafe. "All I know is what's in the scripts, and they drive the people in accounting insane. Oh, and they're never short for extras on set."

They bought some drinks from a beachfront vendor and sat down on a bench facing the ocean. "I'm glad you found me," said Rafe as she sat her camera down beside her. "Maybe I can take some pictures of you and Bronte on the beach."

"Sure." Eden looked at Rafe and bit her lip nervously. "Rafe," she hesitated, "can I ask you something?" She watched as Rafe nodded. "I know we've been through it, and I don't want you to get mad, but I need to know something."

"What about?" Rafe frowned and sipped her drink.

Eden looked at her and then looked out at the water. "It's," she hesitated, "it's about Lauren."

Rafe looked at Eden worried. "Lauren?" she asked warily.

"Yeah," she said quietly, "I just need to ask you something."

Rafe looked fretfully at Eden. "Eden, I," she sighed. "Okay, I guess. You know I'm sorry, right?"

"I know. I just..." Eden took a calming breath, "I just wanted to know. Did you, you know, plan it? Did you go after her?"

Rafe closed her eyes and sighed. "No. No, I didn't. Eden, why are you asking me about this now?"

Looking at her hands, Eden shrugged. "I just... I just wanted to know what happened."

Rafe looked out at the ocean, thinking about everything leading up to her affair with Lauren and her broken relationship with Eden.

She was not by her father's bedside when he died. He kept it a secret how sick he really was. She had been to visit him but had to go on a trip to check on a project in Milano. She had been gone for ten days when she got the call he had died. She flew back to New York immediately.

After making basic arrangements, she went home to Eden, who was in emotional turmoil herself about using the donor Rafe had brought home and about their relationship being good or not. Though she showed some empathy and held her while she cried for her father, Eden still did not want to be close or intimate in any way. Rafe's world was turned upside down because of the issues with Eden she couldn't help with or fix and because of her father's death.

They traveled back to New York to have her father's funeral and have him cremated. Rafe recalled Eden had decided to leave and go home right after the funeral. She was left to begin handling her father's memorial gathering and his affairs alone. They left their disagreement about therapy and the debate about the donor unfinished.

Rafe was grief stricken with the loss of her father and at the loss of Eden's affection. All the people who surrounded her seemed to suck the energy from her, leaving her feeling even more isolated and alone with her grief.

Then she met Lauren. She was listing her father's Central Park home for sale, and Lauren was one of the many agents who had worked in her father's real estate company. Lauren was so full of life and energy as well as very smart. Rafe could see she loved her job and was very good at it too. Rafe was immediately sure she was the right person to work with and would be the best realtor for her. Rafe thought Lauren must have also been very intuitive and could see she was still grieving over her father.

They were deciding what things to leave for staging and Rafe had to stop. Going through her father's things brought back a lot of memories and thoughts about not only him but also her mother. Lauren sat down next to her to offer some comfort and then everything was just a blur. All Rafe knew was she must have lost her mind to give in and do what she knew was wrong.

Rafe thought Lauren must have wanted to comfort her and the need for closeness just pushed everything else aside. Maybe Lauren listened to her and Rafe felt she could talk to her. Lauren must have been telling her things Eden had stopped saying. She was doing and saying all the things Rafe was missing and craving for a very long time. The next thing she remembered was waking up next to Lauren and crying about what she had done.

Lauren's secretary apparently mistakenly used Rafe's home address when sending out the flowers to Rafe instead of the New York apartment address. Because of this, Eden found out about the affair. When Rafe got home, Eden confronted her. Rafe tried to deny it, but finally, she knew she just had to admit the truth and be honest with Eden because she couldn't stand seeing her in pain, and the evidence was sitting in front of her. The next morning, Rafe woke up and found Eden had left the house.

She didn't blame her for leaving. Rafe understood what she had done. She also knew she needed to get away from her own pain. Early the next morning, she flew back to New York to continue taking care of her father's estate, and she also had to face Lauren again.

As she dealt with her father's estate, Rafe found herself in a place she didn't want to be. She knew she had made a mistake, and made it worse by continuing to tempt herself with Lauren.

They both knew it had been an affair, and Rafe told her it had to stop and could not happen again. Lauren understood and left Rafe to finish packing her father's things and taking care of all his other personal business.

Rafe still didn't know if she could have gotten through it all without Lauren. Well, maybe she could have if Eden had helped her. But she knew it was still no excuse for what she had done. Rafe knew Lauren was hurt, but she understood when Rafe told her she loved Eden and had to make things right if it were possible.

When she came home, everyone thought she had gone to New York to continue the affair with Lauren. When they all confronted her about it, she met them with silence and didn't deny it. She didn't see the point. Eden had already packed up everything she owned and moved completely out of the house. Well, almost completely. She left the painting Rafe had done of her when they first met. Rafe felt by not taking it, Eden wanted no memory of her in her life anymore, and she really couldn't blame her. But Rafe could not bring herself to remove the painting after Eden left. It was the only way to keep some part of the woman she loved with her at the time.

Rafe looked at Eden and knew she couldn't repeat everything again. It wouldn't help anything, and she didn't want to hurt her again. "Eden, I just lost control," Rafe admitted and held her hand to her head because thinking about that time and of what she had done caused it to ache. "I made a mistake, I really did. I was just in a bad place. I never wanted to hurt you. I know there was no excuse. I don't want you to think about that, Eden. Please, if I could take it back, I would."

Eden looked at Rafe and could see her misery. "I believe you. I'm sorry I brought it up. I just needed to know if you planned it."

Rafe was still confused about whey she was bringing this up again. "Why does it matter? I did it. It's just as bad either way."

Eden nodded her head in agreement. "It's bad but..." she took a breath, "I think if you had planned it, it would have been worse." She looked up and saw Rafe looking at her in confusion. She leaned over and kissed her softly on the lips. "Thank you for answering my question."

Rafe, not sure what to do about the kiss, just looked out at the ocean again. "Are we still okay? I thought we were past this."

"We're past it, we're okay," Eden reassured her. "It was just something I needed to know." She smiled a Rafe. "Are you going to take our picture?"

Still puzzled, but letting it go for the moment since Eden had, she stood. "Let's go down by the water."

47

AS SHE WAS reading through scripts and making notes to prepare for the Wednesday afternoon meeting, Eden Kingsley was buzzed by the receptionist.

"Ms. Kingsley, Michael Archer is here to see you," came the voice through the speaker.

Eden sighed and sat her work aside. "Thank you, send him in please," she told her receptionist. Eden took a breath and prepared herself for what was coming. She got up, straightened her clothes, and went to the door.

Michael walked in and closed the door behind him. He grabbed Eden up in his arms and kissed her then pulled back from her and smiled. "I've been trying to call you for days. Did you get my messages?"

Eden pushed him away and went back behind her desk to have something between them. "I got them," she confirmed pushing down her anxiety. "I was hoping you would get the message I didn't want to see you."

Michael frowned and looked hurt by her words. "Eden, why? We had a great weekend. I want to see you again."

Eden shook her head sadly. "I didn't know you were married. I don't want to be with someone who's married."

"Is that all?" he said nonchalantly. "I thought you were a free spirit about these things,"

"What would make you think that?" she asked confused.

"Well, because you were with a woman and your baby's father is a donor and all the other things you told me."

"Well, you thought wrong. I'm not a free spirit," she said coldly. "I made a mistake. I never wanted to be 'the other woman' for anyone."

"My wife and I have an understanding. She's okay with whatever I do," Michael insisted with an easy smile.

"That's nice for you," Eden said not believing him. "I don't feel the same way your wife does, and I don't believe for a minute she's okay with you screwing anyone you want."

Michael laughed. "Eden, you're overreacting."

"Overreacting? I've been in your wife's shoes, and I know how much it hurts. I'm not overreacting," Eden argued as the pain she felt from being treated like he was treating his wife pushed forward making her angry. "I don't want to see you again."

"I'm not hurting my wife," Michael pressed. "I'm sorry if you were hurt by someone, but what I do and what was done to you are not the same."

"You're right—what you're doing is worse," Eden declared her empathy going out to his wife. "You're intentionally cheating on your wife. You actually plan to hurt her. And Michael," she said calmly even though on the inside she was fighting her anxiety at this final confrontation, "don't tell me if she found out she wouldn't be hurt because we both know you're lying to yourself. Get out!"

48

THE LUNCH CROWD had thinned at The Kiki Bistro when Julia Hawthorn arrived to have a late lunch with Abby and Eden. She'd had a great day at work and even scheduled several promising appointments. Going with Eden to her studio party was turning out to be great for business and her checkbook.

It was exciting dealing with movie industry people rather than all of the people who worked in the computer tech and international trade companies. She spotted her friends and headed over to join them.

Abby looked up from her menu and saw Julia walk to the table. She barely waited until she sat down to include her in their conversation.

"Hey! We're just getting started here," Abby told her. "So, how was the thing you guys went to last Friday?" she asked.

"It was very interesting." Julia smiled and arched her brows. "The serving staff was all dressed in costume. It was a Greek theme and let's just say, according to the studio's prop department, the Greeks weren't really into clothes that covered a lot. I'll have to talk with Letty and see if she can do a Greek Myth night here some Thursday night." She grinned knowingly at Abby. "But Eden got to have dinner with a big shot director."

Abby squealed in surprise and patted Eden on the back. "All right, Eden! Is he cute or just rich?"

Eden smiled weakly not wanting to talk to them, or anyone, about the huge mistake she had made. It was enough she had to confront Michael and break it off with him this morning. Dealing with the unwanted comments from Abby and Julia would only make her feel worse. "He was cute. I don't know if he was rich. It was just dinner," she said calmly and looked down at her menu not wanting to admit to anything more.

Julia laughed. "Some dinner!" she smirked and looked at Abby. "She was absent most of the night and let Rafe have Bronte for the weekend." She winked. "So, are you going to see him again?"

"No," answered Eden flatly. "I had a work thing over the weekend," she lied weakly, but the girls paid no attention to her words. She was saved for the moment as the waitress came and took their orders. Eden took the opportunity to change the subject. "I saw Rafe Monday on the beach. She was taking pictures of all the people."

Abby looked at Julia and raised her eyebrows and Julia shrugged. She let Eden slide about her weekend with the director for now. "It's good you guys are getting along."

"Yeah." Eden smiled. "She took pictures of me and Bronte on the beach too. I forgot how intense she would get when she works. She's the same way taking pictures. I can't wait to see how they come out."

Julia looked at Eden unable to hide her curiosity. "So, you're starting to spend more time with her?"

Abby went on high alert. "Does this mean you're going try to work things out with her?"

"We really haven't talked about it," said Eden shyly.

"What about your new director guy?" asked Abby. She was glad for the opportunity to bring him up again.

The waitress arrived with their lunches and sat them on the table. Eden could see Abby was not going to give up on getting information about Michael. "He's just a work colleague," she said as she picked at her food with her fork. "He's a great director to network with, and I hear his wife is very nice."

Julia's eyes widened at Eden's description of the director. She was sure he and Eden had gone off together for some privacy she was sure may have been a little work, but not for the studio. Apparently, she was wrong.

"Oh, married," said Abby relived. Maybe she could still get Eden and Rafe together again. "So, what about Rafe?" Abby picked up her fork and pointed it at Eden. "We know you still love her, Eden, and she's been so," she paused thoughtfully, "calm lately. I think she's trying to tell you something."

Eden just picked at her food. Abby was so confident about how she should feel. She wished she could be just as confident about her feelings.

Since it looked like there were no third parties involved, Julia decided to gently push her knowledge about Rafe into the conversation. She didn't think Rafe would mind, and she had resolved to just be a friend. "I think Rafe would like to spend more time with you and Bronte. Abby may be right. You should think about it."

Eden nodded her head fighting the turmoil inside herself. She couldn't even think about being with Rafe right now. She could barely face her after the huge mistake she was trying to live with. She kept looking down at her food and nodded her head. "I'll think about it." She pushed her plate away. "I've need to get back to the office," she said. "I have a meeting."

49

AFTER LEAVING WORK, Eden Kingsley went home and showered, but it didn't help make her feel any better. She was a shaking mess after Michael had left and it took a lot for her to make it through lunch with the girls then the rest of the day at work. It was a relief to finally to be able to go home.

Flynn had come over, and Eden was sitting across from him at her kitchen table in tears and shaking with anger at herself after telling him about Michael. "I really messed up," she sobbed as she wiped a tear away with a tissue.

Flynn looked at Eden with sympathy, not sure how to console her. "He should have told you."

Eden wiped her eyes and blew her nose. "Why should he? I practically jumped into his arms," she said. "I should have asked around. I should have asked him more questions when we met."

"At least you ended it," Flynn said as he pushed the tissue box toward her.

"I guess." Eden sniffed as she took another tissue. "Why is this happening? Rafe can go out and find someone, and it seems like whoever she finds loves her. She would still be with Greer if she had stayed. I go out and I just... screw up!"

"Eden, Rafe didn't sleep with Greer within the first hour she knew her, and they had a lot in common," Flynn said as he went to the sink to make a glass of water.

"I guess," Eden conceded thinking of the painting Greer had done of Rafe. She turned to look at Flynn. "What about the others?"

Flynn brought over glasses of water for both of them and sat down at the table. "She picked them up at a bar," he explained. "It's what they were there for. And almost all of them approached her first," he paused, "and she didn't expect anything from them but one night."

"That doesn't help," Eden snapped scathingly then regretted her harshness. "I'm sorry. I just really don't know what I'm doing anymore."

Flynn took a sip of his water and tried to think of a way to help Eden and make her understand she was not entirely at fault. "Eden, love like you had with Rafe is rare," he said as he held onto his cold glass. "Like love at first sight. From what I've been told, you guys took things slow even though you two knew you wanted to be together almost right away. Abby said you guys saw each other for almost four months before you, you know. She was joking about Rafe and said it was a record for her. I don't think you can expect it to happen again without taking things slowly like you did before. You guys were lucky." He shrugged and then sipped his water to wet his dry throat.

Eden looked down at her hands sadly. "I think Rafe knew at first sight. I just knew she was beautiful, interesting, and easy to be around. I don't think I really even knew I wanted her until after we kissed the first time. But then, I knew," she sighed, "and then I couldn't get enough of her. We were lucky." She looked up at Flynn desperately. "Why can't I be as sure again? About anyone? About Rafe?"

"You know," Flynn said cautiously, "maybe you should try with Rafe again and work on your feelings about her for a change."

"Flynn," Eden started but stopped herself. Between him and Abby, she was feeling a lot of pressure, and it was not helping her figure things out. "I'll think about it. But whoever I decide to be with, I'll just need to go slow. I don't want to make another mistake," she said and wiped away another tear.

50

LOUNGING IN ONE of the deck chairs Julia Hawthorn had invited herself over to Rafe's house to relax by her pool and bring news she was sure Rafe would appreciate. She had changed into her swimming suit and was sipping some of Rafe's expensive wine. Rafe was sitting at the patio table putting together a project for work on her laptop. She was oblivious to Julia.

Julia looked back at Rafe working and sat up. "I talked to Eden today," she said as she sipped her wine sure her news would grab Rafe's attention.

Rafe looked over at her for a second as she tried to process what she had just heard. "That's nice," she said and dove back into her project.

"She said you took pictures of her and Bronte on the beach the other day," Julia continued.

"Uh, huh," Rafe mumbled concentrating on her work.

"Do you still want her," she asked her smiling.

Rafe looked up confused. "What?"

Julia walked over and sat down next to Rafe. She looked at her with a big grin. "I think I was right about her being jealous," she said excitedly. "I think she's open to spending more time with you. She said she would think about it."

Rafe looked up at her still confused. "I didn't get that vibe from her at all," she said shaking her head in disbelief. "When we talked," she paused, "she wanted to ask me about Lauren."

Shocked, Julia could not believe her ears. "Lauren? The woman you had the affair with in New York? That Lauren?"

"Yes, that Lauren," Rafe said dryly. "She asked me if I planned it." She could see the surprise on Julia's face. "I was just as surprised as you," she said and leaned back in her chair. "I thought we were through what happened, but apparently, she still thinks about it. I was pretty sure she was reminding me of the reason she wasn't coming back," she shrugged, "but then she stayed and let me take pictures."

Julia took a sip of her wine and considered what Eden might be thinking. "Maybe she just needed to talk to you about Lauren for some closure." She looked at Rafe thoughtfully. "Her exact words when I asked her about spending more time with you were 'I'll think about it,' and she said it after she had just finished talking about how great you've been lately."

"After the conversation I had with her," Rafe said wryly, "thinking about it may be all she'll do. I can only wait and watch."

51

EDEN KINGSLEY SPENT the rest of the week trying to sort out all the feelings and anxieties she had and what she was going to do about them. She felt good spending time with Rafe, but it still also hurt every time she looked at her because of the affair and everything else they went through. She could see Rafe was trying to get along, but it didn't take the sting out of the fact Rafe cheated on her or help with her feelings about needing to be in a relationship with a man. She felt as if she was caught between feeling like she wanted to try with Rafe and the fear of trying—because it might just hurt both of them in the end.

She knew she pushed Rafe away and hurt her when she said she thought she needed to be with a man. Then leaving without a word after Bronte was born. But she felt, by staying in her house, it would hurt Rafe more to see her dating Jake and bring him home. It would have hurt both of them more. It was one thing Jake pointed out she could not disagree with even though she wished she had never met him. She was also beating herself up because the last two men she thought she wanted to be with turned out to be disasters.

Then there were all the things she was keeping from Rafe. All the things Jake had done, not to mention he was part of the Stewards, the group who filed the injunction. She didn't know how Rafe would react if she knew Jake had been part of everything from trying to take Bronte to the vandalism of her car she was sure he was responsible for in some way. Nothing similar had happened, so she wasn't positive. She hoped it wasn't him. It seemed he still didn't know she had the information she had given to Katheryn.

It was Friday and Eden was supposed to be working from home, but so far, she had not really accomplished anything. She was happy Flynn had the day off and was here keeping her company this afternoon. He was helping with Bronte and helping her talk through things when she was able. She watched Flynn and Bronte playing on the floor and smiled. It seemed like Bronte was her only sanity. Making sure she was happy and safe was the most important thing for her right now.

Outside her house, an unfamiliar car pulled into a parking space in front of the apartment. A serious woman with a briefcase got out, then made her way to Eden's door, and rang the bell.

52

ACROSS TOWN AT the CCAD, Rafe Salvaggio was in the photo lab at the Conservatory's photography department. Her photography class was working on a black and white film project, and they were printing their photos in-house in the state of the art darkroom.

Rafe was using her free time to get her project done. She was standing in the darkroom using the black and white enlarger and focusing a negative of Eden and Bronte at the beach she wanted to print.

Her cell phone rang, and she reached for it in the red darkness of the room. "Hello," she said and listened to the frantic voice on the phone. "Flynn? What's going on? Who? Children and Family Services Department? What do they want?" She listened again, "Abuse? Eden? That's fucking absurd!" she said in disbelief. "No, I'll be there in twenty minutes. Don't let anything happen." She hung up and looked around, her knowing she didn't have time to clean up properly.

Luckily, another student was using the lab. "Hey, Sadie," she called out, "I just got an emergency call, and I need to leave right now. Will you take care of my things?"

"Sure, Dean Salvaggio," Sadie agreed. "I hope everything's okay.

"I'm going to find out right now," she said as she took her film out of the enlarger carriage and slid it into a plastic sheath. She put her things in a pile and headed to the darkroom door.

"Thanks. Just put everything in my storage cupboard. I'll get it back to it next week."

It didn't take Rafe twenty minutes to get to Eden's apartment. It took breaking a couple of traffic laws to do it, though. Rafe rushed up to the apartment door and knocked firmly and then walked inside without waiting for anyone to answer.

She turned to her left and found everyone in the kitchen sitting around the table. She took the scene in at a glance and noticed Eden's ashen face first, then Flynn who was sitting uncomfortably beside her. She looked at the other side of the table and saw a stiff-backed matronly looking woman sorting through papers with an old brown briefcase beside her and a clipboard on the table in front of her.

"Eden, what's going on? Are you okay?"

Flynn stood up quickly and rushed over to Rafe with his eye on the door. "I guess I'll go now you're here," he said nervously. He didn't like the stern woman at the table and could tell she had a big problem with him being there.

"Thank you for staying, Flynn. I'll talk to you later," said Eden appreciatively.

"Call me if you guys need anything," Flynn called back to Eden as he rushed out the door.

The child services agent had turned her attention to Rafe and looked her up and down with judgmental eyes. "Who might you be?" she asked with authority.

Rafe stared back at the woman and frowned. "I'm Rafe Salvaggio, Bronte's other parent. Who are you?"

"I'm Ms. Verdish," the woman said without expression, "I'm a caseworker with the California CFSD." She turned back to her paperwork and shuffled through them again. "Yes, your name is listed here," she said not looking at Rafe. "You'll need to stay and answer some questions."

Rafe walked over to the table where Eden was holding Bronte. When Bronte saw her, she reached up for her and Rafe took the baby from Eden. "Hey, B Girl," she cooed and gave her a kiss before sitting down in the chair next to Eden. "I had no intention of leaving," she said coolly to the woman.

Ms. Verdish cleared her throat and ignored the look of contempt Ms. Salvaggio was giving her. "As I was telling Ms. Kingsley, I am here because a child abuse complaint was filed in our office on behalf of Bronte Kingsley."

Eden reached out and tapped the papers in front of Ms. Verdish. "Salvaggio-Kingsley. She has both our last names," she pointed out.

Ms. Verdish looked at the paperwork. "I only have the one name listed here, but fine, I'll change it." She wrote down the information on the clipboard. "Ms. Salvaggio, you say you're the child's 'other' mother. Just exactly what does 'other' mean?"

"She's adopting Bronte," Eden cut in seeing Rafe was getting frustrated. "We got pregnant when we were together."

Looking up and over her readers, Ms. Verdish blinked at them. "She is adopting her?" she repeated. "So this adoption hasn't taken place yet?"

"No," said Rafe as she shifted Bronte on her lap, "but it should be finalized in a few months."

The matronly woman looked back down and wrote something more on her clipboard then looked up at them and folded her arms on the table. "I'm here because this is listed as her primary address. Is that true?" She waited, and both Eden and Rafe nodded their confirmation of this piece of information. "Good," she said and made a check mark on one of the papers. "Okay, let's see," she said as she looked at her clipboard, "the allegations filed are excessive force when disciplining and neglect."

"This is ridiculous!" Rafe blurted out angrily. "Eden isn't abusive or neglectful. Who filed that the complaint?"

"The complaint was filed anonymously," she said as she took off her readers and looked at Rafe, "and the incidents reported have you, Ms. Salvaggio, listed as the abuser and Ms. Kingsley as an accessory by allowing it to happen."

"Me?" scoffed Rafe infuriated. "That's insane!"

Eden saw Bronte was getting restless and could feel the heat of Rafe's emotions, so she took her from Rafe and carried her over to her play area shaking her head. "No, Rafe would never do anything to hurt Bronte. She's never even been spanked by either of us."

Rafe watched Eden give Bronte a toy and then rejoin the table. "We don't believe in corporal punishment," she informed the social worker.

Ms. Verdish looked over to observe Bronte and then wrote something more on her clipboard. "I see she has a bruise on her leg. Why don't you tell me how it happened?"

"It's nothing," insisted Rafe. "We were at the beach playing, and she fell while I was chasing her around. She was fine. She got back up, and we played some more." She looked over at Eden and saw her nodding in agreement.

Clearing her throat, Ms. Verdish consulted her notes once again. "The complainant says they have seen you chasing after her in a park, and when she wouldn't stop, you pushed her so she would fall and you could catch up to her."

Rafe glared at her in disbelief sat back in her chair. "That's crazy. She's seventeen months old. I can catch her without resorting to violence. She simply falls down sometimes like thousands of kids do every day."

Ms. Verdish adjusted her glasses and looked back and forth between Rafe and Eden. "I noticed as soon as you came in the door the baby reached for you. This could be a sign of pathological dependency to the abuser. She could be seeking to comply and seek approval to avoid your abuse. It could also be considered emotional abuse," she said as she tapped her pen on the table.

Eden was so appalled at the social worker's remark, she was almost speechless. "No, no," she replied shaking her head, "It means she loves her," she assured the woman.

Rafe couldn't believe what she was hearing. This was outrageous. "With all due respect, Ms. Verdish, what the hell are you talking about?"

"Most abused children are fiercely loyal to their abuser," Ms. Verdish said as she looked directly at Rafe. "And by your responses," she continued, "you don't seem to have a lot of control over your temper."

Eden put her hand on Rafe to calm her as she saw she was about to say something she might regret. "That's just not the case here," she said quickly. "When it comes to dealing with Bronte, Rafe doesn't have a temper. I've never even seen her get upset with her over anything."

"Unfortunately, Ms. Kingsley, you're not with them all of the time, so you really can't say for certain," Ms. Verdish informed her.

"Oh, no, I think I can," protested Eden. "Neither of us abuse Bronte. Rafe is even better with her than I am."

"Interesting," Ms. Verdish said absently and made a note on her clipboard.

"What?" Rafe demanded.

Ms. Verdish ignored Rafe and looked at Eden. "Ms. Kingsley, are you being abused by Ms. Salvaggio too?"

"What?" Eden said shocked. "No!"

"I wasn't speaking of physical abuse, more about emotional abuse," Ms. Verdish clarified. "It seems you have a very low opinion of yourself, you seem protective of Ms. Salvaggio, and you allow her to answer for you and to do most of the talking. Is it why you separated?" she asked curtly.

"No, it isn't," shouted Rafe, "and our reasons are none of your business!"

Ms. Verdish looked coldly at Rafe. "More hostility, Ms. Salvaggio?"

"Only if you continue making absurd accusations," Rafe quipped as she stared at the social worker angrily.

Ignoring Rafe, Ms. Verdish looked at her clipboard again. "Next, there is the issue of neglect," she announced. "This is also directed to you, Ms. Salvaggio. It states you seldom have food in your home and there are child hazards throughout the house. I suppose I'll have to visit your home too and possibly make a report with the court if you really are trying to adopt."

Rafe shook her head at what she was hearing. "The court has already sent someone to see my house for the adoption process. You can look too if you want, but I can answer those allegations. It's true. I don't have a lot of food in my kitchen. I only have Bronte a few times a week. The rest of the time I'm working," she explained. "Keeping a lot of food would be wasteful. I buy food as we need it. As far as the child hazards, Bronte has learned what to touch and what not to touch. She's a very smart child," declared Rafe and crossed her arms.

"She has learned what not to touch?" repeated Ms. Verdish with a frown. "It sounds like you have some unrealistic expectations of a seventeen-month-old. What happens when she becomes more curious, and she touches something that could be dangerous? Are you going to take the chance?"

When she was a child, there were all kinds of dangerous or fragile things around . She taught Bronte not to touch in the same way her mother taught her. Rafe looked at Eden concerned. "Am I expecting too much?"

"No, I don't think so," Eden said placing her hand on Rafe to reassure her. "I can't think of any heavy sculptures or dangerous things you have at the moment that would hurt her if she touched them."

Ms. Verdish took a deep breath and began to scribble again on her clipboard. "I'll make a note to look further into the matter." When she was finished writing, she began putting her clipboard into her briefcase. "I think I'm finished here. I've had a look around the apartment, and it seems fine, though a bit sparse."

Eden flushed with embarrassment. "I just moved in not long ago," she tried to explain, but the social worker had already turned her back to her.

Ms. Verdish glanced around. "I see," she said unimpressed. "Well, you have the basics. I've seen the child, and she seems healthy, bruises aside. So, I'll make my report and turn it into my boss for review. Then a decision will be made about inspecting your home, Ms. Salvaggio, and if any further action needs to be taken."

"Further action?" Rafe pressed.

"Yes, counseling, psychological assessment, removal of the child," Ms. Verdish said stiffly. "Though removal would only happen if abuse can be proven."

"Should we be contacting a lawyer?" asked Rafe with concern.

"What you should be doing, Ms. Salvaggio, is making sure another complaint isn't filed," stated Ms. Verdish harshly. "In the eyes of the department, you are *not* a family member, and serious actions can be taken against you. In this type of case, if you are abusing the child, we will file a restraining order against you on Bronte's behalf, have you arrested, or both if necessary.

Rafe looked at Ms. Verdish icily. "I am not abusing and have never abused her, and I am a family member. I don't like to be threatened, Ms. Verdish," Rafe said coldly. "I will be contacting my lawyer, and I will be the one filing a complaint about you."

"Like I said, I'll make my report," Ms. Verdish smiled arrogantly. She turned and headed for the door with Rafe and Eden close behind. "You'll be hearing from our office soon. Have a nice day," she said politely and walked out the door.

Rafe closed the door hard behind the awful woman and locked it. It took everything in her to hold back the anger boiling inside of her, and her eyes were blazing as she turned them on Eden.

"What the hell is this all about? Who is doing this?"

"I don't know," she said shakily as she went to the table and picked up the copy of the complaint the social worker left with her. "I can't believe someone would think we're hurting Bronte. This is some kind of mistake. Whoever did this just didn't know what they were seeing."

Rafe went into the small living room where Bronte was playing on the floor and sat down on the couch. "It doesn't sound like a mistake to me," she said, trying to keep the anger from her voice. "It sounds like someone is doing this on purpose. Maybe it's the people Katheryn warned us about. If they file another complaint, and I can't prove it's a lie," she hesitated, "the CFSD will file the restraining order."

Eden sat down next to Rafe and looked at her earnestly. "I'll just ignore it."

Rafe looked up at her in alarm. "Eden, you can't ignore it," she protested. "If you do, they may take her and put her in foster care or somewhere. I think we need to talk to Katheryn," she said as she lay her head back on the couch and closed her eyes, her head throbbing. "This is so fucked up."

"This is just one complaint," Eden said and tossed the paper on the coffee table. "We have a lot of friends who know us. They can tell the caseworker we would never hurt Bronte."

"We? Eden, all of the complaints were about me," Rafe said as she looked down in despair. "They're saying these things happened when you and our friends weren't there." She lifted her head and looked at Eden with worry in her eyes. "You don't believe I abuse her, do you? You know I could never hurt her."

"No, I don't think you would ever hurt her," Eden said as she shook her head at the possibility. She ran her hands through her golden hair hating herself because she was so sure Jake was behind this, and she didn't know what she could do about it. "Rafe, you don't think they'll really try to take her from us, do you?"

Rafe leaned forward and put her hands to her head to rub her temples. "They can't take her away from you. You're her mother, and you haven't done anything wrong."

Eden looked at Rafe and could see the pain she was in. She wanted to help her and comfort her, but at the same time, she was afraid to go down that path. She put her hand on Rafe's head and smoothed her hair. "They can't take her away from either of us," she said softly as her emotions swept through her and Eden's heart went out to Rafe. She moved Rafe's hand from her temple and kissed her there. "Rafe, they can't," she said hoping to ease her pain and show her she cared about her and was on her side.

Rafe felt Eden's kiss and looked up into her eyes. She couldn't stop herself this time and lost her resolve. She kissed her deeply then whispered softly, "Eden," she pulled her close and kissed her again unable to hide the hunger she felt for her.

Breaking away from Rafe's kiss, Eden moved to kiss her neck and then rested her head on Rafe's chest, taking comfort in the warmth and her scent. It felt so good to be in this place with her.

"Rafe, will you stay and just," she hesitated, "just hold me for a while?"

Kissing the top of Eden's head with a secret joyous smile, Rafe whispered, "Yes."

53

AFTER A WHILE of just sitting together with Rafe, and fighting with the inner turmoil of all the emotional and feelings she was having, Eden Kingsley decided she wanted Rafe to stay longer. Eden couldn't help her feelings of empathy for her and everything happening to her. She wanted to feel empathy for Rafe and understood those feelings.

What she was unsure about were the other feelings she was not supposed to be feeling. She was not supposed to want to be close to her or feel the warmth from her body. She was not supposed to be thinking about how her scent made her body react, and have her thoughts go down a road she had told herself, and everyone else, she didn't want to go down because of the affair. Somehow, as she sat close to Rafe, even those thoughts were on her mind. Her body wanted to go rogue and kiss her or touch her. Those feelings made it so she couldn't help thinking maybe Flynn was right, and she should try with Rafe again.

Then there was the guilt she was feeling over all the things she hadn't told her about Jake and why the social worker came in the first place. Ultimately, both her guilt and her need to show Rafe she cared led her to the decision she should ask Rafe to stay for dinner at the very least. As they watched Bronte play, she invited Rafe to dinner, and she accepted gladly.

When they finished eating dinner together, and Bronte had finally fallen asleep, they took her to her room and put her to bed. Rafe had decided Bronte should stay home because of all the things the social worker had said and the complaint accused her of doing.

"Rafe, are you sure you want to do this," whispered Eden. "It is your night to have her."

"I think this is best," Rafe said just above a whisper. "I don't want to take any chances. I don't think she should spend the night with me until this thing blows over."

Eden closed the bedroom door and went to the kitchen while Rafe sat on the couch in the living room. She brought Rafe a glass of wine and sat next to her. "I still can't believe this is happening. I'm so sorry."

Rafe looked around Eden's sparse apartment and was surprised she had so little here. "I'll send you some things over."

"Things?"

"Things," she confirmed, "like pictures and some more furniture, so your place doesn't look 'sparse,' as she put it. Do you need me to increase the amount of money I give you for Bronte? Are you doing okay?" she asked concerned and thinking maybe Eden needed more help since she was on her own. "If you need to use Lydia more to watch Bronte, I'll pay her."

"You don't have to," Eden reassured her. "We're doing fine."

"I want to," she said as she took a drink of her wine and looked at Eden, giving her a small smile. "At least let me send some things for the apartment."

Eden smiled back in appreciation of her thoughtfulness. "Hey," she said suddenly, "you've never had dinner over here before. I'm glad you stayed."

"Me too. I really like your cooking." Rafe leaned her head back on the couch and closed her eyes. "Katheryn says we should just wait this out, but I wish I could do something about it now."

Touching Rafe's arm to comfort her, Eden felt the softness of her olive skin. "I wish we could too," she whispered.

Rafe could feel Eden's hand on her arm and the hot surge running through her body. She opened her eyes and looked into Eden's eyes. "Eden," she breathed fighting the urge to pull her close like she used to do.

"You look so sad," Eden whispered and brushed Rafe's hair from her eyes.

"I am sad," Rafe said heavily, "because I'm not kissing you." This time, she didn't stop herself and leaned in close, kissing Eden sweetly. When she met no resistance, she put her arms around Eden, pulled her close, and kissed her deeply, losing herself at the feel of her body in her arms. "Eden, I've missed you so much," she said in a throaty voice. She moved her kisses to her neck and shoulder and slipped her hands under her shirt to feel her warm skin against her hands.

Gently Eden pushed Rafe back. "Rafe," she swallowed as her heart beat hard, and Rafe's presence overwhelmed her senses. She felt the dizzy almost drunk feeling only Rafe caused and tried to regain control of herself. "I need to go slow."

Rafe looked into Eden's pleading eyes and kissed her again. "Okay, we'll go slow," she promised softly. She kissed her again and slowly ran her hand down her face and over her breast to unbutton her shirt. "You smell so good. I missed your smell," she said and kissed her again. "I'll go slow. I'll make love to every part of you."

Eden gave a small laugh and pushed Rafe back again. "No, Rafe. I meant I need us to go slow," she explained. "I think we should take our time. Spend time together first."

"How slow?" Rafe asked with a furrowed brow, unable to hide her disappointment.

Seeing Rafe's disappointment, and the way she looked at her with those liquid steel gray-blue eyes, Eden melted a little as she bit her lip slightly then smiled. "Let's start with kisses. Just kisses, for now," she said and leaned in and kissed Rafe gently over and over again.

"Just kisses," said Rafe between kisses. "Can I kiss you anywhere? I want to kiss your neck," she breathed, "and your chest," she whispered, "and your breasts. I want to kiss all of you."

Eden held Rafe's face in her hands. "No," she said softly knowing what Rafe's kisses could lead to, "just here," she kissed her lips, "and here," she kissed her face and forehead, "and here," she kissed her neck, "and here, she kissed her shoulder, "for now," she whispered heavily. Her body shuddered with desire like it did for no other as Rafe poured her hot kisses over her neck, face, and lips.

54

EDEN KINGSLEY LAUGHED at the sight in front of her. Rafe Salvaggio was trying again to set up the giant lopsided stuffed bear beside Bronte. She had won it in a carnival and was trying to take their picture together. It had been two weeks since the social worker's visit, and they still hadn't heard anything from them. Katheryn said it was a good thing, but to stay vigilant.

Things were going well, more than well, between her and Rafe, and Eden was glad. She watched as Rafe got her photo, and Bronte pointed to the merry-go-round. She happily followed them and sat on the blue horse with Bronte as Rafe took more photos. The ride ended and Eden climbed down with Bronte and gave her to Rafe to put into the stroller.

"I think that's enough spinning rides for me today," said Eden a little motion sick.

"I can take her again if she wants to go." Rafe happily buckled the stroller harness around Bronte.

"Let's get a drink and sit down. It's hot out here," suggested Eden. They bought drinks and Eden led them to a shaded bench. "Here you go, Bronte," she said as she handed her a small cup of water. "Let's cool off."

Rafe sat down and watched as Eden got Bronte settled and took a drink for herself. "You're so beautiful," she said looking intently at her. She reached out and ran her fingers down Eden's cheek and neck, and then leaned in to kiss her.

Putting her hand to Rafe's chest, Eden pushed her back breaking away. "Rafe, I'm a mess. I'm sweating."

Rafe took her hand and pulled her close. She wrapped her arm around Eden and kissed her on her cheek and licked a small droplet of sweat from the hairline next to her ear, and whispered, "I like you sweaty. I want to take you home with me," she said as her eyes twinkled and then kissed her on the lips again.

Eden pushed Rafe back again gently. "Rafe, don't," she said, and she looked away from her.

Taking Eden's hand from her chest, Rafe kissed it. "I'm sorry. I didn't mean to push you."

"I just need to take things slow," she said looking into Rafe's eyes for her understanding.

"I know," Rafe said looking back into her amazing brown eyes with the golden specks in their centers. "I love your eyes." She pushed Eden's hair back. "I loved looking at them in the mornings. Sometimes, they were this bright, beautiful golden brown color. Then, when you came home, they were a darker brown like a light milk chocolate with little golden specks. And sometimes, when we made love, I could see more of the gold come out around your pupils," she whispered. "They have always mesmerized me from the first time I saw you. I'd like to see them in the morning again."

Eden broke Rafe's gaze and looked down. "Rafe."

Rafe pulled Eden's face up by her chin. "I know. I'm sorry. We're going slow." She smiled at the beautiful woman she loved. "Just kisses." She kissed her softly. "For now." She kissed her again and then looked into her beautiful eyes. "I love you, Ede. I love you," Rafe whispered.

Laying her head on Rafe's shoulder, Eden closed her eyes at hearing Rafe calling her that intimate nickname again. It was something she thought she had lost, but she was not sure she should have it back. She hated herself for not being able to say those words back, but she just could not bring herself to say them. "I know."

55

AFTER SPENDING THE day having fun at the carnival Rafe Salvaggio and Eden Kingsley had stopped by The Kiki Bistro to pick up some dinner takeaway and were talking with Letty and Ephraim at the counter.

Jude had joined Abby, who was at her usual table with the gang. She looked up and spotted Rafe and Eden. "Hey, there's Eden and Rafe." Jude pointed toward them with her chin.

Stacey checked them out and took a bite of one of her fries. "Do you think Eden's ever gonna switch back so they can get back together?"

"It's not about switching," Abby said to Stacey with annoyance. "It's about who you're attracted to or love. I know they love each other. Eden just has to remember why she was with Rafe in the first place.

"She will. They're good together," said Flynn following Abby and Stacey's gaze.

"Why were they together?" asked Stacy with a scoff. She just did not see it.

Abby ignored Stacey. She knew nothing about Rafe and Eden. She wiped her mouth with her napkin. "All I know is the good Rafe is back, mostly," she said thoughtfully. "Except she won't take the damn blue woman down off her wall."

"I like it," Jude muttered with a shrug.

Abby gave her a look of disdain. "You would."

Erica exchanged a look with Jude and snickered as she set up her camera equipment for the video they were going to shoot after dinner.

"What do you mean, mostly?" asked Stacey looking at Abby curiously.

"I can't put my finger on it," Abby said conspiratorially, "but she seems like the same old Rafe we know and love but different somehow."

Jude rolled her eyes. "That clears things up. You know what I think is fucked? Rafe feels like she can't be alone with Bronte."

"I know," said Flynn. "It's because of those CFSD people. I can't believe someone would say she hurt Bronte." He kept to himself the fact he and Eden suspected Jake had filed the complaint.

"Yeah," agreed Stacey. "Julia had to leave early the other day so Rafe came over to see if I would hang out with them until Eden got there."

"She's not having Bronte stay overnight for a while either unless someone's there," said Flynn nervously hoping he was not crossing a line by telling them such personal details.

"What?" exclaimed Abby. "That's crazy." She looked over at Rafe and Eden.

"Did Rafe just kiss her?" Erica asked not believing what she just saw through her camera lens.

"Oh, my god. She did!" squealed Stacey.

"Are they back together?" Abby asked. "What's going on?"

"Shut up, Abby. Here comes Eden," said Jude.

Eden walked up to the table pushing Bronte in her stroller and waved. "Hi guys," she said, and everyone acknowledged her.

Abby looked at her bewildered. "So, what's going on?"

"Oh," she said and turned to point at Rafe, "we've just been to the little carnival by the beach. It was really fun." She sat down and looked at Bronte. "Wasn't it?"

"No," said Abby in frustration. "I mean what's with the kissing? Are you guys," she raised her eyebrows, "you know," she looked at Eden knowingly.

"Abby, leave them alone," said Jude and gave her a hard look.

Abby crossed her arms miffed. "I think we should know if they're back together." She looked at Eden. "Are you?"

Eden looked at the table of waiting faces, and her anxiety began to edge into her mind because she had no answer yet. "We're just talking."

"Uh! And kissing, apparently!" said Abby scandalized.

244

Eden shook her head and held her hand up hoping to stop Abby from talking. "We're going slow."

"And kissing?" pressed Abby.

"Abby, give it up. It's none of our business," Jude said and looked up at Eden then grimaced a silent sorry.

"I think it's nice," added Flynn, and Erica nodded her agreement.

"Nice." Abby huffed. "Whatever."

Flynn tried to help Eden by changing the subject. "Eden, did you get the stuff Rafe sent over all set up?"

"Most of it," replied Eden with a nod glad of the change of subject.

Abby latched on to this new information. "What did she send you?" she asked inquisitively.

"Just some more furniture and art for the walls," Eden told her. "She was really upset about the social worker, so she's trying to fix everything she made a negative comment about. She said my apartment was sparse, so Rafe is filling it up."

"The whole abuse thing is messed up," said Jude. "Let us know if we need to do anything for you, give a character witness or something."

"Thanks, Jude. It means a lot." Eden smiled appreciatively at her.

Rafe made her way over carrying food in a carryout bag. "Hello," she said smiling at everyone. She turned to Eden smiling brightly. "Ede, did you tell them about the little carnival?"

"Yes," she said, her face flushing pink at Rafe use of the endearment of her name again, and turned back to the table. "We had a lot of fun. You guys should check it out."

"I shot some great pictures," said Rafe still smiling.

"So you guys really aren't going to give us any more information?" Abby asked accusingly.

"About what?" Rafe asked as she looked at the faces around the table.

"She saw you kiss Eden," Stacey informed her.

"Oh." Rafe grinned.

"Oh? That's it?" demanded Abby irked at the grin on Rafe's face.

Rafe ignored Abby and changed the subject. "Are you guys going to come to my lecture at the Conservatory?"

"Nice. Change the subject," Abby complained. "I'll be there. I may blog about it if it's interesting."

"I hope you can use it." Rafe nodded. "We can use the positive press."

"We'll all be there," said Stacey.

"Yeah," agreed Erica. "I'll probably be there with my equipment." She looked at Abby. "I'll be back. I need to get some things from the car," she said and took off quickly.

Rafe smiled at them and looked over at Jude. "Jude, I have those photos for you at the house. They turned out great. I hope you like them."

"Thanks, I appreciate you taking them," Jude said perking up at the news. "The ad agency was going to charge me a couple of thousand dollars for two or three shots. What do I owe you for them?"

"Nothing. It was my pleasure. I really enjoy photography more than I thought I would."

"Why's she taking your picture, Jude?" asked Abby.

"It's nothing," Jude said with a shrug. "We're trying to get some gigs with the studios and other places doing all of their massages and relaxation sessions, so we have to make up new marketing materials. Rafe took pictures of the crew, our equipment, and products."

"You should definitely use the drawings you did too. Mixing the photos with the drawings will soften the look of your marketing materials, and they won't look overly institutional," suggested Rafe.

Abby looked at Rafe and Eden sitting so close to each other, and Eden with her hand on Rafe's leg. She could not stop herself. "Rafe, I can't stand it. Are you two together or not?"

"I can take your picture too if you want, Abby," Rafe said ignoring her question. She picked up the camera hanging from her neck and took a moment to focus and look through the lens.

Impatient, Abby threw up her hands. "Are you going to take it or what?"

"Abby," Rafe said patiently, "you can't rush a masterpiece." She snapped the picture at Abby's shocked face then put the camera down and looked Abby in the eyes with an impish twinkle in her own. "Any more questions?"

Abby broke from Rafe's gaze and tried to rub the spots out of her eyes. "No," she said softly.

"Good," said Rafe curtly.

Eden watched their exchange and shook her head with a small smile. "Rafe, we have to go. I'll call you about the schedule." She got up and turned the stroller toward the door. "Thanks for the great day."

"I'll walk you out." Rafe got up and handed Eden her takeout bag then followed her outside.

After Eden had stowed the takeout bag under the stroller, Rafe gave her a passionate kiss goodbye. As Eden turned away, Rafe grabbed her hand and pulled her back to kiss her again. When they broke away, Eden laughed and ran her hand down Rafe's body, and then turned and pushed the stroller down the sidewalk toward her car.

"I have to go too. I'll see you at home," said Flynn to Stacey and Jude hurriedly and then made his way out.

Rafe walked back in smiling, sat down, and picked up an unused fork and stabbed the last fry on Abby's plate and ate it. "Stop looking at me like that, Abby."

Abby continued to stare at Rafe suspiciously. "What are you doing?"

"Picking up dinner and hanging with you." Rafe smiled as a waitress brought her food in a takeout bag.

"Abby, leave her alone," said Jude noting the signs Abby was not going to let go of the issue.

"No, I need to know, Rafe," Abby demanded. "I know how you can be. What are you doing with her? Are you just leading Eden on or are you serious about her?"

"Leading her on?" asked Rafe looking at Abby quizzically.

"Abby, they're taking it slow," said Stacey. Abby was the one who said they loved each other and now she was making a big deal out of a few kisses. She didn't get it. "Why are you asking her about a few kisses?"

Rafe smiled up at Abby and pointed at her with her fork. "She's just a really funny girl."

Jude could tell Rafe was not going to talk about it with Abby, so she tried to distract her. "Abby, tell us about the new place you want us all to try Thursday night."

Not liking the change in subject, but accepting it, Abby looked at Jude. "It sounds like a really cool place," she said. "You go in and choose the food you want, and you get to cook it yourself. You can cook it by following their recipe or make up your own. They have a chef who kind of watches over you as you cook. You bring your own wine and can eat on their outdoor patio. It's supposed to be really fun."

"An interactive dinner?" asked Stacey.

"I guess," Abby said peevishly. Both Stacey and Rafe had gotten on her nerves. She turned her attention to Jude. "It'll be fun."

"I don't know," Jude said uncomfortably. "I don't cook."

"We'll help you," offered Abby, "and the chef is there."

"It sounds nice," said Rafe liking the idea of being with Eden again while out with their friends. It could be the next step for them. "I'll surprise Eden with it. Thursday?"

"Yep, seven sharp," confirmed Abby.

Rafe got up, leaned over Abby's shoulder, and whispered in her ear so the others couldn't hear. "I'm very, very," Rafe whispered breathily, "very serious."

Abby looked up and saw Rafe's smile. She smiled back with relief as Rafe grabbed her takeout bag and walked away. "See you Thursday, Rafe." Abby looked at Jude and Stacey with a frown. "Julia was right," she said musingly.

"About what?" Jude asked as she dug into her pocket for her keys.

"About what Rafe calls Eden," she grumbled. "I guess I just never noticed. She calls her Ede. I just always thought it was Edy."

"That's probably what she's trying to say." Stacy laughed.

"Yeah, probably," agreed Abby with a slight scowl. She did not like agreeing with anything Stacey said.

Jude just shook her head and chuckled just as Erica came back inside with her equipment.

56

OUTSIDE EDEN'S APARTMENT, Flynn Ogden was sitting in his dark blue Chevy truck just beyond the yellow security light watching. It was part of his nightly vigilance. They might not be thinking about Jake and the Stewards, but Flynn just could not forget.

Randomly, he would drive around the complex looking for anything or anyone suspicious. After making his rounds, he parked so he could see Eden's apartment and waited patiently until the lights were turned out.

He watched for another hour and then started his truck and made his way home, hoping it would be another lucky and quiet night.

57

WAITING FOR THURSDAY evening was almost painful. To Rafe Salvaggio, the week went by much too slow. But it was finally here, and she was excited about surprising Eden with flowers, wine, and an invitation out to dinner with everyone tonight. She looked at the clock on her phone and knew Eden had probably been home for a while. She needed to get there so Eden would have time to get ready and they could figure out who was coming over to watch Bronte. She was confident Lydia would come over as long as they were not going to be out too late. If they were, she could call Letty to keep Bronte, but Rafe did not think that would happen on a weeknight.

Rafe was wearing her father's driving cap and driving his Maserati Ghibli Spyder convertible to Eden's apartment with the top down. It was a great day to have it out on the street. The sun was out, the sky was clear, and the temperature was warm, but not too hot. She wanted to remind Eden of the time when they first met and when they started to fall in love. Hopefully, after dinner, Rafe would take her on a romantic ride down to the coast road—if Eden said yes.

Listening to the radio at top volume to songs from her youth, Rafe knew all the words, so she sang along. She was excited and happy about how things were going with Eden, even if they were going slow.

They had time, she thought and smiled happily.

She had spent the last few evenings at Eden's just holding her and kissing her and talking softly to her until she had to go home so they could both get some sleep, and so she could regain control of herself. Eden's taste, her silky golden hair, her smell, her soft skin, everything about her was so familiar, so perfectly what she wanted, and what she so desperately missed. Eden, Eden, Eden, Eden, Eden, she will have her back, her family back, Bronte and Eden.

Love was in her life again, and it showed in her every movement. Just the thought of Eden and being near her made Rafe's smile brighten, and her heart beat faster. *We'll go slow, just like we did when we first met, and everything will be right again.*

She would be patient and use every fiber of her being to hold herself back and control the passion inside her aching to be released until Eden was ready again. Eden was worth it. Worth the wait. Every day, every hour, every minute that went by just built the hope and love in Rafe's heart.

She smiled to herself because everyone had been wrong. They had even made her doubt herself. It wasn't a waste of time to wait for her. She hadn't let her heart be led by fantasy or her mind be fooled with wishful thinking. She and Eden really were going to be together again, and she would have her life back again.

As Rafe got closer to Eden's apartment, her stomach clenched her heart beat faster, and her mind filled with fantasies all for Eden. She pulled into the apartment parking lot and moved forward slowly looking for an empty guest space close to Eden's door. She looked up and could see the archway to Eden's apartment door—to her paradise—to Eden.

"What the hell?" she said to herself as she slowed the car and lifted her sunglasses to be sure of what she was seeing. Her heart skipped a beat. "*Merda!*" she hissed slipping angrily into her Italian.

Jake walked out of the archway in front of Eden's apartment tucking in his shirt and adjusting his pants. Rafe stopped her car and watched him get into his car. He took his time and finally pulled out of the parking space and headed for the complex exit. Rafe looked at Eden's doorway again then toward Jake's moving car.

With rage building inside her, Rafe down shifted and popped the car into gear, then stepped on the gas, and took off to catch up with him. She sped past him hitting a speed bump hard and pulled in front of his car forcing him to stop before he could get out of the parking lot. She ripped her seat belt and threw her sunglasses and cap off. She got out of her car and angrily approached him.

Rafe beat on Jake's window until he rolled it down a crack and yelled into the car. "What the fuck are you doing here?"

Jake smiled through the small opening. "Hello to you too, Rafe," he said calmly. "A more fitting question is what are you doing here?"

"Fuck you!" said Rafe in a rage. "Tell me what the hell you think you're doing! Are you harassing Eden?"

"Harassing Eden?" Jake laughed. "No, harassment is what you're doing," he said pointedly.

"What the hell are you talking about?" she demanded, infuriated by the smirk on his face.

Jake opened his car door and got out of the car confidently. "Listen," he said leaning on his door. "I think this has gone on long enough." He pressed his lips together and shook his head. "Eden may hate me for a while if I tell you, but I know she'll get over it eventually. Besides, you were bound to find out sometime, and maybe finding out now will save you some pain and money later."

"Find out what?" she demanded as she moved threateningly toward him. "Just tell me what the fuck you're doing here! Eden doesn't want you around anymore!"

"I think you have it backward." Jake laughed. "Rafe, you're such an easy play," he said sadly. "I didn't believe you would be, but Eden was right all along."

Rafe clenched her fists in rage and spoke through her teeth angrily. "What the hell are you fucking talking about!"

Jake shook his head again and sighed. "You are clueless, aren't you?" He looked into Rafe's angry face. "Rafe, Eden is still with me," he said pointing to himself. "She never really left me."

"You fucking liar!" she seethed. "She said you two were history, and she was never going back to you!"

"Please, just calm down," Jake begged. "Listen, this thing Eden's doing," he paused, "it's over because I'm going to tell you exactly what's happening." He leaned back on his car. "Like I said, Eden is really going to hate me for doing this now, but it looks like I have no choice."

"Do what? And don't tell me to fucking calm down!" she commanded.

"This whole thing." He waved in the air with his hands. "Her getting close to you and pretending she likes you. It's all part of the plan."

"Plan?" Rafe repeated shaking her head. "What the hell are you talking about? She's not pretending anything. She still loves me. I know it!"

Jake laughed and took a deep breath. "Oh, Rafe, she doesn't love you. She loves me." He looked at her and licked his lips. "I'm the one she sleeps with at night. I'm the one she wants. She wants a man, Rafe." He glanced over his shoulder toward Eden's apartment. "I was just in her apartment. I was there all last night. I've been there almost every night after you leave. She's almost insatiable." He laughed shyly. "You can really get her worked up." He looked down and saw his shirt was still untucked, so he fixed it. "I was just in there now because she called me telling me she needed me again. I had to leave work early today and meet her so we could make love. She isn't expecting you."

Rafe shook her head as Jake finished adjusting his pants and shirt, her mind reeling and pain showing on her face. She could not believe him. "No!" she said shaking.

"Yes." Jake nodded. "I'm so sorry. You weren't supposed to find out yet."

"Fuck you! I don't believe you! Eden wouldn't lie about something like this!"

Jake looked at her sadly. "You really don't know her very well anymore, do you? This can't be a surprise to you," he said with a look of disbelief. "Look at what she did when she left you for me. Look at all the things she was doing to you with all her complaints and accusations. Hell, from some of the things she's told me, she's probably been thinking about this before she even got pregnant using your friend's sperm." He scoffed and ran his hand over the back of his neck. "You really can't see she's been hiding something from you?"

Rafe could feel the vein throbbing at her temple. Of course, she could see Eden was hiding something, she had told Greer her suspicions. But she had never imagined it would be something like this, something so noxious and serpentine.

Jake saw Rafe's hesitation and continued with his caustic words. "Rafe, all of this is to make sure you never get Bronte and can never be around Eden again. There's a reason behind just about everything that's gone on since before the injunction was filed," he said sympathetically.

"The injunction?" repeated Rafe confused and she could feel herself bristle at the thought of it.

"It's part of all of this," he said emphatically.

"No. You're a fucking liar!" She jabbed her finger in his face. "I'm going to kill you! Stay the fuck away from her and Bronte!"

Jake leaned away from her to avoid her hand. "I'm not a liar, just listen."

"I'm not listening to you! Fuck you!" she screamed in his face. She could not believe Eden would do this to her or their family.

"I know you think you're right, but think about it," he said controlling his frustration at Rafe and having to deal with her. "She doesn't want you," he said evenly standing his ground. "She doesn't love you. Has she ever said it?" He waited for her to think about it. He could see she knew Eden had not told her she loved her. "Has she spent even one night with you? No, she hasn't, because she's with me. She just does little things she knows will give you hope to string this thing along. Looks, touches, kisses, and she always tells you she wants to take it slow. It's a means to an end, Rafe."

"What end?" Rafe shook her head at a complete loss. "What the fuck are you talking about?"

Jake shrugged and rubbed the back of his neck again. "Like I said—to get you out of their lives for good."

"No." Rafe shook her head. "No." She looked at him suspiciously. "You're fucking with me! You helped with the injunction. She didn't know anything about it!"

"I'm not 'fucking' with you, as you put it," Jake said calmly acting as though he clearly hated to use a curse word. "I'm doing you a favor!" Rafe was about to turn away, so he stepped in front of her. He wanted to make sure his words got through her thick skull. "Listen, I can prove it." Rafe gave him a burn in hell look, but he pressed on. "I know about everything." He gave a nervous laugh. "She really is ruthless when it comes to you." He paused to let those words ring in her ears. "I know about all the kisses and touches she knew would drive you mad, the injunction, the opening up by the pool, the abuse allegations only implicate you—it's all part of it." He frowned and then looked at her sympathetically. "Even when she was toying with you by the beach, when she asked you about Lauren, she was reminding you of what you did to her, and telling you what she was doing to you." He paused and looked over his shoulder at Eden's doorway then back. "Rafe, she planned it all, and I've been helping her."

Rafe was taking in his words and looking at him in shock. *How could he know about those conversations*, she thought as she clenched her fists. She shook her head and forced out her words. "I don't believe you."

"Okay," said Jake thinking fast about what he could say to convince her everything he said was true. "Oh!" He snapped his fingers and pointed at her. "She said you described love like a fire that couldn't be put out and any little thing could bring back the flame." He watched her eyes burn with anger as she recognized her own words. "We were making love when she told me, and she laughed about it as she went down on me." He knew those words would get her attention and almost smiled.

Rafe looked at him with shock, and Jake could see her face flush with anger. Jake quickly continued before she erupted.

"She told me all about how you were asking her questions, and how she told you she didn't know yet about still having feelings just for men. She said she couldn't answer you and said she didn't know anymore and she was still figuring things out."

Jake looked at Rafe and could see she recognized the words. "She was lying to you, Rafe. The only thing she's been trying to figure out is how to make sure you stay out of her life forever. You have to believe me," he said emphatically. "She knows you want her back now, and she's been using it against you. How would I know you both said those things if she didn't tell me?"

Rafe leaned on her hands against Jakes car and closed her eyes, her vision failing and her mouth going dry. *He would not know,* she thought. She was dazed he knew private details of her conversations with Eden. She did not want to believe him, but she knew his words about what they had said were true. So how much more of what he was saying was true? "I," she choked, "I don't know how—"

"She told me," Jake insisted sadly. "It's the only way I could know."

Rafe's face paled, and her body weakened as she faced him. "This isn't Eden."

"It is her," Jake said and watched as she finally began to believe him. "I may not know anything about cinematic arts, as you pointed out to her, but Eden," he said and then drove air from his mouth, making a harsh sound, a cross between a bark and a laugh, "she should get out of the script development business and start an acting career. She could be an academy award winner." He laughed nervously hoping he had not gone too far. "She has you totally and utterly fooled."

Rafe's heart was pounding against her chest so hard it throbbed in her ears, and she could barely hear him as she leaned on the car again and whispered. "No."

"I'm sorry this is happening to you," Jake said hanging his head sorrowfully. "I told Eden it was too much, but she's determined you have nothing to do with her or Bronte. And only then, if you pay a lot of money to her for the privilege, since now she knows she's out of your will. She's already had you furnish her apartment. I wondered why she didn't take anything from our apartment and picked such a cheap apartment when we looked for this place together. I thought she was being frugal, but really, I guess it was so you'd feel sorry for her." He watched Rafe lean silently against the car then reach up and put her hand against her temple. "Rafe, I hate what she's doing, and I'm going to help you," he said with sympathy. "I'll tell you what she's planning next, and you can prevent it from happening. Okay?" Rafe remained silent. "She's trying to get you to do exactly what you're doing. Coming to her apartment without an invitation, showing up and surprising her, and all of the other thing you'll probably end up doing," he revealed gravely.

Rafe's head was throbbing. She still didn't want to believe him. Anger was the only thing giving her strength to keep standing. "Why?" Rafe choked the question out softly.

Jake took off his sunglasses and cleaned them on his shirt. He put them back on and looked at her anxiously, desperately wanting her to believe him so he could save his mission. "So, right before the injunction hearing, she can have a restraining order filed against you. Once she does that, and the judge takes into account the abuse allegations and all of the other things, it will seal the injunction and stop the adoption completely."

"Why?" Rafe's voice broke. "Why didn't she just say this was what she wanted when she was asked months ago. I don't understand. It doesn't make sense."

"To be honest, I don't really know all of the reasons why she's doing these things," Jake said sounding sympathetic. "I guess she just wants to make absolutely sure things go her way. She wants to take away any power and control you may have over their lives—forever."

"Power and control? No," she said and started to go to her car. "I'm going to talk to her. I don't believe you!"

Jake followed her quickly. "Rafe," he called and stepped in front of her. "Rafe, I have no reason to lie to you. Go ahead, go talk to her. She's in the apartment right now taking a shower." He looked back in the direction of the apartment then back at her. "Rafe, just think about this, please. If you couldn't see she was being deceitful all this time, what makes you think you'll know if she's telling you the truth today when she tells you I'm a liar?"

He took a breath and held his hands up in front of him as Rafe looked at him pale and angry. "I know you don't like me, and I get it, but you have to listen. She isn't going to admit what she's doing. Why should she? If you go in there threatening her and accusing her of these things, she'll absolutely get what she wants. She'll have a reason to file the restraining order at any time, even if the current investigation is closed. There will be a precedent."

"I can't," she hesitated, "I can't believe you." She shook her head and walked around Jake.

Jake followed her closely. "Rafe, if you just stay away from her, she won't be able to do what she's planning. She has a lot on you with the abuse case, and she has some photos. They may be enough to win the injunction against the adoption but may not prevent you from having visitation rights. It may cost you a lot of money, but at least you'll still get to have Bronte in your life."

"What are you saying?" she asked through clenched jaws.

"I'm saying there's hope for you, even if you lose against the injunction," he said convincingly. "But not if she gets her restraining order." He stopped to let his words sink into her stubborn head. "Take my advice, don't go to her apartment uninvited or otherwise, and try to stay away from her. Don't fall into her trap." He looked at her earnestly. "I promise I won't tell her we talked. Like I said," he looked toward the apartment again nervously, "I don't agree with everything she's doing. She won't know you're onto her, and you can at least save some kind of relationship with Bronte. Don't take the chance of losing Bronte completely by confronting Eden. Believe me... she's ready for you."

Rafe was reeling from the memories of all the things that had happened over the past weeks. "Everything was a lie?" She was talking to herself more than to Jake.

"Yes," Jake confirmed. "Yes, everything was a lie. I'm sorry," he said putting his hand on her shoulder consolingly. "Rafe, don't make what I can guarantee will be a fatal mistake. Just stay away from her, and it'll be okay. You'll have something with Bronte at least. I'm sorry she's doing this to you," he paused then exhaled and shook his head, "but Eden really doesn't love you, she loves me. She loves me," he repeated for good measure. He turned and walked to his car. He got in quickly then looked back over at Rafe as he started his car. He held back his smile of triumph until he pulled around Rafe's car and drove away slowly.

Rafe got in her car and sat with her hands in a death grip around the steering wheel. Jake's words were playing back in her head. Every memory they had made was turned into a lie cutting further into her heart.

How could she confront Eden? Rafe could see everything Jake said had to be true. There was no way he could know all those things they said to each other unless Eden had told him.

It was all planned. There was too much at stake so she couldn't confront her. One mistake and her life would be over.

She could not take the chance. Confront Eden and risk everything, walk away and save one small piece of her heart. Bronte.

She closed her eyes and slowly leaned forward until her head was resting on the steering wheel. Her body shook in despair. Everything, everything, everything was a lie. Eden loved Jake. She never loved her. Everything was a lie, everything was planned, and she had left herself wide open. Everyone had been right about Eden after all.

Rafe's heart shattered.

"*Vaffanculo,*"[12] she said softly. "No, no, please," she begged. "It can't be. Fuck! Why?" she asked in misery and shaking her head. "No, no, no, *No, NO!*"

Her grip on the steering wheel tightened as she lifted her head and a traitor tear streamed down her face. She scraped away the tear and pushed her burning anger forward to deny any daring to follow. She looked toward Eden's apartment, and the image of Jake walking out buckling his pants played in her mind.

Eden never left Jake.

"*Vaffanculo,* Jake," she growled as she started the car. She shifted into gear and then stepped on the gas, and the tires squealed as she sped out of the parking lot. Her mind was reeling, and her heart felt like it was being crushed inside her chest. "Fuck you, Eden," she said softly. The hot wind dried any escaping tears as she felt the knife twist in her heart and engulfing her body and mind with merciless pain.

---

[12] Fuck you!

58

FIVE BLOCKS AWAY, Jake Thompson was still grinning as he drove his car down the street. The connection on his hands-free mobile phone was ringing, and he was waiting for someone on the other end to pick up. A voice answered, and Jake reported.

"It's taken care of. It was so easy. It was like God had intervened."

"Just give the report," said the voice.

Jake gave a short laugh. "I had to pee, and I came out of the neighbors' apartment, and there she was." He laughed and heard the echo through the car speakers. "I told you making a new friend of her neighbor would come in handy. I had to think fast on my feet when I saw Rafe speeding toward me." He smiled, very proud of himself.

"Will the Mission Subject be more isolated and easier to control now?" asked the voice.

"Yeah, they'll both be totally isolated from each other from now on," he said confidently.

"So, you're sure you were successful?"

"Oh, I'm positive."

"Are we now back in control of the situation?"

"Afirmitive. We're back in control of the situation," he confirmed. "I told you I'd find a way to stop them from getting close."

"Then your Mission is still open," the voice said formally.

"I understand, good," Jake said trying not to show his relief. "Have Mason keep up the surveillance and sending me the tapes. By the time the court date comes up, our plan will be unstoppable, and there'll be so much hostility and distrust between them the judge will never allow the abomination of an adoption to happen. If I play my cards right, I'll rescue the child, and I may even be able to pull Eden back into the fold. I'll check in again later." Jake smiled again as he disconnected the call and turned to take the exit onto the highway.

59

WITHOUT SENSATION OR memory of how, Rafe Salvaggio got her father's car back to the storage garage and found her way home in her own car. She pulled into her driveway and made it to her front door where she stumbled inside devoid of any kind of awareness of her body's automatic and habitual movements.

Inside her house, she dropped the flowers and the wine on the floor, locked the door, and blindly made her way into her bathroom. Coming out of her black haze she looked in the mirror at her pale face and colorless lips, then closed her reddened eyes to block the sight of her pain.

The memory of Eden's kisses on her face, neck, and mouth flashed before her as Jake's words rang in her ears.

"She wants you out of their lives forever... she is still with me... she laughed about it as she went down on me. She loves me... she doesn't love you..."

She understood now it never meant anything and it was all just a charade.

Suddenly, Rafe's head spun, and her stomach knotted as hot bile rose in her throat. She put her hand to her mouth, spun around, and vomited violently into the toilet until nothing was left but her body's need to retch. She slid to the floor and stayed there until she could take a deep breath again.

She finally found the strength to pull herself up slowly as every muscle was on fire, aching, tense and weak. She stood shaking and leaned against the sink. She wiped off her mouth with a cool cloth, took a small sip of water, and then weakly made her way to her bed.

She crawled onto the bed and lay down fully clothed and curled her body around a pillow. Her feverish body shook uncontrollably with an inferno of grief she thought she would never know again. She stared into the dark night outside her bedroom window through a hard rain of tears full of pain, fury, and loss as she mourned all over again for Eden. Darkness found her again, and she floated into its depths willingly.

60

EDEN KINGSLEY WAS excited Saturday had finally arrived, and she was at Rafe's house again. She smiled as she took Bronte out of the car for her art lesson. Bronte was excited to see her art teacher, Annie Brown, and all the kids in the art studio. They were both excited to see Rafe again because they had been so busy they hadn't seen her all week. Eden was so happy they seemed to be moving forward, and all the good things she remembered about Rafe were exactly as she remembered them.

They hadn't made a final decision to rekindle their relationship because Eden still wanted to be cautious for the both of them. Being away from Rafe for a while after they spent time together allowed her to try to think clearly so she could figure out all the emotions conflicting inside her. She didn't want to make another mistake and hurt Rafe or herself. She knew taking things slowly like they did when they first met was for the best so they could be sure they were doing the right thing.

She carried Bronte into the studio, and all of Bronte's friends were there getting ready for their lesson. Eden looked around for Rafe, but she wasn't anywhere in the studio. She looked out the window and was surprised when she saw Rafe's car in the driveway. Rafe usually parked in the garage unless prevented by a project she had inside. She carried Bronte over to Rafe's house and knocked on the door sure Rafe would want to be there for the art lesson.

There was no answer when she knocked on the door, so she tried the door handle, but it was locked. "Maybe Mama's in the backyard," Eden said to Bronte. They went around back and saw Rafe was not outside this morning. Eden tried the patio doors but they were locked too, and the shades were pulled closed, which was very unusual when she was home in the daytime. Thinking maybe she just missed Rafe by walking around the house, she returned to the studio.

When Eden got back inside the studio, Rafe still wasn't there, and Eden went over to Annie. "Hey, Annie, have you seen Rafe?" she asked the young teacher.

"No, she's usually here before I am," she said. "Maybe she had to go somewhere. Jude isn't here either, so maybe they're just running late."

Eden shook her head. "Her car's in the driveway, and I don't think she would miss a lesson." She couldn't believe Rafe would miss this. It was something she looked forward to doing with Bronte.

Worried, she looked at Annie. "I think something's wrong. Did she give you a key to the house?"

"No, I just have one to the studio."

"I'll go see if Jude's home," she said. "If Rafe shows up, tell her I'll be right back." Eden switched Bronte to the other hip and made her way around to the front door of Jude's house. She knocked and waited for an answer.

Jude opened the door holding a piece of toast and saw Eden with a worried look on her face. "Hey, Eden, what's wrong?"

"Have you seen Rafe?"

"No, I haven't seen her all week," Jude said and took a bite of her toast.

"Can I use your phone?" Eden asked. "I left mine in the car." Jude pulled her phone from her pocket and handed it to Eden. She took Bronte while Eden dialed and listened as the voice mail came through. "No answer," she said as she looked at Jude. "Do you have a key to the house?" she asked as they exchanged the phone for Bronte.

"No, why?" Jude said putting her phone back into her pocket.

"The art lesson is starting, and she won't answer her door or the phone," said Eden. "I'm worried about her."

Jude looked over at Rafe's house. "Yeah, I was just on my way out to the studio. I think Julia may still have a key," she said and pulled her phone back out. "Do you want me to call her?"

"Would you?" Eden said in appreciation. "I'll just take Bronte to her lesson."

"Okay," Jude agreed and watched as Eden walked back to the studio. "Hey," she called after Eden, "you guys missed a fun dinner Thursday night."

Eden turned back and looked at Jude not knowing what she was talking about. "I didn't know about it," she said absently wondering where Rafe could be. "Let me know when Julia gets here."

61

THE CLASS WAS about thirty minutes into the session when Flynn Ogden and Stacey Randall entered the studio. Flynn immediately spotted Eden with Bronte and his roommate Jude. He headed over to them with Stacey close on his heels. Eden looked up as Flynn knelt down next to her.

"Eden, Julia is over at our place, Abby's with her," Flynn said.

"They were hanging out and shopping for shoes or something," Stacey volunteered.

"Can you guys watch Bronte while I go talk to them?" Eden asked as she stood up and took off her smock.

"Sure, you go ahead." Jude smiled and turned back to watch what Bronte was doing with the yellow paint.

Outside, Abby and Julia were walking toward Rafe's house when they saw Eden exit the studio. They waited for her to catch up with them. "What's going on?" asked Abby with concern.

Eden laughed, nervously averting her eyes and wondering if she was overreacting. "I can't get Rafe to answer her door. I think something's wrong." She looked at Julia. "Can you get us inside?"

"No problem," said Julia as she pulled out her key. "Let's go." She was curious to know what was going on herself. Julia unlocked the front door, and they walked inside.

Immediately, they saw the now wilted flowers and the bottle of wine on the floor. Abby picked them up and put them on the kitchen counter as they walked through the house.

"Rafe?" Abby called out. She looked at Julia and Eden when there was no answer.

Eden walked to Rafe's closed bedroom door, and the others followed. She knocked. "Rafe? Are you okay?" Again, there was no answer.

Eden gently opened the door and walked into Rafe's bedroom, followed closely by Abby, while Julia waited in the doorway. They found Rafe curled up in her bed still wearing her work clothes. Her clothes were now a wrinkled mess. Rafe's face was pale and drawn, her eyes were surrounded by dark circles, and her black curls matted against her face. Eden and Abby knelt down next to her bed.

Eden touched Rafe's face with the back of her hand. "She's so warm," she said softly. "Rafe? Rafe, wake up."

Through the fog of sleep, Rafe felt a cool hand on her face and slowly opened her eyes. She saw Eden and jerked away from her repulsed. "*Non mi toccare!*"[13] she hissed quickly through her teeth pushing Eden's hand away.

Eden reached out and stroked Rafe's face again pushing her hair back. "What?" she said, not understanding what Rafe was saying. "Rafe, I think you have a fever."

---

[13] Don't touch me!

Rafe lifted her head and looked at Eden with hardened red-rimmed eyes. With a clenched jaw and through tightened lips, she hissed, "Don't... fucking... touch me!"

Eden pulled her hand away slowly and looked at Abby in shock. She was speechless.

Abby looked at Eden concerned then knelt by the bed next to her. "Rafe, what's wrong? It's just Eden."

Rafe shifted her eyes to look at Abby, relieved she was here. "Abby, please," she whispered, "make her leave." She closed her eyes again slowly.

Abby looked at Eden not sure what to do. "I don't think she wants you to see her sick," Abby guessed. She was at a complete loss at why Rafe would say something so mean to Eden.

Eden shook her head and stroked Rafe's hair again. "Rafe, it's okay. I've seen you sick before. I can help you."

Rafe grabbed Abby's hand weakly and looked at her pleadingly as her body trembled. "Please," she whispered, "get her out," her throat caught, "out of my room."

Abby looked at Eden with confusion. She didn't understand what was happening except Rafe was sick. "Maybe you should leave," she said softly to Eden. "It's okay, I'll talk to her."

Eden stood up and looked at Rafe with hurt and confusion. Distressed, she slowly left the room and Julia closed the door after Eden was out. Abby felt Rafe's hot face with her free hand and looked back at Julia.

"Abby?" Rafe whispered.

Abby leaned closer to Rafe so she could hear her. "I'm here."

"I'm so sorry I hurt you," she said softly.

Abby looked back at Julia again, still confused, and concerned. "Rafe, I don't know what you're talking about. Come on, sit up. We need to get you out of these clothes. Julia, come here and help me."

Julia went over and helped Abby sit Rafe up, and they began getting her out of her wrinkled work clothes. "My god, Rafe!" Julia blurted as she held her up. "Your body is burning up! Abby, we should get her into the shower. I'll go start it." She went into the bathroom and rushed back out gagging. "Oh, my god! Abby, she's been sick in there!"

Julia took a moment and steeled herself then went back in. She flushed the commode, started the shower, and cleaned up what she could. Finally, she went back into the bedroom where Abby had Rafe stripped down to her bra and underwear.

"Come on. Let's get you up," Abby was saying to Rafe as Julia went over and they lifted her shaking body up. They got her to stand then led her between them into the bathroom. "Rafe, can you get in the shower by yourself?" Abby asked her gently.

"She can barely stand," said Julia. "You'll have to get in with her."

Abby gave Julia a perturbed look. "Fine. Then you go and change her bed sheets." Julia helped her get Rafe into the steamy shower. "Rafe, I'm going to help you clean up. Just let me take my clothes off."

When Abby and Julia let go of Rafe, she was so shaky she was unable to stand. She slid down the shower wall and sat on the floor. "I can't," Rafe said weakly.

"I'll just go take care of those sheets," said Julia leaving the room quickly.

Abby frowned in annoyance at Julia as the bathroom door closed. She disrobed to her underwear, stepped into the shower and held the shower nozzle, avoiding the water as much as possible. She crouched next to Rafe, wet her hair, and then put some shampoo in her hand. "Rafe, I'm going to just, just wash your hair, okay? You have some puke in it, and it's all matted to you." She rubbed the shampoo into her hair and rinsed it out.

Rafe looked at Abby through the water running down her face. "Abby," she said and swallowed, "I didn't mean it. I wasn't..." she stopped and hung her head down.

Abby pushed Rafe's hair back from her face. "It's okay."

"Wasn't serious at all," mumbled Rafe.

"It doesn't matter," said Abby getting the soap from the bottle and not knowing what Rafe was talking about.

"I jumped," Rafe said. She shuddered, feeling a cruel chill run through her body.

"Shhh, it's okay," Abby reassured her. She put the soap on a shower sponge and started washing her as best she could.

"Too soon," Rafe mumbled as she leaned against Abby.

"Rafe, lift your arms," said Abby, frustrated she was getting wetter than she wanted. She didn't understand why she always got stuck with the dirty work. She sighed and lifted Rafe's arms for her one at a time.

"The kisses," Rafe said hoarsely

"The kisses?" repeated Abby thinking Rafe must be delirious. She rinsed her off and turned off the water. "I'm just going to get a towel." She brought back a towel and dried Rafe's hair and face then wrapped the towel around her. She got Rafe's bathrobe for herself. "Julia," she called out. "Come and help me."

"Just a lie," Rafe mumbled.

Julia walked in and saw Abby putting on Rafe's robe. "I got the sheets changed and found some pajamas." She helped Abby get Rafe back to her bed. They put the pajamas on Rafe and got her back into bed where she curled up again.

Abby looked very worried as she got out of Rafe's robe and put her own clothes back on. "Julia, she's really sick. She's just saying random things and is so listless. I'm just not sure what she would want us to do for her."

Julia looked over and could see Rafe was just lying there with her eyes half-opened and feverish. "I think we should leave her alone for a while and see if she stays cooled down. Let's go talk to Eden and let her rest."

Abby looked at Rafe with worry and nodded her head. "Yeah, okay."

Eden had been in the kitchen making tea to pass the time and to help calm down while Abby and Julia helped Rafe. The distress still showed on her face as they came out of Rafe's bedroom and into the kitchen. "How is she?" Eden asked anxiously.

"Well, she's clean and sleeping again, sort of," said Abby as she took the cup of tea Eden offered her. "We should probably make sure she gets some fluids and something for her fever."

"And we know there's nothing in her stomach," added Julia with a grimace. "She may need some food, like dry crackers or something."

"I can get it all for her," Eden assured them desperate to help. "I'm sure there is medicine in her bathroom." She looked over at Rafe's bedroom door. "I wonder how long she's been lying in there sick."

Abby looked at the flowers and wine she sat on the counter earlier. "Did you see her Thursday?"

"No," Eden said as she blew on her hot tea.

"She was supposed to surprise you and bring you to dinner with us Thursday," Abby revealed. "She had the wine she was supposed to bring, and it looks like some flowers for you." She pointed to the items on the counter.

"She must have gotten sick after work on Thursday," concluded Julia. "Maybe she ate some bad cafeteria food at the school."

"So, she's been sick about a day and a half," calculated Abby. "If it's just something she ate, maybe she'll be better after tomorrow and out of bed by Monday."

"I hope so," said Eden still stinging from Rafe's harsh words. "I know she's going to be sad about missing Bronte today."

62

WHEN BRONTE'S ART class was over, Jude, Flynn, and Stacey brought Bronte inside Rafe Salvaggio's house and found Eden in the kitchen. Stacey and Eden took the paint-covered baby into the guest bathroom to clean her up while Flynn and Jude joined Abby and Julia, who were having a beer at the kitchen island.

"Is she going to be okay?" asked Jude as she pulled a beer for herself out of Rafe's refrigerator.

"It's Rafe," Abby said confidently. "She'll be fine."

Jude took a swig of her beer and nodded. "I just hate thinking she's been laying in there all this time sick. I need to get a key to the house since she is here alone so much. If I had one, we could have gotten to her sooner. What if it was something really bad?"

"We can talk to her about it tomorrow or the next day. Here's my key for now," Julia said as she gave her key to Jude. "Abby, you should stay with her tonight."

"Me?" squeaked Abby. "Why? Why do I always have to be the one?"

Julia shrugged. "Eden can't. She has Bronte, and what if it's contagious."

"Oh, it's okay if I get sick?" Abby pouted over her beer.

"Of course not," Julia assured her. "It's just, well, you know Rafe, and it seems like she doesn't want Eden here while she's sick."

"You're her friend too, and you were her roommate," argued Abby.

"I'll stay with you, Abby," said Jude trying to hold the peace.

"Fine," Abby relented. "Who's going to tell Eden?"

"Tell me what?" asked Eden as she walked in with Bronte and Stacey.

"Abby and Jude are staying tonight with Rafe so you can take Bronte home," Julia informed her. "Just in case it's catching."

Eden shook her head in disagreement. She was too worried to leave. "We can stay."

"Eden, maybe you should go," said Stacey and nodded to the baby. "You don't want Bronte to get sick."

"I don't want to go," argued Eden. "I want to make sure Rafe's okay."

"I don't think she wants you and Bronte to see her sick," said Abby with a shrug and pushed her empty bottle back on the counter.

"I don't understand," Eden said uncertainly. "I've seen her sick before. Why did she want me to leave?"

"It's probably just her Salvaggio pride," Abby guessed with a roll of her eyes.

"Well, I've got to take off. Come on, Flynn," said Stacey. "We've got heads to load. Let me know if you need anything later." She gave a wave and headed for the door.

"She means prop heads she made for an independent web horror film," Flynn explained as he followed her out. "I promised to help her deliver them."

"Oh, brother," mumbled Abby.

"I'm going too," announced Julia. "I've got a drinks meeting, and I've got to dress. Come on, Eden. I'll help you out with Bronte." She saw Eden about to protest. "I think it's best for Bronte's sake. We don't want her getting sick," she said as she opened the door.

"So, what, you're just leaving me here?" screeched Abby.

"Jude can take you home," Julia said with a smirk. "Besides you're sleeping over."

"I'll take you home," Jude smiled and patted Abby's shoulder.

"Whatever," Abby grumbled as Julia walked out the door.

Eden looked back at Abby and Jude. "Call me and let me know how she's doing."

"Sure," said Jude and lifted her beer bottle.

When everyone left, the tension in the room went with them. The whole situation had been awkward because no one knew what to do about Rafe not wanting Eden to help her.

Abby looked over at Jude who was working on another one of Rafe's beers. "I guess I should go see if I can wake her up and get her to eat and drink something," she said and got up to make a glass of water for Rafe. "Maybe I'll give her some medicine if she's willing to let me," she added as she searched for crackers, and Jude nodded her agreement.

She walked into Rafe's room with the glass of water and crackers and set them on the nightstand. She retrieved the medicine from the bathroom and set it next to the water glass.

"Rafe?" she said softly and touched her on the arm. "Rafe, you need to sit up and drink something." She got on the bed and pulled Rafe up into a sitting position.

"I hurt," Rafe murmured.

Abby sat behind Rafe so she could hold her up in front of her then picked up the glass of water. She reached around and put the glass to Rafe's lips. "Try to drink something."

Rafe drank a sip of water. "Thank you," she mumbled.

"You're welcome," said Abby calmly. "Next are a couple of pills. Open." She held the pills up to Rafe's mouth. Rafe took them, and then Abby gave her another drink to help her swallow the pills. "Good. Are you hungry?"

"No," Rafe said and turned her head to look at Abby. "I'm so glad you're my friend, Abby."

"Oh, god, Rafe!" Abby gagged. "Your breath! Let me get you some toothpaste." She felt Rafe's body start to shake. "Oh, shit! What's wrong?"

Rafe's body continued to shake. "Thank you."

"You're laughing?" asked Abby annoyed. "Thank you for what?"

Rafe laid her head back on Abby. "For being such a funny girl."

Abby rolled her eyes. "No problem." She pulled herself away from Rafe. "I really need to get you some toothpaste."

To be continued in Book Three — Secrets & Rivalry.

NOTES

Poe, Edgar Allen – "Alone" and "The Raven" Poetry Foundation 3.16.2016

http://www.poetryfoundation.org/poem/175776

Translations: For translations of Italian, French and Spanish use: www.Babblefish.com

The chapters in this book were arranged with the intent of saving paper. This chapter style saved 25 pages. Original Total Book Pages 318 — Final Pages 293.

Music mentioned in this book.

No financial incentive was given for the mention of the following artists in this work. The author is a fan and felt mentioning them worked in the story. For the use of their name, credit is given, and links to their work are below.

Enjoy!

Gianna Nannini

Website: http://www.giannanannini.com/en/
Facebook: https://www.facebook.com/giannanannini/
Twitter: @GiannaNannini
YouTube:
https://www.youtube.com/user/GiannaNanniniVEVO

ABOUT THE AUTHOR

C.L. CATTANO LIVES in the Midwestern U.S. with her partner and their dog somewhere between the city and the forest. With a joy for traveling, she and her partner have visited many countries and have a love for meeting people and learning about the places they visit. When possible, she likes to include references in her work about the things she has learned, the places she has been and people she has met while on her travels and in her everyday life.

Cattano has a variety of creative interests including, but not limited to, creating fine art, writing, photography, and supporting women in the arts. She considers herself a 'Jack of All Trades' dabbling in what she terms the 'whimsies of her soul' pulling her toward happiness and fulfillment.

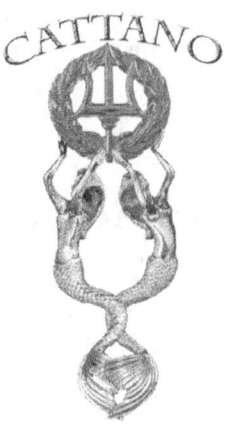

OTHER BOOKS

By C. L. Cattano

Cursed Hearts is a love story transcending time and gender. Separated from by a gift from a bored demon on All Hallows Eve two souls connected

by the power of love have been searching through time for each other and have been incarnated as both men and women.

Over time, the gift became a curse and a game for the demons.

Now the souls have finally met again, and they must fight for a life together.

Will love prevail? Will they finally be able to live together again for a lifetime? They have one night to figure out the riddle and get it right to break the curse.

NOTE: 18+ Lesbian Romance. Some light erotic moments.

Salvaggio's Light Series

Shattered Paradise — Book One
Blue Inferno — Book Two

REQUEST FOR REVIEW

Thank you for reading **Salvaggio's Light** — *An Epic Contemporary Romance Serial.*

I hope you enjoyed book two, **Blue Inferno**. Your honest review will be greatly appreciated by me and other readers. It only takes a few minutes, so I encourage you to go now and leave a review!

Check out the Salvaggio's Light Facebook page to join in the discussions and fun! www.facebook.com/pg/SalvaggiosLight

Join the CL Cattano Mailing List www.clcattano.com

I love getting fan mail, and you can contact me at
clc@clcattano.com